They fell into step together, walking down the hall, just like it used to be when he walked her home after their shifts. It was easy and comfortable, and the nerves she'd been feeling dissipated like the lightest spun sugar on a tongue.

Liam stopped suddenly. "Henriette? You smell like vanilla."

"Occupational hazard." She tipped her head. "Eight months since the last time we saw each other, and that's what you say?"

He studied her for a long moment, like he was trying to see into her soul. Finally, he said, "You want the truth?"

"Always," she said without any hesitation.

"I knew I missed you like crazy," he said softly. "Only until I saw you standing here in my sister's house, I didn't truly understand how much. I'm happy to see you, Henriette."

The emotion in his voice choked her up, surprising her into uncharacteristic muteness.

He smiled slightly, sticking his hands in his pockets. "Nothing to say?"

She opened her mouth to make one of her usual pithy remarks. But instead at the last minute she simply said, "I missed you too."

PRAISE FOR KATHIA

"Put simply, Kathia's novels are like a glass of champagne – heady, addictive and leaving one with a taste for much, much more."

— THE LITERARY SHED

"I simply adore Kathia's novels. Her series are fun and delightful to read. She knows how to add enough drama to the story to make it interesting, while at the same time making it something that could happen in real life. I love how she takes beautiful strong women and makes them even stronger by falling in love."

— A NOVEL GLIMPSE

"In truth, Kathia's super power is creating very real, very relatable characters that sort of just suck you in. Her secondary super power is inserting those characters into fun scenarios and situations that keep the plot moving along quickly and most interestingly."

— ROLO POLO BOOK BLOG

"Kathia is a professional writer who knows how to craft a well-structured story."

"I can't help the ear-to-ear smile I have plastered to my face when reading any of Kathia's books... She makes me laugh out loud, even on a crowded bus!"

"[Kathia's] writing is fluid, with a touch of sexiness and loads of romance, just what you need to relax after a long, hard working day."

"If you haven't read any of Kathia's books, start now. She's great storyteller, and a talented writer."

"Reading Kathia's books is my favorite way to spend an afternoon. (Well.. Okay, my second favorite way, the husband insists I clarify.)"

"If you have not started reading this series, what are you waiting for?"

HANG OUT WITH THE SUMMERHILLS...

YOU'LL HAVE SO MUCH FUN.

Book One: SAY YOU WILL

The Bridgertons meet *Emily in Paris*, in this sexy, modern Brit romantic comedy.

Book Two: LOST IN LOVE

A fun, feel-good romp about a woman looking for a lost tiara, only to realize the real treasure is the cowboy standing in her way.

Book Three: LET'S MISBEHAVE

A steamy, swoony novel about secrets, the healing power of love, and gnomes.

Book Four: STAY THE NIGHT

The perfect summer romance about a stubborn alpha jock and the even more stubborn photojournalist who's determined to win him over.

Book Five: ONCE UPON A DREAM

A modern, feel-good fairy tale about a woman determined to realize her dreams and the unexpected prince charming who helps her.

Book Six: HOW SWEET IT IS

An Editor's Pick for "Best Romance," about a second chance at life and love.

Book Seven: GIVE A LITTLE

She's a billionaire who wants what only what he can give her —both in the boardroom and the bedroom—in this exciting frenemies-to-lovers novel.

Novella: MAKE MY WISH COME TRUE

Beauty smacks beast upside the head in this fun holiday romp in the Irish countryside.

CONTINUE WITH THE NEXT
GENERATION OF SUMMERHILLS...

JUST AS SMART, TWICE AS SASSY.

Book One: THE WORDS YOU SAY

Kick off the next generation of Summerhills in Ireland, with this friends to lovers novel about love and the power of cake.

———

Book Two: THIS COULD BE THE NIGHT

Heart and heat create magic in this novel about two strangers and their one gloriously wicked week away together.

———

Book Three: WRITTEN IN THE SKY SO BLUE

Romance and love spark in this novel about two people who want to burn their pasts and rewrite their tragedies into a happily ever after.

THE WORDS YOU SAY

THE SUMMERHILLS NEXT GENERATION: BOOK ONE

KATHIA

THE WORDS YOU SAY

CHAPTER 1

"The most important thing at a wedding is the cake," Henriette Buchanan said as she cut the mini cake she'd baked specially for this couple.

The bride and groom looked intrigued, but the bride's mother frowned like she smelled something foul. "I think it's the dress," she said in her dour matron's voice.

Henri could hear her cousin Vivienne telling her to be diplomatic, but she took after her father. Diplomacy didn't stand a chance in the face of honesty. "The dress is important just for the day. The food and dancing too, because that's what makes guests happy. But the cake is the taste in everyone's mouth as they toast to your happiness. The cake is what you pull out of the freezer a year later, to remind yourself of the sweetness of your union."

"Humph," the woman said, sitting back in her seat, arms crossed tight across her ample chest.

Why did the mothers have to be this way? In the six months since she'd started her own wedding cake business, she'd dealt with a lot of mothers. Thank goodness her mum wasn't like that. Her mum was one of the loveliest, most accomplished women ever. But then all the Summerhill women were.

Henri turned her body to face the bride and groom as she plated the slices of the first cake. "The wedding is about the present. Wedding cakes are about the future. They go back to ancient Rome, when the groom would take barley bread and break it over the bride's head to ensure fertility. Guests would take home crumbs, to share in the abundance. The first cake I have for you is a dark chocolate mocha."

The groom chuckled, keeping hold of his fiancée's hand as he picked up his fork with the other. "Not barley?"

"I save that one for last." Henri winked at him and sat back to watch their reactions to her cake.

The bride gave a hum that made her man look at her like he wanted to toss her over his shoulder and carry her to a broom closet. Henri smiled. That was what cake was supposed to make you feel: luscious and sexy.

She glanced at the bride's mother. She barely touched the cake, acting like it was laced with arsenic.

Henri rolled her eyes. You couldn't trust a person who didn't like cake.

It'd been a year since her cousin Vivienne had approached her and said she was starting a wedding planning business and wanted to hire her to bake the cake for the first wedding she'd landed. The pastry chef at Papillon, a high-end restaurant here in London, Henri had moonlighted to take the commission.

She'd *loved* it. It gave her license to make something delectable and different while challenging her creativity. It was completely different than making the same desserts day in and day out. Taking that commission helped her see what she wanted to do: to make bespoke wedding cakes.

She'd stayed at Papillon for another few months, though, because of Liam Buckley, the chef she worked for. But Liam deciding to leave and start his own restaurant finally pushed her to set out on her own.

That first bride and groom had left something to be desired, though. They'd sat here with her, in Vivi's Mayfair salon, just like the couple here today. The bride had frittered nervously about what other people would like; the groom left after a couple minutes, announcing that he hated dessert and that they should pick whatever they wanted.

They'd gotten divorced six months later, after the woman found out he was cheating on her. Henri only knew because the woman had just called Vivienne to contract them for her second wedding.

Henri could always tell if a couple was going to last based on how they interacted as they shared cake, especially since the cake was supposed to symbolize the rest of their lives together.

She nodded approvingly at this couple. If they could get out from under the girl's mother, they'd be fine.

She pulled the next little cake toward her. "In medieval times, spiced buns were stacked into a huge tower. If the bride and groom could kiss over the pile without knocking it over, they'd be blessed with a lifetime of prosperity together."

Wiping her mouth with a napkin, the bride grinned at her groom. "Good thing I wear high heels."

"You know a lot about history," the groom said to Henri.

"I come by it naturally. My father restores antiquities, so I've been surrounded by stories from the past." She smiled at them as she cleaned her knife.

The groom nodded. "Your website said that you used to be an architect."

She nodded as she cut into the second cake. "Until I realized I really wanted to bake cakes. But my experience building comes in handy."

"No wonder your cakes are so different than other wedding cakes," the bride said. "Your designs are stunning."

They were. Her brief stint as an architect contributed to her creativity when it came to structure.

She didn't just stack layers; she built cake the way Frank Lloyd Wright did buildings.

She set a slice on three new plates and distributed them to her clients. "In some traditions, every guest has a bite of something sweet, so the couple has a sweet future together. A bad cake is a bad omen. They used to say that a bride who had to bake her own cake would have bad luck in her wedding. This next cake I made for you is French vanilla with violets."

"Vanilla is so plain," the mother said, pushing the plate away.

Henri resisted the urge to roll her eyes—barely.

The bride leaned in, her eyes closing as she inhaled the cake's scent. "This is the vanilla cake that was written up in *Esquire* a year ago, isn't it?" she asked reverently.

"It's a variation. I adjust my recipes based on the couple." It'd been a happy fluke that she'd gone rogue that night in the restaurant and served an additional cake as a dessert special. She'd been bored and wanted to spice things up; the journalist being there was chance.

"Henriette studied at the Cordon Bleu in Paris, you know," the bride said to her mother as she picked up a fresh fork. "She was the pastry chef at Papillon. You remember Papillon, don't you? We went there for Daddy's birthday last year."

The groom dug in. "This is like no vanilla cake I've ever had."

5

Henri shrugged. "Vanilla gets a bad rep for being boring, but I think it's just misunderstood. It's like saying missionary sex is boring. It's all in how you do it and who you do it with, right?"

The mother gasped, but the couple's laughter drowned out most of the disapproval.

"I can't wait to see what the next one is," the bride said as she delicately licked her fork. "I don't think I've ever had cake so delicious."

"The cake is important," Henri repeated, getting the last mini cake ready. "It's symbolic of a couple's relationship. Have you been to a wedding where the cake was dry? What future do you think holds for that couple?"

"When you take a bite of the cake I make for you, you'll taste the perfect balance of the two of you. You'll taste your hopes and dreams, and you'll taste the possibility of all the spice and sweetness waiting for you. If you want a forever love, I put that into your cake. If you want prosperity, a happy family, an easy life, anything, I add that to my recipes. Cake is everything good and joyous in the world, and your life together should start with the absolute best." Henri plated the last cake and set it before the bride and groom. "You'll love this one. It's one of my favorites. Lemon génoise. For you, I've added a touch of hazelnut."

"I love hazelnut," the groom said, digging in. "It's like you're psychic."

"Or the cake whisperer," his fiancée said.

The mother harrumphed. "I didn't get a piece."

Henri leveled her a look. "Are you going to try this one?"

The mother reared back as if no one had ever spoken to her that way. Then she gave a faint nod.

Putting the last piece on a plate, she set it gently in front of her.

"I love all of them," the bride whispered to her fiancé. "I can't pick which one I like more. What do you like?"

"All of them."

The mother frowned at her daughter. "I think—"

"You wanted a four-layer cake," Henri said, cutting in, her attention focused on the couple. They were the ones getting married, after all. This was the beginning of their life together, and she wasn't going to let a meddling mother use *her* cake to bungle it. "I'll do a layer of each flavor. Don't worry about the frosting. I know how to make it work."

"And the fourth?" the groom asked.

"I'll do a special one, just for the two of you to share alone. A surprise. That way everyone can partake in sending you off into a sweet life, and you can celebrate that sweetness together in private." She winked at them. "You'll like it. I guarantee that."

"Yes, please." The bride turned to her mother with steel in her eyes. "That's what I want, Mum."

Her mother looked like she wanted to argue, but the groom lifted his fiancée's hand to his lips and said to his future mother-in-law, "Then it's done, isn't it, Margaret?"

Frowning, the mother crossed her arms and made a disapproving sound, but she didn't say anything.

Good. Henri winked at the groom, who rolled *his* eyes. She set her serving utensils neatly on the table and stood. "I have all your preferences and thoughts about the design and color schemes. If I have questions, I'll be in touch. And you have my email."

The groom stood as well, holding out his hand. "This was incredible. Thank you, Henriette."

"Yes, thank you," the bride added, also standing. Her cheeks were flushed and her eyes sparkling.

Henri smiled. She knew that look—good food was orgasmic. Good food made you want to push your partner against a wall and *feast*.

She sighed silently. If she had someone special, she'd take the leftover cake to him and do exactly that.

She thought of Liam again. Not that that was a surprise—she'd been thinking of Liam a lot lately. Their texting was a poor substitute for seeing him every day like she used to when they worked together.

"All well in here?" Vivienne asked brightly as she strolled into the salon.

Tuning everyone out, Henri focused on cleaning up the dishes. If Liam had been there, he'd have lent a hand. Despite being one of the hottest chefs in London, Liam had never been above pitching in during cleanup. His work ethic was admirable.

She'd always believed that she'd find someone to share that sort of passion with. Someone who shared the same drive—someone who saw what he wanted and *went for it.* Like her parents or her older sister Chloe and her husband Oliver (Henri had recognized the passion between them from the moment they'd met, and she'd only been twelve then).

She'd always wondered if she could have that with Liam. He'd always talked about what he wanted and how he was going to achieve it. She'd loved that.

But they'd worked together, so seeing if they'd have been compatible was out of the question. Then he'd gone back to Ireland to start his restaurant, and she'd gone to France to apprentice under a master génoise baker…

Except now she was back in London, and he'd been contacting her. It made her wonder—

"Right, Henri?" Vivi said loudly.

She blinked, looking up to find all four of them staring at her. "What was that? I was lost in cake thoughts."

The bride and groom laughed. "I wish I loved my job that much," the bride said.

Vivi gestured to the door, gently herding them toward it. "I'll talk to Henri and let you know about the desserts for the rehearsal dinner, but I don't foresee it being a problem."

Not as long as the mother kept to herself, Henri added silently. She loaded the silver tray their grandmother Jacqueline had given her when she'd decided to start her venture and took everything into the kitchen.

Vivi had converted an old café in Mayfair, blocks from the Summerhill South Street house, into a show-room for her wedding planning business. Henri used the kitchen to bake since she couldn't afford a kitchen of her own yet. The office, salon, and everything else was Vivi's domain.

Her mobile beeped with a text. Setting the tray down, she wiped her hands on her jeans and picked it up, grinning when she saw it was Liam. He must have known she was thinking about him.

Really, she'd been thinking about him all the time lately.

Hot Chef

If you catch a flight right now, you can be here in Westport to have dinner at my restaurant tonight. I have morels.

She *loved* morels, and no one made them better than Liam. He had a way with all mushrooms; she used to tease him that it was because he was Irish and of the fairies, so of course he and mushrooms were like *this*.

If only she could go. But her two-month stay in France had depleted her bank account, and it'd only been six months since she'd officially started her business. She couldn't afford it.

Plus, she had her sights set on the bigger picture: the Watford-Roberts wedding. It promised to be the event of the year since there were no royal weddings scheduled. If—*when*—she got the contract to bake the cake for that wedding, she'd be set. Her name would be synonymous with scrumptious decadence. She wanted to be here to act on it when that came through.

<u>Henri</u>
Tempting… Would love to catch up.

<u>Hot Chef</u>
It'd be like old times. I'd be savory, you'd be sweet. Together we'd make the perfect meal.

She smiled, feeling nostalgic. They'd worked so well together in the kitchen, in sync with each other's movements from the beginning. During the course of the night, they didn't have much contact—she'd put earbuds in and do her thing in her corner of the kitchen—but they often volunteered to cook family dinner with each other, and in downtime between shifts, they'd sat together, with her sketching and him reading cooking texts from other centuries, peaceful and relaxing.

It'd been wonderful; she missed it when he left Papillon eight months ago. The restaurant wasn't the same without him. When he'd left, it was like a light went out in that kitchen.

Who was she kidding? Liam *was* the light. Everything about him had drawn her. His golden eyes, his

11

reddish-brown hair that curled over his collar, his broad chest, and his large hands that were capable of creating the most intricate of dishes. And once you got past how incredibly handsome and virile he looked, there was his bold laugh and the sly twinkle in his gaze that conveyed his sharp wit.

And then there was his drive. She'd loved that about him. He'd understood her.

But they'd worked together so acting on the attraction hadn't been an option, because he'd had an absolutely no fraternizing rule in that kitchen. Which was only smart. She'd heard horror stories about the shenanigans that usually happened in the back of the house—like getting cornered in the cold storage by the men. She didn't want to work in that sort of environment.

Plus, the restaurant world was small and tight, and the last thing she needed was a reputation. News of bad behavior got around. As she was trying to get her fledgling business off the ground, she needed people to speak good things about her and her cakes, not gossip about her love life.

Besides, it'd been eight months since she'd seen Liam. Aside from their pithy text exchanges, they hadn't *really* talked. She thought he was hot, but for all she knew he could think of her as an excellent pastry chef that he wanted to hire.

She bit her lip and then quickly typed her response.

Henri
Unfortunately the perfect meal is going to have to wait. I'm just getting business off the ground. Gotta hustle. Can't afford to just hop across the pond. I'm staying with my parents even.

Hot Chef
I could take care of the ticket.

Henri
NO. Aside from giving me a room, I don't even let my parents pay for me. I just need a few more gigs booked and then I'll be okay.

.

Henri
It's very sweet of you to offer though.

Hot Chef
You're breaking my heart, Buchanan.

Hot Chef
Let's make time to talk.
There's a Henriette-shaped hole in my life.

Still smiling wistfully, she was almost done loading the dishwasher when Vivi strode in. Her cousin's heels clacked with purpose on the wood floor, the way they did when she was on a tear. Henri had no idea how her cousin could move that fast in her tight pencil skirt and heels so high. Those thin heels defied construction. Henri hardly ever wore shoes like that, but when she did, she made sure her foundation was sound. (Wedges for the win.)

But she and Vivi, though they were only a little over a year apart in age, were very different people. They both shared the Summerhill blue eyes, but Vivi had the blond hair too; Henri had her father's dark waves. Vivi also inherited the Summerhill way of always looking *just so*, with her hair in an elaborate twist and her eyes subtly enhanced with makeup. If Henri remembered to swipe some mascara on her lashes it was a miracle, and as long as her hair was out of her way, she didn't care what it looked like. She always had a chef hat on anyway.

"Are you texting with Hot Chef again?" Vivi asked, bringing a cup Henri must have forgotten and setting it in the sink.

She put it in the dishwasher and closed it. "How did you know?"

"You get a goofy look on your face." Vivi set the portfolio that she always carried with her on the counter. "Just ask him to come visit you. You know you want to."

Henri snorted. "And what? Ask him to stay with me at my parents' house? And then what? He has a restaurant in Ireland and I'm here in London. I can't afford a long-distance relationship. But as soon as I get a few more gigs and feel more comfortable financially, then I'll see."

"Do you need help?" Vivi asked flat out.

"No." Henri gave her a look. "I'm going to make this work."

"You and your pride. Though I guess all of us from the Summerhill stock are the same." Vivi straightened her necklace, like she did when something wasn't right.

"The tasting went well," Henri said to change the subject.

"They raved about your cakes. Speaking of, do you have any left?" Vivi pulled out a barstool and perched at the counter. "I'm dying to try what you did this time with the vanilla one."

"I made two, just in case." She pulled the other small cake from under the island in the center of the kitchen and set it on top.

"Just a small piece."

"I know." She cut a sliver of cake, knowing her cousin would only have a couple bites and leave the rest. Vivi was overly careful about how much she ate. Henri pushed the plate and a fork toward her.

"Hmm." Vivi lifted the plate and inhaled the cake's aroma, like it was a glass of wine. Then, with deliberate intention, she set the plate down, forked a piece, and slowly put it in her mouth. Then she moaned. "This is better than sex."

"Then you aren't doing sex right." Henri folded her

arms. "Do you want to wait until you finish the cake to tell me what's bothering you?"

Her cousin sighed, setting the fork down and looking up at her with her direct Summerhill blue gaze. "I signed the Whitehall-Strangs for the fall."

"Why isn't that a cause to celebrate?" she asked warily.

"They've already booked the Drummond Room."

"Damn it." Henri made a face. "I was counting on that contract. That's the third couple in the past two months."

Vivi lifted her hands helplessly. "It was that article that came out in *Brides Magazine*. They painted the hall as being absolute magic. Everyone wants to have their wedding there, which is fine, except that Drummond Room mandates that the couple has to use their in-house catering."

And that catering included desserts, which included cakes. Meaning she was out another gig for the year, and that didn't bode well for her bottom line. "My cake is a million times better than what they serve."

"I know."

"Starting off your life together with inferior cake is the worst intention ever."

"I know."

She hugged herself tighter, feeling the pinch of her dwindling bank account. "The wankers."

Vivi smiled faintly. "The couple or the Drummond Room director?"

"Both." She plopped onto a stool across from her cousin. Then she picked up Vivi's discarded fork and stuffed a large bite into her mouth. Any couple who didn't want *this* to symbolize their union was daft. At least she still had the Watford-Roberts wedding.

Vivi put her hand on hers and squeezed. "We'll figure something out. Your cakes are too incredible. We just need to make people realize they want your cake as badly as they want the rest."

"And how are we going to do that?"

"Let me think about it," Vivi said with her usual I'll-take-care-of-this attitude that made her such a great wedding coordinator.

"You need to think about it quickly." She'd spent more than she'd meant to in France—the chef had invited her to stay longer and she hadn't been able to turn that down. She was staying with her parents, so at least she didn't have rent, but she couldn't stay there forever. She knew that it took a while to build up a business, but she'd thought she'd be further along than she was. Certainly, she'd thought she'd have more weddings booked.

She'd make this work. Her cakes were excellent, not only delicious but artful. She believed. She just needed enough time—or a big coup—to get her fully on the map.

That had been part of the problem as a pastry chef. Not only did she have to make the same desserts day in and day out (*boring*), but she couldn't be as creative as she wanted to be. Most of the recipes were given to her and there was no leeway for experimenting.

Cake was her art. She'd combined her architect's degree with her love of pastry to create something unique. Her cakes were sculptures—masterpieces—as much as they were scrumptious. She did something most bakers didn't do.

She couldn't see herself doing anything less.

Frankly, everyone in the family did exceptional things—both her immediate and extended families. To list all her cousins' accomplishments would take days, and then there were her aunts and uncles. Even her brother-in-law Oliver was renowned for breeding roses. Anything less than utter success wasn't acceptable.

"I don't want to go back to just making treacle pudding all the time," she said softly.

"You won't." When she didn't reply, Vivi frowned at her. "Really, Henri, I won't let you down."

Henri nodded. She wasn't going to let herself down either.

CHAPTER 2

*L*iam strode into his oldest sister's home office. "I've been thinking about my life."

"Isn't this a conversation you should be having with Áine?" Maeve said without looking up from her laptop. "She's more equipped to deal with life crises."

"I'm not having a crisis. I know what I want." And that was Henriette Buchanan. "But I've been thinking about your life too, and I have a solution for both of us."

Maeve looked up, her brow arched. "My life needs a solution?"

"Yes." He took a seat across from her. "Three words for you. Dad's old company. It's had your knickers in a wad for the past week."

Her face immediately took on a fierce scowl. "I'm

going to figure out a way to win the bid. I have two weeks to figure it out."

That was his sister: determined. She always found a way, but normally she was more neutral. She was emotionally involved in buying back the company their dad had started, and she herself said you couldn't bring emotion into business. "You said the CEO told you he wasn't going to entertain an offer from you because you weren't married."

"Can you believe that? Money is money, and this is the business Dad started." She banged her fist on her desk. "Our *name* is on the fucking company. I sold him the company thirty years ago, for fuck's sake. Why can't he sell it back to me? It shouldn't matter if I don't have a husband."

"But it does to him." Liam took a deep breath, mentally crossing his fingers. "So I think you should have a wedding."

She looked at him like he was a recalcitrant child instead of a thirty-five-year-old man. "Sorry?" she said in a tone that suggested she was anything but.

He smiled. "Well, specifically, I need you to order a wedding cake, but I started thinking bigger and realized having a wedding was the answer to both our problems."

She closed her laptop and focused completely on him. Even working from home, she looked every inch the chic woman who'd been touted as the wunderkind of finance when she'd first started out twenty-five years ago.

Frankly, if he didn't know she was forty-seven, he'd have taken her for being that youthful still. She was utterly beautiful, with milky skin. Her fiery red hair, free of its usual twist, hung shiny and sleek past her shoulders, and her warm brown eyes watched him carefully.

"Before we tackle me getting married," she said, "maybe you can tell me why you, of all people, need a wedding cake."

He rubbed the back of his neck. "You're going to think I'm daft."

"I already do, darling." She smiled that crooked smile of hers that lit her eyes that she never showed anyone outside of her inner circle, which, as far as he could tell, only included him and their middle sister Áine.

Seeing her smile reinforced why he was here. He wanted to help Henriette, but he'd realized that this was the perfect opportunity to help Maeve too. This was the simplest way he could do both.

Well—*simple* might be overstating it, but still. He relaxed in the chair, rotating the tension off his shoulders.

Without Maeve, who knew where he'd be today? She'd raised him and Áine. Selling off Buckley Sinks & Taps after their parents had died, she'd turned that money into a fortune and ensured their futures.

Without her, Áine wouldn't have been able to become a psychiatrist as easily, and he certainly wouldn't have been able to go to culinary academy in the States.

The dynamics of their relationship had changed as he'd gotten older, becoming more equal, but she was still there for him. "Do you remember how, when I was sick of working for ingrates and wanted to strike out on my own, you helped me come up with a plan of action?"

"Of course."

Her help hadn't been monetary—she'd helped both him and Áine invest their share of the proceeds from the sale of their dad's company so that they would always have options. He was grateful for that beyond belief. Most restaurateurs he knew were always strapped for cash and struggling—especially in the beginning, like Henriette was now. Because of Maeve, he had the luxury to not only pursue his dreams but to make them reality.

Because that had been his dream: to have his own restaurant, where he could cook whatever he wanted, whenever he wanted, for whomever he wanted. He'd been fed up with being restricted to only certain recipes, and he'd been especially done with patrons telling him how to cook his food. He'd been fed up with *hustling*. Food wasn't supposed to be draining. It was supposed to fill you up. Food inspired connection and joy.

But it hadn't the way he'd been doing it.

So eight months ago, he'd left London and come back to Ireland, to Westport. Now he had his own place, making what brought joy to his soul, cooking for the people he wanted to nourish. If they didn't want what he served it, he told them to leave.

A lot of people had told him he'd never be able to get away with that, but he had, to great success. He'd only been open for six months, but *A Ghrá*, his little restaurant, was booked two months out, and he was in the black.

He'd done the hard work, but he knew he owed getting the word out to Maeve. One invitation to a well-connected food critic and now, his restaurant was quickly becoming known as one of the best in Europe, despite being located in the hinterlands of County Mayo. It'd been all he'd dreamed about since the first cooking show he'd seen on the tele as a child.

Now it was his turn to be there for Maeve. Henriette too, at the same time.

And, if he was lucky, he'd actualize the second part of his dream: a family with Henriette. Because if the past eight months had taught him anything, it was that career success was great but it paled unless you had someone to celebrate it with you, and the only person he wanted to celebrate with was Henriette Buchanan.

He'd been with her practically every day for over a year at Papillon, and he hadn't realized that he'd been falling in love with her until he'd left London. Talk about daft.

He'd been attracted to Henriette from first sight. He'd been the chef at the most popular restaurant in London, and she'd come in to interview for the open pastry chef position.

He remembered the stunned moment he'd set eyes on her. He'd been expecting a prissy half-French pastry chef, but instead this goddess walked in, tall and willowy, with shiny dark hair and bright blue eyes that hinted at the secrets of the universe.

Then she'd started to talk and he'd fallen for her snarky wit. He remembered asking her what her favorite cake was; she'd replied, "All of them. Cake is like sex, isn't it? Trying new things keeps it exciting."

When she'd whipped up a lava cake for him as a trial, dotting it with a shocking pairing of a tomatillo sauce, all he could imagine was licking it off her skin.

The lava cake? The best he'd ever had. It'd been love at first taste.

Not even he'd ever made lava cake that rivaled Henriette's, and that was saying something because he was excellent in the kitchen.

He was excellent in other rooms too, and he bet Henriette was as well.

Not that he knew for a fact. They'd never even held hands.

He'd had to hire her—whatever magic she'd woven into the cake that day couldn't be denied. The problem was that in hiring her, it put her off-limits. He had a strict respect policy in his kitchen, and that meant no fraternizing.

In the beginning of his career, he'd worked in kitchens where the drugs and harassment were out of control. Having two sisters, he hated the way women were often preyed upon and vowed that there would be none of that in his kitchen. He made sure his kitchen was creative and without negativity. No drama, no funny business. They were there for culinary excellence.

Which meant he couldn't ask Henriette out.

Which meant in the beginning he'd spent a lot of time with her and their coworkers, and sometimes other chefs, at after-shift drinks, talking to her over a pint. The more time he spent with her, the more he'd fallen for her and her quirky intelligence. He'd brought a plush chair into the kitchen for her because she liked to curl up and draw during her breaks. Some of the team liked to play poker in between shifts, but Liam had quickly realized sitting next to her reading was his happy place.

When they cooked family meals together, it was magic.

They'd only worked together for a year, and it'd been eight months since he'd seen her, but he couldn't get her out of his mind—or his heart. Sure, he had his dream, but he'd quickly realized that his dream was missing one essential ingredient: Henriette.

"Liam," Maeve said, bringing him back to the

moment. "You're woolgathering. You were explaining to me why you want me to order a wedding cake."

"There's a woman—"

"The start of any grand Irish tale," Maeve replied with a quirk of her brow. "Apparently this woman is linked to the cake."

"She was the pastry chef at Papillon. I think you met her when you came in."

"What's her name?"

"Henriette Buchanan." He took out the brochure he'd printed off Henriette's website from his coat pocket and set it on the desk, pushing it toward his sister. "She creates bespoke wedding cakes now."

Maeve picked up the printout and scanned it. "I want to say I see, but I really don't."

"I've kept in touch with her since I left Papillon. She'd left to go to France to apprentice with a master, but she's back and I want to see her. I've hinted that she should come here, but she can't afford it. She's trying to get her business off the ground."

His sister leaned back in her chair. "And so you want to throw some business her way."

He nodded. "She makes the best desserts I've ever tasted. Better than my pastry chef here."

Maeve's eyebrows rose. "That's something, coming from you. Are you planning on asking her to work with you?"

"I don't allow fraternization in my kitchen. I can't break my own rules." Besides, working in a restaurant full-time didn't make Henri's heart happy. When she used to talk about sculpting structures out of cake, desserts both delicious and beautiful, she'd light from within. Making wedding cakes was perfectly brilliant for her. "I can't order a cake from her for the restaurant; it wouldn't make sense. But if you ordered a cake from her, she'd profit from it, and word would get out that Maeve Buckley contracted her, so she'd instantly be sought after. And she'd have to assemble it in person, so I could spend time with her here, where she can experience Westport." His restaurant was here, so her liking to be here was important. He wanted to show her she could be happy here too.

"You believe in her," Maeve said, studying him.

"She's one of the best pastry chefs I've ever met. I want to help her." He rested his elbows on his knees, his hands open in front of him. "I also want to help you. This would benefit you both at the same time."

Her expression darkened, and for a second her brown eyes became dark, like a shark's. "I shouldn't have to change my life to cater to someone's old-fashioned ideas of how people should live. In that man's mind, there's something wrong with me for never having been married."

"Yes, but you still want the company back," he pointed out.

"It was Dad's dream," she replied simply. "I never would have sold it to that old coot if I'd seen a different choice."

His heart expanded with love for her. He felt a pang that he'd been too young to help her back then, but it only reinforced his determination to be there for her now. "You were eighteen, Maeve. What were you supposed to do? Dad wouldn't have faulted you. He'd have been proud."

She hummed, tapping her fingers on the desk, the way she did when she was thinking seriously.

"Have a wedding, Maeve." He leaned forward, willing her to see the brilliance of the idea. "Say you were keeping your relationship under wraps. Let word of the wedding get out. Then you'll have a shot at the deal, won't you? But on the wedding day, you can postpone it for a while before you eventually cancel it."

"Saying what?"

"That there's a family emergency. That you're called out of town for important business." He shrugged. "There's any number of excuses that would be acceptable to anyone."

Gripping the armrests on her chair, she appeared to think it through. "It has merit, except for one problem," she said finally.

"What?"

"I'd need a groom for this scenario to work," she said as if he were a simpleton.

"I was thinking about that. How about Andy?"

"*Andrew?*" She gawked at him for a full ten seconds before bursting out in laughter. Her head fell back, her hair glinting like fire in the sunlight coming in from the window behind her.

Maeve hardly ever laughed anymore. He blinked at the sudden realization, feeling a tightness in his chest. "Why is that funny?"

"He's our *plumber*," she said as if he were an idiot. "I've seen his arse."

Liam shrugged. "Wouldn't that be a requisite for the man you were going to marry?"

"I will not pretend to marry Andrew." She tapped her fingers on her desk as she stared at him. "But your idea about having a wedding *does* have merit. It'd have the added benefit of quashing the rumors about something being wrong with me and the suppositions about my love life."

He leaned forward. "So you'll do it?"

His sister studied him for a long moment. "You actually feel confident about this plan?"

He shook his head. "Not at all. It's hardly flawless, but it accomplishes everything easily. I want to see Henriette, but she needs to feel on more solid ground, and this is how I can help her get there. She's brilliant at what she does. It helps you as well, and, in all honesty, it brings me closer to what I want."

"I can't believe I'm actually entertaining this idea. It's insane." Maeve leaned back in her chair, arms folded. "Do you even know if she was ever attracted to you?"

"I know how I felt being around her." He remembered one night when he was walking her home from late-night drinks out with the crew, and how at her door she'd turned around and tripped, falling right into his arms. For a moment, before she drew herself out of his arms, he'd seen the look in her eyes and felt her breath hitch, and he'd wondered...

He'd almost kissed her that night, despite his rules. It'd been what had finally pushed him to leave his comfort zone and open his own restaurant. "I couldn't have felt how I did around her if there wasn't something there."

"So you're willing to gamble thousands of pounds to fly her here to bake a cake to find out if she's interested in you?"

"She's worth it," he said, unwavering.

Maeve met his stare, obviously considering. He knew better than to say anything—she'd taught him everything he knew about negotiation and being persuasive. Sometimes you had to lay everything out and then let the other person meet you. This was one of those cases.

"This idea is absolutely mad," she said again.

"Yes."

She shook her head. "When is this—*my*—wedding to take place?"

"What are you doing in three weeks?"

Swearing, Maeve jumped to her feet. "*Three weeks?*"

He stood too. "You said the bidding for the company opens in two weeks. Make the wedding for after the bidding is over. That way you can close the deal and then postpone the wedding."

She hummed, her arms crossed defensively.

"If the wedding is in three weeks, Henriette would have to come here right away," Liam continued. "The sooner she's firmly on the map, the better. I can convince her she needs to stay here, to get everything ready for the wedding. Incidentally, your cake needs to have at least five layers, with a lot of detail work with the icing. Something that'll take a long time to assemble and finish, because I need time to woo her properly."

She pressed a hand to her forehead. "If you're using words like 'woo,' this is serious."

"That's what I've been saying." He'd meant it when he said there was a Henriette-shaped hole in his life. He missed her.

He hoped that she felt the same. It came down to one thing: reminding her how good they were together and showing her how their friendship would translate into a relationship. Plus, he had to show her that she didn't have to be in the fast lane to succeed. She could have everything she ever wanted, right here out of Westport—and maybe some things she hadn't realized she wanted, like he'd discovered.

He wanted to have the privilege of being able to kiss her whenever, wherever. He wanted to cook with her, and then he wanted to take her to bed. He wanted to go through life holding her hand. He'd always felt so easy around her, settled and calm even while expectant and excited. He'd never felt that with anyone, and he knew that he'd never feel it with anyone other than Henriette.

Maeve watched him with her all-encompassing stare that withered the hardiest of bollocks. Then, in a soft voice he'd never heard from her before, she said, "You love her."

He blinked in surprise. "What did you think this was about?"

"Sex," his sister said in her customary direct way.

"I don't want sex." He frowned. "Well, I do, but I also want the quiet times, and the laughter, and everything in between. I want Henriette, in my life, until the very end."

"Henriette, the cake baker. The sweet to your salty." Maeve retreated behind her poker face. "What are you going to do if she doesn't love you?"

"I can't consider that, and in any case I have to try." He looked his older sister in the eye. "Will you help me?"

Maeve rolled her eyes. "Of course I'll help you. I always help you."

He heaved a sigh of relief. If Maeve was going to help, it was a done deal. "We need to order the cake right away. Like next week. Not being with her the past eight months has shown me I don't want to spend another minute without her."

"You're such a romantic, just like Dad was," his

sister said softly. "You think she'll drop everything and come here to bake a cake?"

"That's why I'm having you call instead of Áine. You can get people to do anything." It was less flattery and more statement of fact. When Maeve asked for something, people jumped through hoops to provide it.

"A wedding cake is a lot of cake," she said. "If I'm canceling the wedding, what are we going to do with it?"

He grinned. "We eat it," he said. He'd had four years to think of every creative, naughty way of eating cake there was. He just needed Henriette to put all those thoughts into play.

CHAPTER 3

*a*fter Liam left, Maeve sat in her office and thought about the entire preposterous visit.

He was wrong. She couldn't announce having a wedding and then postpone it. First off, she'd done that before, in her twenties. People's memories were long, and if she postponed this wedding, they'd expect she'd cancel it like she did the last one.

Second, current CEO of Buckley Sinks & Taps, Terrence Walsh—the man she'd sold her dad's company to—wanted her married, period. He had definite ideas about who he wanted to pass the company on to: someone Irish born who had a vision of how the company could help the economy here—a good family person who had "proper Irish values." He'd made it very clear in their meeting last week that he'd consider selling the company back to her except for one thing: that she'd never been married. She'd gotten the impression that, in his mind, there was something wrong with her for still being single. Even being divorced was preferable than never having been married.

Which was absolutely ridiculous.

She'd known male colleagues who'd had promotions fall through because of their lack of family—some companies expected their executives to live a certain way. She just never thought it'd be an issue for her given she had her own holdings. Her money was as good as a married person's.

Plus, her dad had started the company. That their name was on it should have given her an edge. Her dad had had such grand ideas for it too. She remembered going into the manufacturing facility with him and him telling her all the ideas he had for creating sinks and fixtures that would bring whimsy to everyday life. "Life is short, *a leanbh*. While we have to be practical, it doesn't mean it can't be beautiful."

She remembered the red sink he'd brought home to install for her. She'd loved that red sink. She'd had Andrew install one similar to it in her bathroom now.

Buckley Sinks & Taps had gotten away from that principle in the almost thirty years since she'd had to sell it to Walsh. It'd made sense, because the Irish market hadn't been ready for her dad's eccentric vision back then. But now it was the perfect time to bring back that whimsy her father had envisioned. Maeve knew how to do it—and how to expand their market worldwide.

She just needed to convince Walsh to accept her bid.

Liam was right: if Terrence Walsh thought she was married it'd be a done deal. She was a Buckley, had a track record at helping companies excel, and lived in Ireland. She tapped her fingers on her desk. The problem was a half-assed wedding wasn't going to be feasible.

However, if she went along with Liam's mad idea (she couldn't believe she was actually considering it), she'd have to go through with the marriage, and stay married for a year or two before she got divorced, in order to maintain appearances. She couldn't have the wedding scheduled to take place after the bidding. She needed to be married by the time she put in her offer.

She was genuinely thinking of getting married in order to make this deal.

Any other company and she'd have said, "Fuck it," and moved on, but this company was her father's dream. She'd grown up walking through the facility and talking with the workers. She'd learned everything she knew about manufacturing there, next to her father.

That was his greatest dream: for the two of them to run the company together. "*A leanbh*, I had the vision to start this business, but I know you're going to take my dream and turn it into the most brilliant reality," he used to say to her.

But instead, when he and her mother had died, she'd taken the easy route and sold the company.

It'd afforded her the ability to raise Áine and Liam without any struggle. At the expense of betraying her father's vision.

"I'm seriously considering getting married in order to buy an Irish *sink manufacturer*," she repeated out loud, hoping hearing it would highlight how daft an idea it was, but all she could think was that it was her dad's company and she wanted it back.

"What was that?" she heard a masculine voice say.

She startled, turning to look at the doorway.

Andrew, their plumber, stood in the threshold, looking at her askance. He held his toolbox in one hand and his car keys in the other.

She frowned at him, suspicious. "Did Liam send you?"

He arched his brow like she was mad. "No. You asked me to come look at your shower. The drain's still giving you problems?"

Right. She nodded. "Yes. Thank you."

He still looked at her skeptically. "I'll just go up then?"

"Please."

She watched him leave, thinking about Liam's suggestion. Andrew was tall and handsome, she supposed, with his thick black hair and green eyes, but she didn't feel an iota of attraction for him. Not that she needed that for an arranged marriage, she supposed.

She put a hand to her head. She was actually considering this. What would her dad say if he knew?

He'd probably laugh and say, "*A leanbh*, life is a grand adventure, isn't it?"

Who could she marry?

She couldn't just marry anyone; she wasn't going to put her hard-earned money in jeopardy. She'd watched her contemporaries get fleeced in divorce, even after very short marriages.

If only she was dating someone, or if she had a good friend who'd be willing to help her. She could hardly imagine being in love like Liam was.

Holy fuck, she envied her brother.

Had she ever wanted someone with the intensity of emotion that he wanted his Henriette? Someone she wasn't sure he'd even kissed yet. Liam was very strict about his "no sex" rule in his kitchen.

Ordering a cake to woo his lost love… God, it was so Irish of him.

Everything practical inside her said that it was a doomed proposition—that once they got together, once they had sex, it wasn't going to be as good as he thought. And even if it was, it'd be a flash and a bang and then over. There was not a chance it would last forever, the way Liam believed it would. Her experience had certainly proved that.

And yet Liam had always had the right of it in

THE WORDS YOU SAY

everything that he wanted. He'd believed he'd be one of the most sought-after chefs in the world, and he was. He'd said his restaurant, despite being in the wilds of County Mayo, would be one of the most popular restaurants in all of Europe, and it was well on its way to being just that. Why would she doubt that this woman he wanted was the love of his life? Liam had said it himself: she'd taught him to identify and go after what he wanted, just like their dad had taught her.

When had her little brother surpassed her?

She snorted. He was hardly "little" any longer. He was twelve years her junior, yes, but he'd grown into a large man, like their father had been: tall and wide, the same riveting gaze and shock of unruly hair. Liam and Áine had been six and eight respectively when their parents had died in the car accident; their memories of their parents were faint at best. Sometimes she wondered if that was a bad thing, not to remember your parents. Today, seeing Liam and being reminded so sharply of their father, she was glad he and Áine couldn't remember, because it still hurt.

Neither did she want them to feel the crushing pain of heartbreak like she had when she'd broken off her engagement. She knew she was protective of Áine and Liam, but that was the way she was wired.

Apparently, that was the way Liam was wired too. She couldn't believe he'd come up with this mad plan to help her.

Before she made any kind of decision regarding

what to do, including ordering a wedding cake, she picked up the phone to call Evan Ward, her private investigator. Better to have some information on Henriette first. She may have met her when Liam worked at Papillon, but she didn't remember who the girl was.

She and Evan had known each other a long time—over twenty years. He'd retired from British special forces young, after an injury, and had gone into business for himself. Security, of course. She'd been put in touch with him shortly after he'd just started working in the private sector. Aside from her family, he was the only person she trusted without question.

He'd saved her from making the biggest mistake of her life.

She'd been twenty-seven, about to be married, when the pandemic had put a halt to the wedding. She'd remembered being disappointed that she'd had to postpone it, but then Evan had come to her with a dossier on her fiancé. Evan had said things happened for a reason, so when he was given the window of opportunity, he ran with it. He wanted her to have all the information on the man she was going to marry, so she could make an informed decision about whether she wanted to reschedule the wedding.

Once she'd read the report, she'd canceled all the arrangements and flushed the engagement ring the bastard had given her.

One time, she'd asked Evan how he'd known to check, and he'd replied, "I had a feeling."

Ever since, she'd trusted his feelings implicitly. She trusted *him*, and trust wasn't something she gave very easily to anyone aside from Áine and Liam.

Evan had prevented her from making a mistake once. Maybe he'd help save her from making a mistake here too.

Before she called him, she steeled herself. That first moment she heard his voice always struck her. It was deep and masculine and hit her in just the right places. Not that she ever let on to that.

Or that fact that she found him *very* attractive. He was absolutely gorgeous, and the years had only made him more so. Chiseled, direct, intelligent. He had dark hair and dark eyes that noticed everything. And his hands... They were the kind of hands you wanted to feel all over your body.

But it was his character that drew her most. He was kind to everyone, and he listened. He never made her feel silly or insignificant, and he always delivered what he promised. He always told her the truth, even when he thought the truth might hurt. And then he always made sure she was okay after.

She could marry him.

"No, I couldn't," she mumbled, shaking her head. He was off-limits. She wasn't going to jeopardize a relationship she valued so much with a cockamamie idea, so she suppressed the feelings and placed the call to him.

"It's Saturday," Evan said the moment he picked up his private line.

"Have I caught you at a bad time?" She knew he wasn't married, but it suddenly occurred to her that he could have someone over. Over the past twenty years, they'd become more than colleagues—they'd become friends of sorts. She would have known if he had someone, right?

"If it were a bad time, I wouldn't have answered the phone," he replied.

"You always answer when I call," she pointed out.

"Precisely."

She tapped her fingers on her desk, trying to figure out the subtext on that one pointed word. "Why do I get the feeling that you're saying something I'm not understanding?"

"Because you're a smart woman." There was a rustle in the background, and then he said, "What do you need, Maeve?"

"I need a background check."

"Potential new hire or business associate?"

"A romantic interest."

There was an audible pause on the other end of the line.

"For my brother," she clarified quickly. "I want to make sure the woman he's interested in isn't hiding anything."

He made a sound, something like a hum. It was a sexy sound, an intimate sort of sound that made her flush.

But, like always, she pulled her thoughts away from anything too personal, because they were colleagues and she never crossed the professional line she'd drawn. She was a woman; the moment she dallied with any man in her sphere, all her credentials would be lost. A man could have sex with whomever he wanted and he was a stud in the boardroom. If a woman acted that way, she was called names and her leadership was questioned.

Evan never crossed it either, even though sometimes, alone in the dark of night, she almost wished he'd try.

Maeve shifted in her seat. She wondered what Áine would say about her lusting after one man while thinking of marrying a stranger. Áine would probably prescribe her a vibrator and tell her to take a long vacation. Her sister had always been very practical.

"Her name?" he said, oblivious of the sexy thoughts she was trying not to have.

"Henriette Buchanan. She lives in London."

"Occupation?"

"Pastry chef."

He hummed again. "Do you have any other details about her?"

"Only that she and Liam worked together at Papillon in London before he left last year."

"Got it." There was a rustle of paper and then silence. "Is there anything else you need, Maeve?"

Her womanly parts tingled at the question even though she knew he didn't mean it like *that*. Still she couldn't help a hum of her own as she pictured the intense look he got in his eyes, focused all on her.

"Maeve?"

"No, that's it for now," she said.

"I'll call you back." He hung up.

She set her mobile down, used to his abruptness.

It was less than five minutes before he rang back. "Maeve, the girl is so clean that there's barely anything on her. She graduated in architecture and after a few years at a top London firm, she went to the Cordon Bleu to become a pastry chef. Her father is Phineas Buchanan, artist and restorer, and her mother is Viola Summerhill, owner of a well-respected art gallery in London."

Maeve sat up. "She's a Summerhill? Related to Beatrice Summerhill?"

"Yes. Her niece."

She respected the hell of out Beatrice Summerhill. She didn't know the woman well, but she'd looked up to her all these years. "You'll send what you have on Henriette?"

"Yes, but like I said, it's not much. That said, she feels genuine."

Maeve eased back, relieved. "Thank you, Evan."

"Where are you?" he asked, sounding like he was settling into a seat.

"Westport." Her home was up the coast from Westport, on a nice bit of land on the sea. She'd bought it this year. It made sense, since Liam decided to move to Westport to open his restaurant—she could go back and forth between him and Áine in Dublin easily. And she'd heard rumors that the CEO of Buckley Sinks & Taps was thinking of selling, so she wanted to be in place to make a move.

"You spend more and more time there," Evan said. "You like it."

"It's close to my brother. And it's peaceful." She looked out the window. Life felt simpler here.

Life.

She shook her head. She'd been questioning her life choices lately, all because of Walsh and his damned ideas about what a person's life should look like.

She wondered what Evan would think if she told him about that. She wondered how he felt about *his* life. He was a couple years older than her and he'd never been married either.

Instead, she asked, "Where do you go when you need refuge? Do you have a batcave you keep?"

He chuckled. "You know me so well."

When he laughed like that it did things to her.

"I have a place not far away from where you are," he said.

"Really?" She sat up, frowning. "Why didn't I know that?"

"You never asked."

"Does that mean if I ask you'll tell me?"

"Ask and find out," he replied in a low voice.

What did that tone mean? She was in business; she studied peoples' mannerisms and voices for subtleties and clues to their inner thoughts. Evan's tone was intimate and not one that he often used with her. "I can ask any question, and you'll answer me?" she asked.

"Yes."

"What happened to the international man of mystery? You normally keep things close to the vest."

"We've known each other long enough, don't you think, Maeve? We've always been honest with each other. I don't have anything to hide from you."

"There's a difference between honest and personal."

"You don't do personal."

She sat up straighter. This day was getting stranger by the minute. "You say that in a way that—"

When she didn't finish her thought, he said, "In what way?"

Like he wanted *personal* to be an option. "Any question?" she asked doubtfully.

"Yes."

She arched her brow. *Well then.* "Boxers or briefs?"

"Neither," he replied.

She closed her eyes, pressing her fingers to the bridge of her nose. *Don't imagine that.*

She couldn't help it. She could see it so clearly, unbuttoning his pants and reaching in to feel silky skin and hard flesh. She flushed, knowing she shouldn't think about him like that. He was off-limits.

He chuckled again as if he knew where her naughty mind went. "I'll talk to you later, Maeve," he said, and then he hung up.

She sat back and stared at the phone. What just happened?

CHAPTER 4

*H*enri assembled the last of the macarons she made for her parents and arranged them on a plate. She would have made génoise to keep her skills honed, but her mum loved macarons, and her dad loved anything that brought her mum joy. She'd made salted caramel. The flavor matched her mood: salty and a little singed at the edges.

This morning she'd found out that she'd lost the Watford-Roberts contract.

She wanted to tell herself it was okay, that it was just a wedding, but she couldn't make herself believe that. The media coverage would have put her business firmly on the map, and losing that was catastrophic. She had no idea when another wedding that socially important would come along.

So she'd decided to meditate, her way: to put on her

earbuds and make something that made her happy. Today that was macarons for her parents.

She'd given up her flat when she'd gone to Lyon for the apprenticeship. When she'd come back, her parents had invited her to stay with them. She'd expected it'd be for a month or so till she found a new apartment, but here she was, six months later, still living with them.

They didn't mind—she knew that. In fact, they liked having her around. But she didn't take it for granted, and she liked doing small things that showed them how much she was grateful for them.

After she tidied the kitchen, she still felt at a loss. Her mum was out, but her dad was upstairs in his atelier, so she decided to go talk to him. He gave the best pep talks. Folding her apron and putting it away, she jogged up the stairs to the third floor.

Her mother had owned the house from her previous marriage, but when she and Henri's father had gotten together, he'd moved in and they'd made it their own. They'd converted the attic into a workspace for him, with skylights and all the space a painter and restorer needed.

There were three places Henri felt at home: her kitchen at Vivi's showroom, her father's flat in Paris where she'd stayed as she attended the Cordon Bleu, and his atelier here in this house.

Henri had happy memories of being in his atelier. She'd read that a person couldn't remember anything before the age of three, but she knew she remembered sitting at his feet as a baby. She could feel the wooden toy he'd carved for her in her hands; she could see the sunlight filtering in; and she could hear him singing to her softly in French. She used to take naps on his couch. After she'd become an architect, she used to sprawl in there and work on her designs, and in the past six months she'd done the same with her cake designs.

He did less restoration work these days, taking only special projects that came his way. Painting held his focus, to her mother's delight, though she always insisted that he didn't have to sell his artwork through her gallery.

Of course he did, though. Finn Buchanan and Viola Summerhill were partners in every sense of the word.

Henri stopped at the top of the second flight of stairs, looking into the atelier. The afternoon sun streamed in, illuminating the dust in the air. Jazz played from an old record player, and she recognized the music as Marcel's, an old friend of her father's from Paris, who'd passed away when she was little.

Papa stood in front of a large canvas on an easel, hand flying with energetic brushstrokes. Even from behind, he looked as vital as ever. His dark hair, the same color as hers, had a lot of gray in it now, but otherwise he hadn't aged. Neither had her mother, for that matter.

There was comfort that they'd be around a long time.

He turned and looked at her, a smile lighting his face the way it always did when he saw her. "Darling," he said, lowering his paintbrush. Then his brow furrowed, and he *really* looked at her. "What's wrong?"

She sighed. "How can you tell, just like that?"

"You're my daughter," he said as if she were daft. He tossed the brush onto his worktable and picked up a rag to wipe his hands. "Before you were born, I promised myself I'd know every one of your expressions, so that I could help you with whatever you needed."

"Oh, Papa," she said, sighing again. "Have I told you how much I love you?"

"I can always stand to hear it again." He nodded to the couch. "But first tell me what has you upset. You were fine at breakfast."

"I found out I lost another cake bid," she said, dropping onto the cushioned seat. "They decided to go with a local bakery that does the most pedestrian cakes you can imagine. Marks & Spencer does better cakes than this baker. Their marriage is doomed."

Her father chuckled as he joined her. "I've always wondered what you would say about the wedding cake your mother and I had."

She'd seen pictures of it. It'd been simple but luxurious, one large sheet with four layers covered in fresh flowers. She, of course, hadn't been able to try it firsthand, but she fancied that she'd shared it *in utero* since her mum had been pregnant at the time. "Aunt Bea said it tasted the sweetest, because Mum was the happiest she'd ever been. I believe her."

Papa ran his hand down her ponytail. "I don't think you're just upset because those people's marriage is doomed. What really has you worried?"

"That I'll have to go back to working in someone else's kitchen. That I'm not going to make it. That I'll have to live in my old room forever. That I'll have to live an ordinary life making plain desserts."

"Darling, of all the things I've worried about concerning you, none of them have ever been that you won't have what you want," he said with calm certainty.

"It doesn't feel like that right now." She made a face. "Not even baking helped, and usually that cheers me up."

He lifted his nose, smelling the air. "Did you make macarons?"

"Salted caramel," she affirmed.

"Your mum's favorite." Papa chuckled, a twinkle in his eyes. "I should have asked you to move home sooner."

She sighed. "I remember when Chloe had to come home to stay when she lost her job, before she met Oliver. She was so upset about it, but I was twelve and didn't understand why she wasn't happy, because I thought it was great that she was home. But now I get it. She felt like she wasn't getting anywhere either.

It's a terrible feeling thinking that you're failing at life."

Her father held her chin, raising her gaze to his. "You are not failing, Henriette Buchanan. You're setting the foundation for your future. It doesn't happen overnight, and you don't want to scrimp. Decide what you want and don't settle for anything less. Do you need me to visualize with you?"

That was why she loved her papa so much. "Yes, please."

He closed his eyes, his brow faintly furrowed. She watched him for a moment, the way she always had when they did this together, before she closed her eyes too. She pictured what she wanted: a vast kitchen, a beautiful tower of a cake on the counter, an open magazine with her picture in it. She pictured a man coming up behind her, his arms stealing around her waist as he kissed her neck. Then, to her surprise, a couple little kids ran through the kitchen, laughing, throwing themselves at their legs.

She opened her eyes and blinked. That was a surprise.

"Did you see it, darling?" Papa asked.

"Yes."

"Then it'll happen." He nodded his head once, definitively, as if it would be because he declared it so.

Her father would never lie to her, so him telling her it'd happen fortified her. She scooted closer, wound her arms around his, and burrowed her head in his chest.

He smelled like oil paint and bay rum from his soap. She inhaled him, drawing comfort from the familiarity and his strength. "Thank you, Papa. I'm so grateful for you."

"I thank your mother every day for giving me Chloe and you," he murmured into her hair. He kissed the top of her head. "You're a masterpiece. Don't ever forget that."

The sound of the floor creaking had them both looking up.

Her mother leaned in the doorway of the atelier, her eyes warm with love as she watched them. She was wearing a body-hugging dress in a blue that matched her eyes, its neckline high and adorned by a simple diamond pendant. Her hair was piled on top of her head, a few wisps curling at her nape. She looked elegant and sexy.

Based on the low hum her father gave, he thought so too.

Rolling her eyes, Henri stood up. "I should go so you two can *take a nap*," she said wryly.

Her mother laughed lightly. "We can *nap* later."

"She baked you macarons," her father said, sprawling back on the couch like he was at his leisure.

Her mum arched her brow as she went to him. "Is that a new code word?"

Henri's mobile rang. She lifted it out of her coat pocket and frowned at the screen. It was a private number, blocked. Given that there were only a handful of people who called her, she figured she should answer this. "I think I need to take this. I'll call out before I come back," she said, shooting her parents a look.

They were already snuggled together, grinning like they were teenagers about to be left alone. Secretly delighted, she shook her head as she left the studio, closing the door emphatically. She could hear them laughing as she sat on the stairs.

"This is Henri," she said into her mobile.

"Henriette Buchanan?"

She arched her brow. "Yes. Can I help you?"

"I'd like to order a wedding cake. My name is Maeve Buckley. My brother Liam gave me your number."

"Liam." Henri's breath caught in her throat. Thinking about him made her go hot and shivery. She hadn't heard from him since the last text exchange they'd had. She'd hoped that she hadn't pushed him away. This seemed like a good sign. You didn't recommend someone for a job if you were done with her, especially one for family. "He used to talk about you and your sister all the time when we worked together. We met a couple times, I think."

"I went in as often as I could. I like to support my brother's ventures. I understand you're Beatrice Summerhill's niece?"

"Yes, she and my mother are the best of friends. You know Aunt Bea?" she asked with surprise.

"We've crossed paths in business. I admire her greatly."

"It's a small world." She couldn't believe Liam's sister was calling her to order a cake. She shook her head, ready to accept the order just based on the fact that she'd most definitely get to see Liam again. "When is your wedding?"

"I need the cake on the twentieth."

Henri blinked. "That's in a couple weeks."

"I realize that may be difficult to accommodate with your schedule, but I feel like we can come to a mutually beneficial arrangement to expedite the affair," the woman said very smoothly. "I need a large cake, for two hundred people, with different levels. I've seen some of the photos from your online portfolio, and I'm leaning toward an original design with at least five levels decorated with lace icing."

That would require a lot of man hours. In two weeks... "You're in London?"

"Ireland. In Mayo, just outside Westport. Close to where Liam's restaurant is."

She often drove to see Chloe and Oliver in Cork. Westport probably wasn't much farther away. She supposed she could drive there so she could take her pans. "I'd have to charge travel and lodging in addition to the normal cake fees." She did a quick estimate in her mind, trying to come up with something fair that would still cover her costs. She said it, adding, "Of course, that's an estimate that could change depending on the complexity of the cake and design you select."

"That sounds reasonable," the woman said, as if spending a small fortune in sugar and icing were part of her normal routine. "Then you're available for the period of time, Henriette?"

"Yes, and please call me Henri."

"Henri, then. And I'm Maeve. You'll stay at my estate, of course, and you'll have access to the kitchen here. If you need anything special, Liam can help you acquire it. He knows all the vendors in the area."

"Who's catering your wedding?"

There was a pause. Then Maeve said, "I'm planning on just having cake and a champagne reception. If I decide to have anything else, Liam will do it. I trust that'll be okay for you?"

Okay? It was like Christmas come early. Working with him had been the happiest thing about being at Papillon. "That's brilliant. He's an excellent chef."

"I think so," she said, a bit of warmth coming into her voice. "If you need anything, contact him. I imagine you'll see him constantly when you're here."

There *was* a god. She looked up at the ceiling and mouthed, *Thank you.* "It'll be nice to catch up," she said, as if her knickers weren't melting at the thought. "I'll need to come right away"—she cleared her throat—"so that we can do a tasting. I'll send you my preliminary questions, and if you can return them right away, I can plan the cakes that I think would suit you and your fiancé. If I can be there by Wednesday, do you think you'd both be available for a tasting on Thursday?"

"Both of us have to be there?"

Henri frowned at the change in the woman's tone of voice. "That's my one rule, that the couple do the tasting together. The cake is a very intimate thing, a tangible expression of the flavor of your relationship. It's important, and I like to make sure both the bride and groom are represented in the final product."

There was another pause, and then Maeve said, "You mean that."

"I wouldn't say it if I didn't. The cake sets the tone for the entire marriage."

"I'll make it work," the woman said.

Henri arched her brow at the resoluteness of that statement, but she figured that if Maeve was acquainted with Aunt Bea, then she was a busy woman, and, therefore, her fiancé would be too.

Still, some things were important, and she wasn't willing to budge on this point. "I'll send you my questionnaire, as well as a contract, and expect them back by end of day tomorrow. I'll include the estimate, though I'll adjust that depending on the cake you two ultimately decide you want."

"Brilliant. I'm looking forward to meeting you, Henri," Maeve said.

"Likewise." She hung up the phone and stared at it. Then she gave a mighty yawp. "I'm coming back into the atelier," she called to her parents as she hopped up.

Opening the door, she peeked inside, just in case. They still sat on the couch, wrapped in each other. Her mum looked flushed, but at least they had all their clothes on properly.

"That was a good call?" her dad asked.

"The visualization worked." She grinned. "I got a big order, for a very fancy cake. And it's for someone Aunt Bea knows."

"Who?" her mum asked.

"Maeve Buckley."

Her mother blinked. "Bea's mentioned her. A very successful businesswoman. Very smart."

"She's getting married in a week and a half."

"I didn't realize that. She has wide-reaching connections. That should be good for you."

She hadn't considered that. Added to the cake and seeing Liam again, it promised to be a sweet couple of weeks.

"Buckley," her dad said suddenly, his brow furrowing. "Isn't that the last name of the chef you worked for at Papillon?"

"Yes, it's his sister." She felt her cheeks start to flush and she tried to downplay it. "Liam recommended me for the job. I'll need to go to Ireland this week."

"Hmm," was all Papa said, though he looked at her like he suspected there was more to the story.

There wasn't more to the story, and she didn't think there would be. She was going for a commission; she wouldn't do anything that made her look unprofessional, and Liam wouldn't either.

But she couldn't wait to see him. She felt like jumping up and down with excitement.

She waved at her parents as she headed out of the atelier. "I need to make a list of equipment I need to take with me. You can carry on."

Her mother snorted. Her father grumbled, but Henri didn't hear him. She was already making a mental list of everything she'd need to take with her.

She did a quick inventory of her underthings, just in case, and winced. She should have listened to Vivi when she said she needed a few sexy pieces to wear beneath her chef's togs.

CHAPTER 5

"*T*able six wants another lamb entrée."

Liam looked up from where he was plating his version of a ham and cheese sandwich, made with rashers on brioche, which he'd baked fresh earlier. He glared at Marie, his server. "What was wrong with the one they ordered before?"

"It was so delicious they had to have it again." She shrugged as she added the slip to the line of orders.

He eased his expression. "Tell them to leave a favorable review online and I'll expedite it."

Marie grinned as she picked up the appetizers for another table. "Is that the way of it?"

"Yes." He jerked his chin toward the door. "Go before the *fois gras* gets cold."

She rolled her eyes but got on with it. When the door to the floor opened, the kitchen was flooded with the sounds of people enjoying themselves. Liam smiled, taking a moment to enjoy the sound before returning to the rashers and cheese sandwiches he was assembling.

He had a group that had reserved his tasting room a couple months ago with a request for a seven-course chef's menu. He wanted to try out the elegant little sandwiches on them, thinking he might add them to his appetizer menu.

Henriette used to love when he made her these sandwiches. She'd been the one to suggest adding a bit of his homemade marmalade to it, to round the flavors and give it depth. She'd been spot-on, but then she always was.

He wondered what she was doing tonight.

He wondered how he was going to approach seeing if she'd be interested in him.

He wondered if she could be happy living in Westport.

He shook his head. If he could engineer a seven-course meal, he could engineer romance and convince her that there was more to life than the hustle and bustle of London. He just needed whatever he did to be fit for a queen. *His* queen: Henriette.

How was he going to romance her? He had absolutely no idea.

Before he made extensive plans in that direction, he needed to talk to Maeve to see what she'd decided. He hadn't wanted to push—pushing Maeve never yielded the results you'd expect—but it'd been a couple days since they'd talked. She had to have made a decision by now.

Finishing the little sandwiches and plating them, he dinged the bell for them to be picked up, checked on his sous chef and the rest of his team to make sure they had everything they needed, and then went to his office in the back.

Getting out his mobile, he texted his sister.

Liam
Have you decided?

Maeve
I hired her officially today. She's coming Wednesday.

He sat on the edge of his desk, oddly relieved. And excited, because he was going to see Henriette again in two days.

He needed to arrange for Deirdre, his sous chef, to take over the restaurant so he could take the time while Henriette was here to be with her.

His text buzzed.

Maeve
What does how my bedroom looks have to do with cake?

He grinned as he replied.

Liam
Henri thinks a person's private area says a lot about who they are.

Maeve
And what does that have to do with cake?

Liam
When she bakes, it's intimate. She needs to understand who you are.

Maeve
I thought I could order the cake to get her here and then have a few more days to decide on the rest of the plan, but she needs my fiancé here for the cake tasting.

Maeve
What am I going to do about that?

Liam
Didn't you say Dad used to say if something was important to you, if you felt it deep in your heart, you'd do everything in your power to make it reality?

Maeve
He did.

Liam

Don't you want his company back?

Maeve

Yes.

Liam

So what are you willing to do?

Maeve

Scrounge around for a husband, what else?

Maeve

Damn you.

Liam

This is going to work.

Maeve

If not, Áine can get us a discount for a double room at a nice sanatorium.

Chuckling, he put his mobile away and went back to the kitchen to start the fifth course in the tasting menu.

As the night was winding down, Andy popped his head into the kitchen. "I hear this is the place where a man can come get something halfway decent to eat."

Wiping his hands on a towel, Liam jerked his head

to the small table in the corner. "Sit your arse down and I'll find some scraps for you."

With a wry grin, Andy went to the sink, washed his hands, and then helped himself to a beer from the refrigerator before taking a seat. He laid the book he had tucked under his arm on the tabletop and set the beer next to it, opening the other refrigerator for a chilled glass.

Liam had met Andy through Maeve, when he'd needed some work done in his cottage. He'd contracted the plumber to take care of some issues with the pipes, and he'd been so fair and efficient that Liam had hired him to take care of the restaurant as well. They'd become fast friends.

All men had a code, and Liam understood Andy's. Which was why he'd suggested to Maeve that she marry him—Andy would never hurt her. Maybe he'd talk to Maeve about reconsidering Andy.

Andy decanted his beer into the glass and took a long draught. Sitting back, he crossed his legs and lifted his glass to Liam. "Sláinte."

The plumber came into the restaurant a couple times a week, always alone, always sitting at the table in the kitchen. He usually ordered the steak, though Liam did different preparations of it so it wouldn't bore his friend. "Your usual?" Liam asked.

"Surprise me," Andy said, opening his book.

Liam shook his head. You wouldn't know it to look at Andy, but he had an extensive library of first editions at his cottage. When Andy wasn't fixing pipes and such, he was reading. He read more than any other person Liam had ever met, including Áine—which was saying something. Andy always had a dusty old tome with him. One time, Liam had asked him what he preferred to read, and Andy had said, "Everything."

Liam checked the dessert and cheese courses for the tasting room and then began making dinner for Andy and himself. He put together a trio of sandwiches for them: the rashers and cheese, a hot roast beef, and a spicy pork belly with pickled apple. For the side, he made crisps and a celery salad with a light anchovy dressing. He took the two heaping plates to join Andy.

His friend closed his book and surveyed his plate. "You may be shite as a handyman, but in the kitchen you're magic."

"You're such a charmer." Shaking his head, Liam fetched silverware and a couple beers, with a glass for himself.

Andy took a bite of the first sandwich and groaned. "Brilliant," he said after he'd swallowed. "You putting this on the menu?"

"Thinking of it." He began with the roast beef. There was missing something. He frowned, wondering what it was. If he had Henriette try it, she'd know right away. She'd probably say something outlandish, like cinnamon—and she'd be right.

They'd spent hours together in the kitchen. He knew details about her that he didn't know about his own sisters. Romancing her should be easy, but he'd been trying on ideas for the past couple days and he hadn't come up with anything compelling. She was coming Wednesday, presumably until the "wedding" so that didn't give him very much time to woo her.

"You're quiet for a change," Andy said, looking at him over the rim of his pint glass. "Problem?"

"Not exactly." He chewed on a crisp, pondering Andy. "If you were going to go on a romantic date, where would it be?"

"The bookstore," he answered instantly.

Liam arched his brow. "Let's assume the person I'm trying to romance isn't bookish like you."

"I guess not everyone's perfect." Andy grinned. He pointed at the spot on his plate that had held his salad. "This celery thing was, though. How do you do it? It was damned celery; it shouldn't have been that delicious, but I'm tempted to ask you for more."

He pushed his plate closer to Andy's and transferred half his salad to his friend's. "I'm serious. I need some ideas for romantic outings."

"If you're coming to me, you must be desperate." Andy popped a crisp into his mouth and chewed, his gaze faraway in thought. Then he shrugged. "What does she like to do? Take her to do it."

Henriette liked to bake, and she liked to experience new flavors. But they did that as part of their jobs. He wasn't certain it'd be a path to romance.

Unless…

He sat up. He knew where to take her. He picked up his glass and held it up to Andy. "You, my friend, are a genius."

"I know." Andy clinked his glass and took a sip. "But I'd still take her to a bookstore."

CHAPTER 6

*M*aeve paced back and forth in the kitchen. She'd actually agreed to go with Liam's mad plan. She'd ordered the wedding cake. Now she needed to get engaged.

Groaning, she pressed her hand to her forehead. Where was she going to get a fiancé in three days?

Where was she going to get a fiancé that she could *marry* in three days?

She mentally ran through the men she knew. She was used to coming up with a "plus one" for events that she went to, but she kept her time with those men in public. She didn't trust them enough to invite them to her home, much less into her bed.

Not that whoever she married would be in her bed. It'd be a marriage of convenience.

There had to be someone who'd benefit from a short-term marriage, who wouldn't be a threat to her bank accounts. She just couldn't think of anyone who fit the bill.

But she knew who'd be able to get her a list of viable candidates: Evan Ward.

She winced, imagining his reaction when she asked him to make a list of men she'd be able to marry. But he was the only person she trusted to give her his unfiltered opinion. He'd protected her all these years. He wouldn't let her down.

At least imagining his face at her request would give her relief from imagining him not wearing boxers or briefs. *That* had been occupying her mind since she'd talked to him last.

The electric kettle on the counter began to hiss, an explosion of steam coming from its spout. She felt like that—like she could explode. Exhaling, she turned to make her tea.

She heard the heavy steps of work boots coming her way. She turned right as Andrew loomed in the kitchen doorway. "Maeve, I've done all I can for your shower, short of ripping out the pipes and replacing them all with ones that are up to spec."

She crossed her arms. "I can't believe the pipes aren't up to spec."

He shrugged. "They installed narrow pipes because it was less expensive. They're fine, unless you put in a showerhead like the one you put in there. Then they can't handle the flow of water."

Because the showerhead that had been in there before had barely trickled water. "I like it strong."

Evan would have come back with a clever quip, but Andrew's expression didn't even change. "Then you're going to have to live with the drainage issue unless you want me to rip out your pipes and replace them properly."

She made a face at him. "You spent two days here, and that's all you can give me?"

"No, I can give you this too." He held out a piece of paper to her.

"What is it?" she asked as she took it.

"Your bill." He grinned at her, giving her a saucy wink as he left.

Shaking her head, she took the bill—and her tea—and strode down the hall to her office. She closed the door and paced some more. Why had she told Liam she'd do this?

Because she loved him and he wanted Henriette, so she'd do whatever she could in her power to facilitate that. Also because he loved her and was trying to help her get what she wanted.

And she wanted Buckley Sinks & Taps back.

If only arranged marriages were still in vogue.

What she needed to do was have some choices vetted. Which meant she needed to call Evan.

What would Evan say to her request?

She winced.

Trying to come up with the words that would make

her request logical and not completely mental, she picked up her mobile.

Evan answered on the first ring. "Twice in as many days, Maeve?"

Her arms broke out in goose pimples at the low intimacy of his voice. "I need to hire you. I need help with a situation."

"Do you need protection?" he asked, instantly business. "I made sure your home in Westport has a decent security system. Are you using it?"

"No. Yes. I mean, everything is fine. Mostly." She took a deep breath. "I need a fiancé."

"Hold the line, Maeve."

She heard him murmur something to someone. He must be at his office. She waited, listening to the ambient sounds as he seemed to be walking. Then the background noises stopped, as though he stepped into his office. She pictured him there, the stark luxury of the leather and wood furniture that decorated it, the way he always loosened his tie and undid his top button when he was in there alone, which she only knew because he'd admitted it when she'd caught him unaware one time.

"Okay, repeat what you said to me," he said.

"I need a fiancé by Thursday." Then, to be clear, she added, "And I need to get married in two weeks."

The stillness on the other end of the line was deafening.

She sat down, frowning. "Are you going to say something?"

"Why do you need to get married?" he asked in his direct way.

"Because I want to buy a company."

"Explain, Maeve," Evan said.

"When I was eighteen, I sold my father's manufacturing business, Buckley Sinks & Taps."

"To raise capital to be able to raise your brother and sister," he said. "I've always admired you for that."

"You have?" She blinked in surprise. Shaking her head, she focused. "It's being offered for sale in two weeks, and I want it back, but the current head won't sell it to me because I'm not married. He wants to sell to someone traditional."

"Being married doesn't make you traditional. I have married clients who have wild lifestyles."

"Do red rooms require security?" she asked, smiling for the first time all day.

"Surveillance sweeps," he said, humor in his voice. "Buying your father's old company is so important that you'd consider marriage?"

She swallowed the emotion in her throat and told him the truth. "To anyone else it's just sinks and faucets. To my father, it was a dream to show people life didn't have to be beige, that life didn't have to be mundane, even if you didn't have much. It was his way of making a difference in people's lives, and I sold that dream."

When Evan spoke, his voice was quiet. "Maeve, you were eighteen. You had no choice."

"It doesn't mean I can't make it right." She closed her eyes. Thirty years, and she could still feel the guilt and sadness as she signed her name on the purchase agreement. It'd been as devasting as the day she'd buried their parents.

"Why Thursday?" Evan asked suddenly.

"Henri is coming to sample cakes on Thursday."

"Henriette Buchanan."

"Yes. She's the one making my wedding cake."

"I thought you wanted her researched because your brother is interested in her?"

Maeve dropped onto the settee by the window. "I did. Liam came up with this mad, mad plan. I get married to enable my acquisition of Buckley Sinks & Taps, Henri comes here to make a fancy cake and get the notoriety from baking for Maeve Buckley's wedding so her business takes off, and Liam gets his lady. It's all worked out. I just need a man who'd be willing to marry me."

There was more silence on the other end. Then Evan began to chuckle.

She closed her eyes, the deep sound of his low laughter hitting her in places nothing but herself had touched in forever. Then she forced herself to adopt a strict tone. "This may be amusing to you, but I'm quite serious."

"So you've concocted this plan—"

"No, my brother concocted this plan," she repeated. "I'm just going along with it because I'm as daft as he is."

Evan chuckled some more. "I've heard a lot of unbelievable things in my line of work, but this takes the cake, so to speak."

"This isn't funny," she said. Absurd, certainly, but not funny. "Are you going to help me vet a husband or not?"

"I already know who I'd suggest."

She blinked in surprise. "You do?"

"Yes," he said, his voice firm with belief. "You need someone who'd be willing to sign a contract to protect your wealth, preferably with wealth equal to yours. You need someone who has enough gravitas in society, to be seen as worthy of you. You need someone discreet, who'd respect you and your reputation. You need someone who can benefit from a marriage like this."

Of course he'd have the situation analyzed and distilled in the span of minutes. He was the smartest man she'd ever known, sharper than even herself. "And who is this paragon of a man, and why haven't you introduced him to me sooner?"

"You know him, Maeve. It's me."

If she weren't sitting down, she would have fallen over. "Sorry?"

"If you need to marry someone, marry me." His voice was soft but steady. "Do you trust me?"

"Of course," she said instantly, not having to think about it.

"Then marry me. I'm successful. We run in the same circles. We've publicly known each for a long time and are seen together often, so it won't look strange that the wedding is so sudden. They'll just think we've been private about our relationship. It'll quiet the occasional conjecture about my personal life as well. If you're determined to do this, I'm your best candidate."

She shook her head, unable to process. "You'd marry me?"

"Yes," he said, unwavering.

She'd been trying to imagine having a husband, but she hadn't been able to see it. She could see Evan in her bed *very* clearly. She just wasn't sure that was a good thing.

Her heart pounded. She felt sweat break out on her skin, like it had when she'd signed her very first multi-million-dollar deal when she was twenty-four. She put a hand to her forehead. There was no going back if she said yes.

But she didn't want to say no, for more reasons than just her dad's company.

"Maeve?" Evan prompted.

She took a deep breath and said, "Yes, I'll marry you, Evan."

CHAPTER 7

"*A*untie Henri, Auntie Henri!"

Henri looked up from the boot, where she was loading her bag back into the rental car, to see her ten-year-old niece Lily running her way.

Given that Oliver bred roses, she'd once asked them why they'd named their daughter Lily. Chloe had just shrugged and said it was the less obvious choice.

"Auntie Henri," the girl repeated, throwing her arms around Henri's waist, making her stagger a bit. For being so slender, Lily was surprisingly stout. Chloe said Lily got her earth from her father; Henri didn't doubt that.

That was the only thing Lily got from her father, though. Her blue eyes and blond hair were just like her mum's. Obviously, Henri didn't know Chloe when she was a little girl, but whenever she looked at Lily, she thought Chloe must have looked just like that at her age.

"Daddy said that we can visit Mr. Casey's horses today." Her niece jumped up and down in her excitement. "Do you want to come with us?"

"I can't, poppet." She tugged on Lily's braid. "I have to go on to Westport today to bake a cake."

Lily's eyes got round. "I *like* cake. Can I come with you?"

Chloe came out of the house, a fond smile on her face as she looked at them. "Lily love, your Aunt Henri has to leave."

"I know," Lily called. "I want to go with her. She's making a cake."

Chloe laughed as she joined them, sliding her arm around Henri's waist. "It's going to be a grand cake too."

Henri leaned into her sister's embrace for a moment. "Lily, I'll stop back here and bake you a special cake. How's that?"

"Yes!" She danced around, her thin arms flailing like the muppet she was. "I'm going to tell Daddy."

They watched her run to the path that led to Oliver's greenhouse, screaming for her dad. Henri shook her head. "Good thing you don't have neighbors."

Chloe laughed, then she sobered. "I was so quiet when I was her age. I promised myself she could express as much as she wanted to."

"You're good parents, Chloe." Henri kissed her cheek.

Chloe escorted her toward the driver's side of the car. "You don't need to bake her a cake when you come back. Just bring a slice if you can."

"I promised her a cake. I'll bake her one, if it's okay to come stay on my way back." She'd stopped to spend the night with Chloe and her family, partly to break up her trip and partly because she just missed her sister. They'd stayed up late, drinking wine and talking about boys—something they'd never gotten to do because of their age difference. Usually, she only did that with Vivi. It'd been nice. She told her sister about Liam and how excited she was to see him. Chloe, of course, only talked about Oliver.

"You're always welcome here. For as long as you want." Chloe leaned on the open door. "Do you need anything before you go?"

"No." She hugged her sister.

Chloe embraced her tight, and then she held her at arm's length. "You know I expect status reports regarding Liam."

The butterflies in her stomach took flight as she got into the car. "I don't know that he's interested in anything more than collaborating on desserts."

"If he's been texting you all these months, he's interested. I bet Vivienne would tell you the same."

She made a face. "Vivi has all sorts of advice."

Chloe laughed. "I can't wait to hear what she has to

say. Didn't you say that she's the one who started calling Liam 'Hot Chef'? I wish I'd thought of that. It's apt."

"Vivi has a way with words."

"It's truth. I remember meeting him last year when we were visiting Mum and Finn and Oliver took me to Papillon. He definitely made a chef's hat look good." Chloe waved her hand, like she was trying to cool herself.

Grinning, Henri buckled her seat belt. "Wish me luck."

"You don't need luck. You've got this, the cake and the man." Chloe closed the car door and waved as Henri drove off toward Westport.

It was a four-hour drive from Cork to where Maeve lived in Mayo. Henri thought about the questionnaire that Maeve had emailed back to her and the preferences she'd stated. It was going to be challenging, doing the cake she wanted in the short amount of time. Usually the amount of detail work for a cake decorated that elaborately took at least a couple weeks of prep work and sometimes a helper. She didn't have a helper or that kind of time.

She thought Liam would know someone, or maybe he'd even help in a pinch—they used to work so seamlessly together. The thought that they might be in the kitchen again, in tandem, made her so happy.

As she drove, she thought about complementary flavor combinations for the sample cakes. She'd been flirting with saffron in her mind for a bit. It wasn't conventional at all, but given the questionnaire and what she'd found out about Maeve Buckley from Aunt Bea, the woman wasn't conventional. After all, she'd waited until she was in her late forties to get married for the first time.

Henri couldn't wait to meet Maeve's fiancé. He had to be a special man to convince a woman like her to take that sort of plunge after resisting all this time.

Aunt Bea was shocked to hear that Maeve was getting married, but she said she'd heard Maeve had been living in Ireland for almost a year exclusively. Henri figured that she'd moved there to be close to Liam.

From everything Liam had told her about his sisters, it seemed they were very close. When he spoke about them, it was with affection and humor. She remembered he'd told her that their parents had died in a car accident when he was six and that Maeve had raised him and his other sister.

They'd all been celebrating a particularly triumphant write-up for the restaurant, and as she and Liam had gone to the wine cellar to fetch more champagne, she'd asked if he'd told his parents yet. He got so quiet that she asked if she'd said something wrong. She didn't think he was going to reply, but then he told her. She'd felt so sad for him when he said he couldn't remember his mum or dad and that it weighed on him sometimes.

She'd wanted to take his hand as he was telling her, but she didn't want to overstep any lines. But she had shed a few tears for him. He'd looked surprised by that, and for a second she'd thought he'd brush them away. But he'd just murmured, "Don't be sad. I had the best in Maeve."

Just for that, Henri vowed she was going to do a brilliant job for Maeve and her fiancé.

She wasn't sure what she expected Maeve's house to look like, but she was both impressed and not surprised when she drove up to a large manor house. It'd been modernized, with large windows all around it and a paved driveway, but with the ivy that clung to the façade, it still had old-world charm.

Henri parked her car behind a discreetly expensive car to the side of the circle driveway. Her uncles Nick and Luca would be able to tell her what kind of car it was just by looking at the wheels, but she'd never been interested in cars. You didn't need one in London.

Sitting in her rental, she noticed a white van as well as a large black Range Rover toward the back of the house. (She knew it was a Range Rover because she could read it on the back of the car.)

"Full house," she mumbled, unhooking the seat belt. She blew out a breath, oddly anxious.

This was it. A big commission that would get her the attention that she wanted. The chance to induct herself into the big leagues.

Seeing Liam again.

"Maybe he'll be paunchy and have lost his hair in the past eight months," she said to herself, trying to calm her heart.

Highly unlikely.

As if sensing her anxiety, Vivi texted right then.

Vivi

I expect constant updates.
Also, brush your hair occasionally.

Shaking her head, she put her mobile away, opened the door, and got out.

The first thing that struck her was the aroma floating in the air. She inhaled. *Coq au vin.* She smiled, wide and delighted. It was one of the first dishes she and Liam had made together.

They'd been scheduled to make family dinner for the crew at Papillon, and Liam had wanted to make *coq au vin.* He'd obsessed about the fact that something was missing. She'd hesitated, but she finally suggested adding a bit of chocolate to it. He'd gawked at her like she'd told him to add dragon's eggs, but then he broke out into a gusty laugh and told her she was brilliant.

Was Liam here? Why would he be? Maybe he'd dropped off *coq au vin* for his sister?

Curious, nervous, hopeful, she strode to the door and knocked.

A woman with dark-red hair opened it. She looked to be in her thirties, slim and fit, wearing an expensive green dress and heels. Henri preferred wearing jeans, but she knew enough about fashion from her aunts and cousins to recognize the posh designer brand.

"You must be Henri," the woman said. She had wise dark eyes, the kind that could look through to a person's soul, which was exactly what she was doing to her right then. "I'm Maeve. Welcome to *Cois Dara.*"

"*Cois Dara?*" she asked, shaking the hand Maeve offered.

"It translates to 'beside the oak tree.' There's a great oak out past the sheep pasture behind the house. It's a lovely walk." Maeve stepped out of the doorway and gestured her inside. "Please."

She stepped into the foyer, the smell of *coq au vin* wrapping around her. Inhaling it, wondering where it was coming from, she looked around. The house was simple but luxurious. She'd been around her father and Aunt Portia long enough to recognize the quality antiques interspersed with modern splashes of comfort. All in all, it was surprisingly homey and welcoming.

"I had a room upstairs readied for you," Maeve said, closing the door. "I think you'll like it, but if you'd prefer a different room, please let me know. It overlooks the gardens out back."

"I love gardens." When she had her flat, she had access to the roof, where she'd put planters to grow her own herbs.

"That's what Liam said." Maeve's smile was reserved. "He insisted you'd love the room."

She felt her cheeks flush at the mention of his name. "I'm looking forward to seeing Liam."

"He's looking forward to spending time with you again," the woman said, turning. She called down the hallway. "Liam!"

There was a clatter and a muffled curse. "What?" was the answering yell back.

Liam. Henri held her breath—she'd recognize his voice anywhere. It'd always done things to her. In the kitchen at Papillon, she used to purposely leave her earbuds out so she could listen to his voice as she baked. His voice had always inspired her to create sexy desserts.

"Come out here, damn it," Maeve called back, hands on her hips.

Henri didn't bother hiding her smile.

He came out, wiping his hands on a dishtowel, an annoyed look on his face. "I'm in the middle of—"

Henri knew the moment he noticed her, because he stopped abruptly and stared at her like he couldn't believe his eyes.

He wasn't paunchy. Or bald.

If anything, he was even more handsome than he'd been when they knew each other at Papillon. He wore jeans and a white shirt, open at the collar. His hair was longer, glinting reddish in the sun, curling over his collar.

There were a few strands of gray at his temples—had they been there before?—which made him look tastily grown up. His eyes were direct and focused all on her.

"Henriette," he said, his face lighting in a big smile.

She couldn't help answering it with one of her own. She wanted to run to him and hug him, but that'd probably be weird since the most they'd touched before was brief glancing brushes on the occasions they worked together.

"I have a couple calls to make." Maeve cleared her throat. "Liam, can you help Henri get situated?"

"Of course." Liam stepped forward, his hand extended. "Welcome to Westport, Henriette."

As Maeve left, Henri put her hand in his, shocked by the feel of his palm against hers. It was large and strong, slightly callused and warm. She looked up into his golden eyes, unable to keep her smile from growing.

"God, I missed you, Henriette," he said softly, his gaze not leaving hers. "I'm happy to see you."

Was he happy to see her, like a friend? Or was he hinting at something more? She tried to read him, but she was afraid she was only seeing what she wanted to see. "I didn't expect to see you here today."

"The kitchen is my domain, even my sister's. Maeve wouldn't know a colander from a pot. I came to make sure you got situated and had everything you needed." He frowned suddenly. "Are you tired? The drive is long.

I should show you to your room instead of making you stand here."

"I'm eager to see the kitchen, actually," she said hopefully.

He laughed softly, relaxing. "That's what I'd want too. Wait till you see it. It's wasted on Maeve, but you'll think it's a dream. This way."

They fell into step together, walking down the hall, just like it used to be when he walked her home after their late-night drinks after their shifts. It was easy and comfortable, and the nerves she'd been feeling dissipated like the lightest spun sugar on a tongue.

He gestured to a doorway at the end, though the scent of *coq au vin* could have guided her. "You're cooking?" she asked.

"*Coq au vin*," he confirmed, glancing at her. "I wanted to make something special for your first night here."

"I can't believe you're making something so intricate when you're working later. When we were at Papillon, I hardly ever felt like cooking outside work."

"I'm taking the next week or so off so I can be available here. It's not every day your sister gets married."

They stepped into the kitchen and she sighed. "This is glorious," she said in wonder. It was everything the kitchen of a large manor house should be: large, with lots of light and counter space, copper pots hanging over the center island, a large range, and a bank of ovens.

She ran her hand over the cool marble countertop of the island, turning to take in the nook with the long wooden table and bench. In the far corner, there was a plush turquoise chair with an afghan on its back and a small side table. It didn't look like it normally belonged there. Was it for her?

Gaping, she whirled to stare at Liam.

He was smiling, a hopeful look in his eyes. "You like to have a comfortable place to sit. I thought you'd enjoy that. If you want it in a different spot, I'll move it."

"You remembered," she said softly, turning to look at it again.

"Of course I did." He cleared his throat. "I imagine you brought your own utensils and tools."

She nodded, facing him again. "My rental is full."

"I'll help you bring it all in, and then I'll show you where your room is." Liam stopped suddenly. "Henriette?"

"Yes?"

The corner of his lips quirked. "You smell like vanilla."

"Occupational hazard." She tipped her head. "Eight months since the last time we saw each other, and that's what you say?"

He studied her for a long moment, like he was trying to see into her soul. Finally, he said, "You want the truth?"

"Always," she said without any hesitation.

"I knew I missed you like crazy," he said softly.

"Only until I saw you standing here in my sister's house, I didn't truly understand how much. I'm happy to see you, Henriette."

The emotion in his voice choked her up, surprising her into uncharacteristic muteness.

He smiled slightly, sticking his hands in his pockets. "Nothing to say?"

She opened her mouth to make one of her usual pithy remarks. But instead at the last minute she said, "I missed you too."

CHAPTER 8

*S*eeing Henriette in his sister's house was powerfully moving in a way he hadn't expected. She'd always been good at pinpointing a missing ingredient in one of his dishes; in this case, the dish was *home* and what'd been absent was *her*.

Walking next to her now, Liam wanted to take her hand. He wanted to kiss her until he didn't know where he ended and she started. He wanted to ask her about her time in France and what the best cake was that she'd made since he'd last seen her. He wanted to tell her about his crew and ask her opinion of his dessert menu because it wasn't as in sync with his menu as he'd like. He wanted to show her the cottage he'd bought, which he'd been waiting to expand until he knew if she'd be willing to share it with him.

He just wanted to sit next to her while she sketched and stare into her lovely, lovely blue eyes.

"I have some thoughts about the cakes I'm going to make for Maeve and Evan to try tomorrow," Henriette said, stumbling a bit on the runner in the hallway.

Long-limbed and loose, she was normally graceful and effortless. He wondered if she felt it too: the shift in their relationship. Was that what had her off-balance?

But then what she said registered, and he lost his footing too. Evan? Who the hell was Evan and why hadn't Maeve told him she'd found a fiancé? The only Evan he was aware Maeve knew was... He blinked. "Evan Ward?"

Henriette gave him an amused sidelong look. "Yes, as he's the one she's marrying."

Why hadn't Maeve told him she'd decided on someone? Not that it mattered in the end, because she was going to cancel the wedding, but *Evan Ward*? He essentially worked for her.

"Do you have a problem with Evan?" Henriette asked with her characteristic forwardness.

"No, he's a solid guy." Liam opened the front door and waited for her to go outside. "They've known each other a long time. I was surprised that their, er, relationship took this turn," he said honestly.

She turned her magnificent blue eyes onto him. "Sometimes working together can show how well suited you are to partnership."

Before he could ask her what she thought of them, she was striding toward her car, the boot opening automatically. Her shapely behind wiggled as she stretched and shifted one box to reach for her industrial mixer.

"I'll get that for you," he said, hurrying forward and taking it before she could heft it. "Leave the heavier things for me."

"The rest isn't heavy, except perhaps the bags of flour and sugar," she said, tugging a box toward her.

"You could have asked me to have the ingredients you needed here waiting for you."

She shrugged as they headed back in. "I figured you'd have your hands full with the wedding and your restaurant."

He winced, grateful she was walking in front of him so she didn't see. The wedding was going to be canceled, so he didn't actually have any work to do there. "I'm here for anything you need, Henriette. Just tell me."

"Thanks." The smile she flashed over her shoulder made him momentarily breathless.

And ever hopeful, because he swore he saw awareness in her gaze, more than professional interest. He'd have kissed her to find out, but he didn't want to muck this up. The stakes were too high.

So instead, as he set the mixer on the island in the spot where he knew she'd want it, he said, "What are you making for the tasting?"

"I haven't quite decided," she said as she slid the box on the counter. She began unloading spatulas and pastry bags and an assortment of other utensils. "The answers on Maeve's questionnaire weren't what I expected, so I'm rethinking a few things."

"It's a shame you can't make a large lava cake." He plugged the mixer in and adjusted its position to suit her. He knew how she liked her station. "I love lava cake."

She laughed. "You like it for its name. You and fire go hand in hand. It appeals to your volcanic personality."

He liked it because it was the first thing she'd ever made for him. "I've never tasted a better cake."

"Lava cake is intimate," she replied as she tucked away some of her things in the cupboard below that he'd emptied for her. "It's the sort of cake you take away with you, to share in the privacy behind closed doors. Or so I believe."

Leaning against the counter, he studied her. "You don't know for certain?"

"I've never had anyone I wanted to share that sort of intimacy with," she said, still bent over with her focus in the cabinet.

"Have you looked?"

She straightened, meeting his gaze. "One time I thought I'd found someone, but the timing wasn't right."

"That's a shame," he said, hoping she meant him, but if it was someone else, he was grateful the guy was out of the picture. "Come on. Let's get the rest."

They made a few more trips back and forth until they'd emptied her car. He helped her situate her supplies in the pantry, her large cake pans tucked away for the moment, the smaller ones she needed to make the tasting cakes for tomorrow lined up neatly on the counter.

While she organized what she needed to start, he took her personal bags to her room. Setting them next to the wardrobe, he checked on the flowers that he'd put in there earlier. On the windowsill, he put a small planter of edible flowers: calendulas, pansies, and nasturtiums. Next to her bed, he'd placed a vase of orange and red daisies—one time she'd told him that roses were proper, but daisies were fun and she liked their cheery faces.

On his way back to join Henriette, he spied Maeve's office door open. He poked his head in and knocked on the doorframe. "You have a minute?"

"For you?" She closed her laptop. "Always."

He stepped in and closed the door. "You didn't tell me you'd decided on a fiancé."

Her brow furrowed. "You knew that I needed to have someone by tomorrow."

"But I'd have thought you'd tell me before you decided on someone."

She studied him for a long, silent moment. Then realization lit her eyes, and she nodded. "Henri told you about Evan. Are you upset about Evan, or are you upset that you heard it from someone other than me?"

He perched on the edge of her desk, arms crossed. "What do you know about Evan?"

She adopted the same defensive posture. "I know I trust him implicitly. I know he won't take advantage of the situation. I know he doesn't question my decisions," she added pointedly, "even when they seem outlandish."

"He's your private investigator."

"He's the man who gave me the report that caused me to ditch the crook I was planning on marrying twenty years ago."

"Really?" That stopped him short.

"Really."

Liam had been fifteen then, and he'd hated the guy she was going to marry, but he didn't have the tools or wherewithal to do anything about it. He was a kid—what did he know about marriage except that he didn't trust that arsehole at all. "Then I owe Evan a debt of gratitude."

"You owe him more than that," she replied tartly. "He won't say a word about this wedding or that it's a sham. It's just like you planned. You get a chance with Henriette and I get Buckley Sinks & Taps."

"You really do trust him," Liam said with shock. Maeve hardly trusted anyone.

"I'd trust him with you and Áine," she replied without a single hesitation. "I realized that he's the only person I trust enough to marry."

Liam frowned at her. "But you aren't actually marrying him."

"Yes, I am." She steepled her fingers, elbows on the desk. "For your plan to work for me, I have to get married by the time bidding comes around. It won't be enough to be engaged, and it certainly won't help my reputation to jilt someone again. I need to go through with it and stay married for at least a couple years."

Cursing under his breath, Liam rubbed his neck. "I'm sorry, Maeve. I didn't know I was putting you in this position."

"You aren't. I want Dad's company back." She tapped her fingers on the desk, her gaze far off. "It'll work out. Evan and I have a longstanding professional relationship. We can make this work for us."

Liam froze, gaping at his sister, who was *blushing*. Maeve *never* blushed. "Maeve, you like him."

"Of course I like him," she said, her brow raised. "I'd have to in order to go through this with him."

No, this wasn't a simple matter of liking and trusting the man enough to enter this partnership—she *liked* him. It was right there, in the way her cheeks were flushed and the bright light in her eyes.

He had no idea what sort of code Evan Ward lived by. The one time Liam had met the man, he'd been an enigma.

Fuck—what had he initiated? He wanted a solution to help her, not to break her heart. She'd walled off after she'd ditched her fiancé twenty years ago; he'd been young, but he'd still kept an eye on her to make sure she wasn't hurt again.

He'd wanted her to have the company because she wanted it so badly, but it wasn't worth heartbreak. He didn't care what Maeve said—he recognized that Evan Ward had the power to break her heart.

When had this happened? Maeve was the most grounded person ever, not given to flights of fancy. She wouldn't have woken up and found herself smitten with a man she'd known for over twenty years. She had to have feelings for him before.

Did Áine know?

He rapped his knuckles on the desk. "I need to go to the restaurant to check on things. See you for dinner." He gave her a kiss on her cheek. "Want me to close the door?"

"Please." She picked up her mobile.

And so he was dismissed. He left her office, closing the door, and pulled out his mobile.

First, he texted Áine.

<u>Liam</u>

Has Maeve ever mentioned anything to you about Evan?

She replied instantly.

<u>Áine</u>

Evan Ward? He owns the firm that handles security and investigations for her.

Liam
I know. But have they been seeing each other?

Áine
Maeve doesn't date people she does business with.

Liam
She blushed when she talked about him.

Áine
Maeve doesn't blush either.

Liam
She did. Several times.

Áine
I'm calling.

His phone rang a second later. He ducked into a sitting room and drew the doors closed as he answered.

"Why were you talking about Evan Ward?" Áine asked.

"Because she's marrying him in two weeks."

There was a long moment of silence on the other end, and then Áine calmly said, "I didn't notice any signs of psychotic break the last time I spoke with her. She doesn't do drugs. Has she been drinking?"

"It's my fault," he admitted, rubbing the back of his neck. "I put her up to this wedding."

"Explain how you can put *Maeve*, of all people, up to anything she doesn't want to do."

He briefly explained his idea, hiring Henriette, Buckley Sinks & Taps, and the rest of the situation. Áine listened attentively—it was her job, after all—humming at appropriate intervals.

When he finished, she said, "It's quite brilliant, actually. A possible win-win for all parties."

He shook his head. "I know I should be relieved that you didn't flay me for putting a ludicrous plan like this into motion, but I find myself questioning your sanity for encouraging this. Maeve is bringing some man we don't know, someone we aren't sure she's ever dated, into her home."

"Aren't you taking a chance and doing that with your pastry chef?" Áine asked reasonably. "Besides, Maeve never does anything she doesn't want to do. On some level, conscious or unconscious, she wants this. She wants Evan."

"That's what I'm afraid of," he murmured.

"Maeve would never invite someone into her home that she didn't trust," Áine said quite logically. "But if it makes you feel better, I'll call her after my last client."

"Thank you." It made him feel moderately better, but he still needed to make sure Maeve would be okay in the end. Meaning he needed to meet this Evan and take the measure of him and make sure the man knew he was being watched.

What he needed to do was figure out how to come stay in Maeve's house for the duration of Henriette and Evan's stay.

He chatted another minute or two with Áine. The moment he got off the phone, he sent a text to Andy.

<u>Liam</u>
I need your help. Can you come over to my place later?

<u>Andrew Ryan</u>
Restaurant or house?

<u>Liam</u>
House.

<u>Andrew Ryan</u>
Have beer.

AT PRECISELY A QUARTER PAST FIVE, fifteen minutes after his workday ended, Andy arrived at the cottage. Liam knew it was his him by the usual *rat-a-tat-tat* rhythm of his knuckles on the window by the door.

Before Liam could open it for him, Andy let himself in. "My tools are in the car. I'll only get them after I quench my thirst."

He went to clap Andy on the shoulder in welcome. "Thanks for taking the time."

"Ah, what are friends for?" The big man shook the drops of rain off him and stomped his feet. "It sounded like an emergency."

"Of sorts." He led his friend and plumber into the kitchen. "I need to figure how to flood my cottage."

Andy stopped dead in his tracks. "Have you been tippling ahead of me?"

"I'm serious." He went to the refrigerator and pulled out two bottles of beer and two chilled glasses. Uncapping them, he filled the glasses and handed one to his friend. "What's the best way to cause a problem with the plumbing that would require me to stay elsewhere for a week?"

Andy took a long draught, studying him over the top of the glass. Finally he lowered the beer and nodded. "This is about the woman."

"Yes." Two women actually. Liam leaned against the counter. "I need a reason to be with her at Maeve's house rather than here by myself."

The plumber scratched his head, obviously thinking. "So you'll want damage, but you'll want not so much damage that it'll cost your firstborn to repair it."

"I knew you'd understand." He lifted his glass in a toast.

"A broken pipe in the basement should do it." Andy nodded. "The basement is concrete, so the damage will be limited as long as we make sure we dry it out properly, and the broken pipe will ensure you have no water for as long as it takes to get a replacement."

"How long will that take?"

Andy shrugged. "How long do you want it to take?"

"That's exactly the answer I was looking for." He clicked his glass to his friend's.

"I'm wondering something, though," Andy said after a long sip. "Why not just say there's a problem instead of actually having a problem?"

"I don't want to lie to her," he said simply.

Andy's eyes widened. "You *like* her."

He nodded. "I'm going to marry her, if she'll have me."

"Then we better make this good." Andy set his empty glass down and rubbed his hands together. "You got a hammer, or should I get mine from the car?"

$\mathcal{M}$aeve stared at Evan's text.

<u>Evan Ward</u>
I'll be there in twenty.

She went hot, and then she went cold. She set her mobile aside and opened her laptop to get some work done. She was forcing herself to ruthlessly focus when her mobile pinged with another text.

<u>Evan Ward</u>
I'm hungry, Maeve.

She gaped at the message. What did he mean by that?

What did she think he meant? Evan was a man who

was straightforward and said what he meant. If he was hungry, he wanted food, for Christ's sake.

Probably.

Except she kept thinking about him telling her he didn't wear either boxers or briefs, and then she wondered if the kind of man who'd go naked under his expensive slacks wouldn't have more exotic appetites and, therefore, actually *not* mean food when he said he was hungry.

This was the man she was marrying.

She shook her head, annoyed with herself. She needed to get a grip. They'd been business associates for twenty years—friendly, yes, but just because they were getting married didn't mean that there was anything erotic between them.

She'd remind herself of that often while he was here.

Her mobile rang. Her heart stopped, thinking it was Evan, but she exhaled in relief when she saw it was just her sister.

Áine had her practice in Dublin. When Maeve had been living in London, she'd only seen Áine for holidays, but they spoke often. Since Maeve had been staying more and more in Westport, Áine drove out to spend weekends here in the country, to visit her and Liam. She loved when Áine came to stay—her sister was calm and wickedly funny.

Speaking to Áine before Evan arrived would be grounding—plus, she needed to tell her she was marrying him. So she picked up the call. "You have good timing. I have someone arriving momentarily."

"I heard," Áine said in her serene way. "Liam told me quite the story about a scheme to have his cake and eat it too. And about your virtue being in danger from a certain private-investigator-slash-fiancé."

She snorted. "That's what he said to you?"

"You know how he is. His protective instincts rise up."

"And how do you feel finding out that I'm marrying Evan?" she asked.

"I'm the one who usually asks for an in-depth analysis of feelings," Áine pointed out. "But since you bring it up, you realize this crosses your stark divide between business and personal, correct? Not to mention that you must trust him incredibly, not just by allowing him into your inner sanctum but with your reputation, which, to you, is one of your most treasured commodities."

"I like that you make such good use of your degree," Maeve replied dryly. "Yes, I realize all that."

"And you're still marrying him?"

"Yes."

"Hmm."

She waited for more, but when Áine wasn't forthcoming, she said, "What does that mean?"

"It's like I suspected. You wouldn't marry Evan unless you really wanted to, regardless of what excuses you're using. I wish I'd gotten to meet him before now.

I used to wonder about him, but now I'm really curious. When precisely is he arriving?"

She glanced at the clock. Oh God—he was going to be here any minute. "I need to go, Áine."

"I imagine you do. Maeve?"

"Yes?" she said, looking out the window, feeling something fluttery in the pit of her stomach. She used to get that feeling before her board meetings, when she'd first become so successful.

"One last question."

When Áine didn't ask it, she said, "Well?"

"How attractive is he?"

He drove up the drive right then in a sleek black car. The lights outside flared on, highlighting him in the driver's seat. Even through the car window, she could see his hair, slightly disheveled the way it usually was by the end of the day. He wore a dark shirt, open at the collar, and his hair was closely cropped around the sides but a bit longer on top.

She couldn't see the rest of his body yet, but she knew his shoulders were broad, his chest muscled (his shirts fit him *very* well), and his thighs powerful (though she tried not to stare—unsuccessfully). And she knew that by now he'd have a five-o'clock shadow, which made him look rakish and even more manly, if that was possible.

Her sister snorted on the other end of the line. "I guess I have my answer."

"Goodbye, Áine." She hung up and stood, smoothing her dress as she went to greet him.

He was walking up to the threshold when she opened the door. Her breath caught, but it did that every time she saw him (since the first moment they'd met) so she had plenty of practice disguising it. She braced herself and met his cool gray gaze. "You're earlier than I expected," she said.

"I flew to Knock and rented a car from there." He came to stand directly in front of her, a leather bag in his hand, doing his usual scan of her.

Normally, it didn't bother her—she was used to him surveying her, like he was gauging her well-being. But today, in her home where she didn't invite anyone but Liam and Áine, it felt more personal. Intimate. Proprietary. Like he was a king coming to claim what was his.

Of course he was. He was coming to marry her.

It gave her goose bumps.

It made her nipples harden.

She cursed silently, knowing that he saw everything. "It's cold," she said as cover, rubbing her arms for effect. "Come in."

He followed her inside without comment. He did a quick perusal of the foyer, his eyes going down the hall. He set his bag down, moving toward her as she closed the door. She looked up as she latched it. "I—"

He took her chin in his hand and lifted her face to his. He gazed at her, intense and searching, before lowering his lips to hers.

The second their mouths touched, she gasped. Without thought, she put her hands on his arms (deliciously rock solid) and leaned into the kiss. They still looked at each other, though his eyes had gone half-mast and hot. How had she ever thought they were cool? He watched her, his thumb on the pulse on her neck as if making sure she liked it.

Like didn't do it justice. She'd give a fortune to be kissed like this the rest of her life.

He stepped into her so her back was pressed against the door while he blanketed her. She could feel the length of his hard body—*hard* being the key word—and she gasped again.

He lifted his mouth enough to speak softly, his words caressing her lips. "If you keep squirming against me, your cake maker is going to get one hell of a show."

"My cake maker?" She shook her head, not understanding.

"Henriette Buchanan." He motioned with his head to the end of the hall. "She was coming out of the kitchen."

"So that"—she made a gesture with her hand between them—"was for show?"

"That was how I'd greet the woman I want to spend the rest of my life with," he replied, running his knuckles down her neck as he stepped back. "Unless we were in private."

She bit her lip. She shouldn't ask... "What would

you do in private?"

His smile was slow and wicked.

"I've never seen this side of you before," she murmured, intrigued and beyond turned on.

"You've never looked, Maeve." He picked up his bag and glanced at the stairs.

"I'll show you your room," she said, walking ahead of him.

"Don't you mean 'our room'?" he asked softly, following her.

She glanced over her shoulder at him.

His expression was neutral. "We're getting married. You're not the sort of woman who'd keep a separate room from your man, Maeve."

She stopped on the landing and faced him. "What sort of woman am I?"

Standing on the top step, he was eye level with her. He looked at her with his customary directness, but in his gray eyes there was something more—something she didn't recognize. She wanted to say that it was attraction, but if that were the case, she'd have noticed it before, wouldn't she?

"Well?" she prompted him. "What sort of woman am I?"

"The passionate kind," he said, his voice low. "The kind who wouldn't stand for her lover to be anywhere but in her bed, not just to make love to her but to hold her while she sleeps and when she can't."

How did he know she had trouble sleeping? She

narrowed her eyes. "You know this just by looking at me?"

"Maeve, I've been looking at you for twenty years."

She blinked, feeling herself flush. Because she didn't know what to say, she turned and strode down the hall to her suite of rooms.

The guest wing, where Henri was staying, had four bedrooms. When she'd bought the house, she'd had the opposite end of the house opened up into a larger space for herself, leaving just one spare room next to hers. Mostly, she used it as overflow for her luggage when she was packing for a trip.

At its door, she stopped and faced Evan.

"Take me to our room, Maeve," he said.

She crossed her arms. "I don't take just anyone into my room."

"I know." He smiled. "But I'm not just anyone, and you trust me."

She hummed, wanting to deny it, but he was right. She would have liked to say that she was leading Evan to her inner sanctum, as Áine called it, just because of the plan and the acquisition, but she never deceived herself. She was taking Evan to her room because she wanted him there. Áine was right about that too.

The thought terrified her.

But—heaven help her—she wanted to kiss him again.

"Your room, Maeve," Evan prodded gently.

She turned and led him down the hall.

In London, her penthouse was decorated like one would expect of a successful financier: understated but expensive, with lots of glass and white leather. Her bedroom was luxurious, but it was stark, much like the way she dressed in town.

She didn't miss it there.

Here, she'd indulged in everything she'd ever wanted: rich, bold colors; lots of pillows and soft furry rugs; an elevated bed with steps to climb up to it; and a red velvet fainting couch. It was opulent and luxurious, and every time she entered the room she sighed with pleasure.

Her dad would have loved it. He'd have spun her in the air and said, "*A leanbh*, you done good here."

Evan's quiet footsteps behind her pulled her out of the reverie. She turned to watch him right as he set his bag down next to her closet door. What would he think about her room?

He surveyed the room with the same thoroughness he did everything, taking in the dark turquoise of the walls and the dark fuchsia of her duvet. His gaze traveled over her mirrored bureau and the crystal chandelier hanging in the center of the room.

When he faced her, he said, "I feel like I've stepped into Scheherazade's boudoir."

"You didn't expect my room to be like this?"

"No." His fingers grazed her comforter. "It makes me wonder what else I'll find under the surface."

She hummed, thinking about her lingerie. Not that

she was sure he'd see much of that, unfortunately. What kind of marriage were they going to have? Some lines you couldn't come back from if you crossed, and she'd hate for this lark to do irreparable damage to their relationship. She'd miss him, she realized—a lot.

Feigning calm and assurance, she leaned against her closet door and nodded at his bag. "I know you don't wear boxers or briefs, but I hope you have pajamas in that bag."

"I sleep nude," he said, meeting her eyes.

She did too, but she wasn't going to tell him that. "Not in my room, you don't."

"Ground rules, Maeve?" He cocked a brow. "And in two weeks, it's going to be our room."

"About that," she said. "I—"

He stepped up to her, took her by the waist, and kissed her again.

She didn't think it was possible, but she melted into him even faster this time. There was less shock and more *oh-my-this-is*-good. Her arms wrapped around his neck and she pressed her body to his, humming at the way they fit together.

It felt perfect.

His fingers speared into her hair, supporting and soothing at once. She hummed again, falling into the embrace even more.

He lifted his lips from hers, staying close enough that his breath caressed her skin. "I have something for you."

Her brow furrowed, and she looked down between them, just below his belt.

He grinned, full and amused. "Not that. At least not until later, and only if you ask nicely."

"You smile so rarely," she murmured, staring at his mouth.

"Maybe we can practice smiling more together." Keeping her where she was with one hand, he reached into his pocket with the other and pulled something out.

A ring.

Set in white gold, it appeared to be a large canary diamond with a swirl of diamonds around one side of it, in an assortment of shapes and sizes. It caught the sunlight in the room, casting prisms all over. She had to blink a few times to see it—not just because of the way it shined but because she couldn't believe what she was seeing.

She looked up at him, aware she had to be gaping.

"You already agreed to marry me," he said, taking her left hand in his. "We want to do this right. It shouldn't be a shock that I'd get you a ring."

"And yet..." She swallowed thickly as he lifted her hand and poised the ring on the end of her finger.

He looked at her steadily, solemn, all humor gone from his expression. "I'm honored you trust me with yourself, Maeve. I don't take that lightly, and I never will. I'm not a man who makes fancy speeches, so I'll just tell you that you can always count on me. I honor you, and I always will. I will be loyal to you, I will respect you, and I will never take this for granted."

He slipped the ring on her finger. It fit perfectly.

She opened her mouth, and then closed it, not knowing what to say. Then she tried, "You're supposed to save the vows for the wedding day."

"These were private, between just you and me." He kissed her hand, just above the ring, and then he pressed a sweet, lingering kiss to her lips. "I'm still hungry," he murmured against them.

A frisson went up her spine. He obviously meant food—probably—so she reluctantly withdrew from his arms. "Come with me," she said, flushing a little when she heard the words she'd said in the air between them. So she added, "To the kitchen."

He arched his brow, but he said nothing, simply gesturing for her to lead the way.

Walking ahead of him, she couldn't help holding her hand out to look at the ring he'd given her. It was absolutely beautiful. It was exactly what she would have picked for herself. "I've been looking at you for twenty years," he'd said to explain how he knew her preferences so well. It made her shiver all over again.

The entire way downstairs she could feel his eyes on her, burning a path down her back. She tried not to put extra invitation in the sway of her hips, but by the muffled growl he gave, she knew she wasn't successful.

She felt another blush spread across her chest and face, trying not to think about the night ahead, trying not to think about what might happen in the dark of night in her oasis room.

But mostly she was excited to have Evan here, even if it was only for a little while.

CHAPTER 10

*H*enri worried that her cakes were going to scorch with Maeve and her fiancé in the kitchen. They sat at the table in the window nook, across the room from her, having wine while she was baking her cakes for tomorrow. They were radiating so much heat that Henri checked the ovens a couple times to bring the temperature down.

She'd done three cakes already, but she was rethinking the last two she was going to serve them: the flavors were absolutely wrong. They needed something with spice—cinnamon and cayenne—to match what they had going on. Because what they had going on was *incendiary*. She just had to figure out the perfect complement to their heat; you wouldn't want to go too hot and singe anyone.

If only she could make a lava cake work for one of

the layers. Maybe she'd do that for them before the wedding, for a private moment.

Maybe she'd do that for just Liam. He'd been so enthusiastic about her lava cake.

Then she thought about Liam some more, and she fanned herself. If Vivi was here, she'd confirm that he was putting out signals. Vivi was a connoisseur of male attention the way Henri knew ganache. He'd texted her that he was caught up with an issue at home he needed to deal with and that they should start dinner without him.

Part of her loved the signals and wanted to explore them. The other part of her didn't want to get distracted by them. In building a cake tower, the foundation was important. The same went in business. She wasn't going to allow the foundation of her business to be shaky.

Liam would understand that. After all, he'd spent the last eight months singularly focused on making his restaurant a success. He understood that this wasn't about work: this was about passion.

As if on the same wavelength, Maeve suddenly said, "Have you heard from Liam, Henri?"

She glanced up. "He texted. He might not make dinner."

His sister frowned. "What would be so important that he'd miss dinner?"

Your calling, of course, but it seemed the importance of food ran in the family. "He got everything ready before he left. I'll serve us."

"That's not necessary. I'll do it." Maeve started to get up.

Evan took her arm. "Let Henri tonight. She'll feel more settled getting the lay of the land."

How smart he was. Henri shot him a grin, which he returned with a wink. She *liked* him. Not as much as Maeve, though, based on the way the woman looked at him. As was proper.

No wonder they were getting married so quickly.

Liam had indeed gotten everything ready before he'd left, including the salad. Henri quickly dressed it with the vinaigrette he'd made, cut the bread, and served the *coq au vin*. The aroma of it all enveloped her, and she felt a pang of longing for Liam to be here.

But it was okay he wasn't. This was a good opportunity to figure out what to do for the two remaining cakes, so she set their plates on the table, wiped her hands on a towel, and joined the couple at the table. Talking to them would help focus her ideas.

Her gaze fell on the colossal rock on Maeve's hand. She hadn't noticed it before, but it was one of the most stunning rings she'd ever seen. It wasn't her style, but it suited Maeve to a T. She'd seen a lot of rings in the past six months since she'd started her business.

She'd never thought about what sort of ring she'd want. She didn't consider herself the jewelry sort, but seeing the way Maeve kept looking at it made her wonder how she'd like to symbolize her love.

Evan poured her a glass of wine. "You have an impressive background, Henri. What made you decide to leave architecture to become a chef?"

"Folly. Passion." She flashed him a wry smile. "My parents always told me to follow my heart, and I realized my heart was full of cake."

He laughed low. It changed his entire face, making it welcoming instead of austere, which seemed to be his normal expression. As she understood, he owned a security firm, so maybe that was par for the course.

He was an attractive man, but when he smiled, he was stunning. Henri guessed he must be around the same age as Maeve because they were so in sync, in the way people were when they were in the same place in life. She'd observed that with her parents and her aunts and uncles.

Regardless of his age, he was *hot*, and the way he watched Maeve? Henri didn't know how the woman hadn't ordered her out of the kitchen so they could have sex on every surface available—and against all the walls.

"Isn't dinner to your liking?" Maeve asked.

She looked up, frowning in question. Liam's *coq au vin* was transcendent. "Why would you think that?"

"You shook your head," Evan pointed out.

"I was just thinking about the two of you and your cake," she improvised.

The couple exchanged a look. It was Maeve who asked, "Is there a problem with the cake?"

"I'm rethinking a couple of the options I wanted to give you." She waved her fork at the two of them. "I wasn't expecting this sort of chemistry between the two of you. I didn't get a sense of that from the questionnaire."

Maeve blinked in surprise, but Evan looked intrigued. "Chemistry?" he asked.

"Explosive chemistry," she clarified. "I need to enhance what I originally thought I was going to make to balance that, but I need to be careful not to overwhelm what you have."

"There's more to cake than I realized," Evan said. He leaned back, seemingly relaxed.

But Henri could see that his posture was to disarm from his very sharp gaze and the way he took in everything. "You remind me of my uncle Jon, Aunt Summer's husband. He's a private investigator too."

Evan raised one brow slowly. "In what way do I remind you of him?"

"The way he watches." She smiled. "But then my cousin Luke says all men like to watch."

Maeve snorted.

Evan turned his look on his fiancée. Maeve just gave it back to him.

Hot. It made her think of her parents, and Chloe and Oliver, and her grandmama Jacqueline and grandpapa Declan for that matter. She sighed. *That* was what she wanted for herself. One day, once her business was on terra firma.

"You worked with Maeve's brother in London," Evan said.

She knew a prompt when she heard it. "At Papillon. My cousin Vivi was starting a wedding planning business, and she asked if I'd bake a cake when another baker fell through. I loved it, so I decided to take the plunge too."

"Why wedding cakes?" he asked.

"I love cake, and I love happily ever afters," she said simply, feeling like he'd understand somehow. "This is my way of helping people manifest theirs, because your cake represents your future and you don't want a faulty foundation for the start of your life together."

He studied her, stroking his chin in thought. "You really believe that."

She nodded. "I do."

He turned to Maeve. "You picked the right person to make our cake."

The woman's cheeks pinked. "I can't take credit for that," she said smoothly. "Liam recommended Henri."

Evan turned back to Henri. "Have you been to Liam's restaurant?"

"No." She'd have liked to be able to go there, but this job was so rushed as it was, so she didn't think she'd get the chance. Really disappointing, because after all they'd talked about their dreams when they'd known each other before, she'd have liked to see how his vision came together. She'd have liked to celebrate it.

"The food at *A Ghrá* is excellent," Evan said. "Better than some of the most touted restaurants in London. Liam manages to make it intimate but still a culinary experience."

Maeve frowned at her fiancé. "I didn't—"

"I owe you a date to have dinner there," he said to her with a private smile. He lifted their entwined hands, flipped hers over, and kissed the inside of her wrist slowly. "Are you busy tomorrow night?"

Maeve arched her brow. "Yes."

His lips quirked. "Are you pouting because I've neglected you, love? I'll make it up to you."

"There's no need." She tugged on her hand.

"There's always need." He lifted it to his lips again, this time placing a kiss by the engagement ring. "You're important to me."

Maeve narrowed her gaze.

"I already have a reservation. Wear your red dress," he told her.

She raised her eyebrow in a supercilious look that Henri had only seen her aunt Bea pull off. "Which red dress?" Maeve asked.

"The one you wore to the opening of the August Macke exhibit at the British Museum two years ago."

Maeve blinked at him in surprise. "You remember that?"

"I remember every moment I've ever had with you, Maeve," he replied, his voice husky.

Wide-eyed, Henri watched back and forth between them, like a tennis match. "This is the best foreplay I've seen since my sister was dating her now husband."

"This isn't foreplay," Maeve said.

"We reserve that for the bedroom," Evan replied mildly.

"This is cozy," came from the far side of the kitchen.

Liam. She looked up with a smile, glad he was here. She was beginning to feel like a third wheel.

He sauntered in, his gaze raking over her. She knew her hair was probably frizzy with the heat from baking all afternoon, and that she likely had flour dusted on herself here and there, but the way he looked at her told her he didn't find anything wrong. In fact, she swore she saw blatant male appreciation.

Then he glanced at his sister and Evan. When his gaze fell on their clasped hands, his expression darkened.

Henri frowned at him. Didn't he like Evan? She thought Evan was wonderful. She'd been around enough wankers in culinary school and restaurants to recognize one, and she'd stake her favorite cake pan that he was one of the good guys. He was perfect for Maeve.

Maeve certainly thought so. She shifted her chair closer to Evan's, leaning into his shoulder as she looked at Liam. "Shouldn't you be at the restaurant?"

"Deirdre is manning the kitchen until the wedding so I can focus on you." He gave his sister a look that Henri couldn't decipher. He put the bag in his hand on the floor and walked toward the table. "Evan," he said, holding out his hand.

The older man stood, still holding Maeve's hand with his left hand as he shook with his right. "Liam."

To watch their faces, you wouldn't have noticed anything, but their gripped hands held so much tension Henri waited to hear the snap of bones breaking. She caught Maeve's gaze.

The woman rolled her eyes. Then she frowned at her brother, gesturing to the bag he'd set down. "Are you moving in?"

"Yes, actually." He let go of Evan's hand and took the seat next to Henri, putting his arm around the back of her chair like it was the most natural thing in the world. "A pipe broke in my cottage, so I have no water. I didn't think you'd mind if I stayed here until it's all sorted."

"Hmm," was all Maeve said.

Henri wanted to hum too—not because of his pipe but because she could *feel* him though he didn't touch her.

For the record, it felt excellent.

If only she could snuggle into him, the way Maeve was snuggling into Evan. But they were a couple, and she and Liam hadn't even seen each other in eight months. Plus, she was here in a professional capacity.

This job could reap great rewards, given Maeve's social contacts and the people likely to attend her wedding. Henri wasn't going to flub this, even if climbing on Liam's lap and seeing if he kissed as well as she'd imagined was a tempting proposition.

Evan looked Liam in the eye. "I know that this proposal must have come as a surprise and that we don't know each other well, but I'm looking forward to changing that."

Liam returned the look without blinking. "Me too."

Maeve stood. "I should go up and get a room ready for you."

"I'll help," Evan said, standing too. He gathered their dinner plates and took them to the dishwasher, quickly loading them as Maeve watched. When he turned around, he held his hand out to his fiancée. "Coming?"

Maeve blushed. Without a word, she put her hand in his and they walked out.

Henri sighed, watching them. "They're so lovely together."

Liam, who was also watching them, faced her with a scowl. "What?"

"Maeve and Evan. I haven't worked with a lot of couples yet, but I can always tell the ones who really love each other." She tipped her head, studying him. "It's sweet how protective you are of your sister."

His lips firmed, brow furrowed. Then he shook his head. "I don't want to talk about them. Tell me how your day was. What did you bake?"

"It's what I didn't bake that's the issue." She angled herself toward him. "I still have two more to do for tomorrow and I'm rethinking what I was going to make since I've seen the two of them together."

"Hmm," he said, sounding like his sister.

It made her smile. "I'm thinking spice. Maybe apple with a bit of cayenne. Down to earth but still elegant, with a kick."

"Is apple normal for wedding cakes?"

She laughed as she stood to clear her plate. "No, but those two aren't normal either."

Liam frowned again, following her toward the sink. "No, they aren't."

Leaning in, she lowered her voice conspiratorially. "I saw them kissing."

His expression soured. "Do we have to talk about this?"

She laughed. "I'm just saying it wasn't a vanilla and violets sort of kiss. It was more like passion fruit. You think you can find some for me?"

"Fresh passion fruit, in Ireland?" He looked at her like she was mad.

"Can't you call someone?" she asked, mostly kidding. "You're a chef. You have connections."

He snorted. "Not even I'm that good."

She'd beg to differ, but she didn't have empirical evidence of that. Instead, she said, "It's been a trying day for you, hasn't it?" Henri wanted to put her hand on him, to comfort him, but she kept her hands busy tidying after dinner.

"Not as trying as some days used to be at Papillon." He flashed her a wry grin as he leaned against the counter, arms folded. "Those days I wanted to punch a wall."

"It never seemed that way in the kitchen." She set two mixing bowls on the counter and pulled her notebook, where she kept her recipes, closer.

"Do you miss it?"

Pausing as she flipped through her recipes, she pursed her lips to ponder that. "I miss some things. The camaraderie." Which was code for him escorting her home after their late-night staff dinner and drinks.

"I miss our walks," he said, his voice low. "And sitting together quietly."

She swung her gaze to his. "Me too."

He pushed off the counter and came to stand in front of her. She could feel his golden eyes like a physical touch on her skin. "Talking to you as I walked you home was the best part of my day. I'd spend the entire day in anticipation."

"You did?" she asked, caught in the bold intensity of his gaze.

He nodded. "I love talking with you. You have a unique view of things, and you know the most random things." His lips quirked. "One time you regaled me with the history of sugar and honey. I remember how you told me sugar was medicine, a symbol of privilege, and a mark of oppression."

"Sugar is important," she said, glancing at his lips.

He leaned closer. "I'd agree."

"Did you know until the seventeenth century, there were no honeybees in the Americas, so they didn't have honey?" she said softly. "Their sweeteners came from trees, cactuses, and mashed fruits until the Portuguese accidentally landed in Brazil and began sugar plantations there."

"Because the Ottomans were disrupting the trade routes and Europeans couldn't get their sugar imported any longer." He brushed an errant curl from the side of her face, though he didn't touch her skin.

"Those damn Ottomans." She smiled, feeling the urge to nuzzle into his palm. "You were paying attention."

"I've always paid attention to you." His hand hesitated and then lowered to hold hers.

It was the first time they'd touched. When they'd worked together, there was nothing physical, beyond the occasional accidental brush of their arms.

Closing her eyes, she *felt* it. If she could translate what it was like into cake, it'd be devil's food cake, rich and sweet and tempting. Because she needed the reminder herself, she said, "I need to bake the cakes tonight, so they have time to cool before I frost them tomorrow."

He kept her hand in his. "Want help?"

"Will you be good?"

His slow smile made her heart beat excitedly. "I'm always good."

"You know, I don't doubt that at all." She felt a pang of regret as she withdrew her hand from his, but she pushed that aside and reached for her recipes.

CHAPTER 11

Some of his favorite moments in the past couple years were next to Henriette as she was concocting some sort of magical dessert, the way she was making the final cake for Maeve's tasting tomorrow. Who else would have put chocolate and sage together?

Sitting on a stool across the kitchen island from her, he watched her work as they talked. He poured them more wine, and she'd served him dinner, letting him eat as she finished her last two cakes.

He imagined being at home together would be like this. It made him feel a kind of longing he'd never felt before. Before, he knew he wanted Henriette in his life. This was like sampling what it was going to be like, and it was something he wanted to have every day.

"You got everything you wanted in life," Henriette

was saying, glancing up from mixing her batter. "I'm happy for you."

He folded his arms, studying her. "You don't think you've gotten what you want yet."

"I haven't."

"Why not?"

She shook her head, putting the batter aside. "I don't want to just make cakes that are pretty. I want them to be visually stunning as well as orgasmically delicious. I want people to covet one of my cakes. I want my cakes to be chronicled and remembered years from now."

He nodded. He understood that. "And you aren't there?"

"No one knows about my cakes yet. Right now, I'm an expensive baker in a sea of expensive bakers."

"You need a spotlight," he said. "A marketing coup."

"You understand. I knew you would." She smiled as she pulled the bowl back and began to whip the batter again.

He more than understood—he'd been there. If Maeve hadn't helped him with media coverage, he'd likely still just be one of many expensive restaurants in Westport, struggling to get diners to come in. One properly done article in the right magazine, and he was booked months out.

Doing the cake for Maeve's wedding was going to help. Aside from the word of mouth over the unexpected wedding, his sister had contacts everywhere, and people were always bending over backwards to do her a favor. Liam knew that part was going to work out.

"That was one of the reasons I took this job." Reaching for a small round pan and a spatula, she scraped the batter into it and expertly leveled it before putting it in the oven. "I figured a wedding as large as she was having would have a lot of influential people who'd experience my cake and want to order them for themselves. I know how important this opportunity is, and I'm not going to squander it. I'm grateful that you recommended me for this, Liam."

He looked up from his plate to find her watching him.

She shrugged. "You know any number of pastry chefs who are excellent, who would have been convenient. You didn't have to recommend me."

He set his fork down and moved toward her. "You know why I did, don't you?"

She shook her head, her eyes wide.

He stopped directly before her and took her hand again. It was strong, with long elegant fingers. Artist's fingers. He wrapped his fingers around hers, holding, getting to know the feel of them, trying not to think about them exploring his body.

Not yet, anyway. First he needed to show her how it could be between them.

He lifted her hand and placed a kiss on her knuckles. "You had your dreams, and I had mine. I wanted to get settled with my restaurant. I didn't think I could focus on a relationship properly and get the restaurant off the ground. But I was attracted to you from that first day, when you interviewed."

She leaned into him, her free hand on his waist. "All I could think about as I made that lava cake was licking it off your body."

"I'm glad I didn't know that," he said, brushing her hair back from her face. He trailed his fingers down her neck and cupped her head. "It was hard enough resisting you."

"It was hard?" she asked, her voice husky with innuendo.

"And it is now."

Her lips quirked. Then the humor faded from her expression. "I should also say that I'd like to explore that in great depth, but I don't want to do anything to jeopardize this job. And a wedding is an important day. I don't want your sister to think that I have anything but complete focus on the cake for her and Evan."

"She won't think that." Maeve would be the first to congratulate them, given she'd gone in on this scheme with him.

Maybe he should come clean and tell Henriette about the lengths he'd gone to in order to bring her here. He looked in her eyes as he massaged her neck, loving her reflexive hum. Would she think it was a sweet gesture, the trouble he went through to meet her again? Or would she think that he'd engineered this to get into her pants? That was far from the truth, but he didn't want to chance that she'd take it the wrong way. She was attracted to him, but he didn't want a few nights in bed—he wanted a lifetime at her side.

"I like Maeve," Henriette said, her eyes closed as she arched into his touch. "I can't wait to meet your other sister."

"Áine?" He frowned.

"She's coming for the wedding, I assume." She opened her stunning eyes. "You're all so close, I'm surprised she's not already here."

Fortunately, the timer rang, saving him from having to come up with a reply. He let go of her so she could take care of it.

She efficiently took out the last cake and set it on a rack to cool with the other cake. Setting the hot pan on the stove, she began to put away her supplies.

He rolled up his sleeves to help her finish cleaning up.

"You don't have to do that," she said when he started washing her pans.

"I'm happy to." He smiled at her. "Maybe it'll earn me a taste of your cakes."

"That's not all it'd earn you." She flashed her quirky grin at him.

"In that case, I can be here all week to be your scullery boy."

She laughed. "Liam, there's nothing boyish about you."

Her laugh was the loveliest thing he'd heard in forever, and it hit him right in the center of his chest. He remembered how her laugh used to cause him to stop and search for her, making him wish he could taste the joy of it.

"What?" she asked, taking a pan from the drying rack and toweling it off.

"I love your laugh."

She chuckled. "Okay."

He couldn't help it—he leaned over and touched his mouth to hers. Her laugh died, but her lips opened, softening under his.

He tasted them now like he'd wanted to for so long, nibbling and licking, savoring slowly. He wasn't going to rush this first time. He was going to imprint this kiss on his memory so that even when he was an old man, he'd be able to remember the feeling and her every breathy sigh.

They only touched at their mouths. His hands still held a bowl under the faucet, and he vaguely felt the pan she'd been drying between them.

"Liam?" she murmured against his lips.

He hummed.

"We should stop."

He looked into her magnificent eyes, about to make a case for why they really shouldn't, but in them he saw uncertainty mixed with the desire.

So he kissed her again, quick but thorough, and set

to finishing the dishes. By the time he rinsed the last one, she'd wiped down the counters.

He picked up his bag and strode toward her. "I'll walk you to your room."

She flashed him her half smile as she turned and sauntered out of the kitchen, her hips swaying with the promise of heaven.

Carrying his bag, he followed her down the hall and up the stairs. Pausing on the landing, he glanced down the other wing, at his sister's closed door. He couldn't do anything about that tonight. So he turned right.

Henriette waited for him by her door. Forgetting everything else, he went straight toward her.

He wished he could invite himself in. He wished he could be sure that if they were intimate, she'd want to be with him beyond that.

He wasn't going to risk that she wouldn't, despite the yearning in her eyes. So he dropped his bag by the bedroom he normally stayed in when he spent the night here and walked toward her. He'd call himself an idiot later.

The expression on her face became quizzical. Any other woman would have been hurt or doubting her sexiness. Henriette just looked like she was puzzling him out.

He came to a stop in front of her, close enough that he could smell the sweet scent of baking radiating from her. He had a feeling he was going to get turned on every time he smelled vanilla from now on. "I'd like nothing more than to follow you in, but—"

"This is your sister's house," she finished for him. "And I'm here in a professional capacity."

"Yes, but it's more than that." He smiled faintly, reaching out to push aside a lock of hair that had come out of her topknot. "In the year we worked together at Papillon, did you ever wonder how we'd be together?"

"It was fourteen months, and all the time," she said with her usual candor.

He loved the way she spoke her mind. "Me too. I knew what it was like to walk you home after work, but I wondered what it'd be like to go inside with you. I imagined how it'd feel to take a shower and crawl into bed together. I wondered which one of us would make coffee in the morning, and how it'd feel to hold your hand as we walked to work together."

Her gaze sparkled bright in the low light from her bedroom. "I'd make the coffee. You're beastly in the morning."

"I'm not." He frowned. "And how would you know?"

She flashed her crooked smile, leaning against the doorframe. "One time shortly after I started at Papillon, I went with you to the morning market. It was early, and you hadn't had any coffee yet, and I thought your growling was going to make the cheese vendor cry."

"I don't remember that," he said, crossing his arms over his chest.

She chuckled softly. "It was cute."

She was cute. He brushed the back of his hand against her cheek, watching her eyes close as she nuzzled against his touch. "Henriette, I don't want to go for months without seeing you again."

"I like the sound of my name on your tongue," she admitted, opening her eyes. "What do you want, Liam?"

"You," he said simply. He cupped the nape of her neck, looking into her magnificent eyes.

She nodded. "I want you too."

"How do you want me?"

The corner of her lips lifted, and a wicked glint lit her gaze.

He arched his brow. "That wasn't what I was talking about, though maybe we can discuss that later."

"Why not now?"

"Because I don't want a one-night stand."

She grinned crookedly. "I'll be here for at least a week and a half."

He trailed his hand down her arm, taking her hand in his. He looked down, watching their fingers twine. Her hands were fine, but not delicate. They were capable and artistic, and everywhere their skin touched he felt a spark. "Tonight is the first time we've held hands."

"Does it live up to what you'd imagined?" she asked curiously.

"I couldn't have imagined something this grand," he replied. He drew her closer. "We've had all these moments," he murmured. "It's been eight months since I've seen you, and it feels just like yesterday that we walked through the restaurant's garden to pick herbs together. I know so much about you, but this is just the first time we've really touched."

She watched him, her thumb caressing where they joined. "We can remedy that tonight."

With his free hand, he held her face. "I've been thinking about this. I don't want to look back in fifty years and think that we missed out on anything."

"Then I recommend kissing me immediately." She tugged on his hand.

He held strong. "I want to woo you, Henriette."

Lips pursed, she studied him as she processed that. He could always tell when she was deliberating by the way the space between her eyebrows furrowed.

Finally, she said, "What does that look like to you?"

"Spending time together, like we used to, with more touching. Doing the things we like to do, together."

"I live in London and you live here."

"I know." He was hoping she'd stay longer, but based on the look on her face, now wasn't the time to bring that up. So he decided to shift her focus to what was important. "I'd like to kiss you."

She simply lifted her chin, her eyes wide open and waiting.

Smiling, he held her face. That was his Henriette, always approaching things with eyes and mind wide open. Heart in his throat—a first for him—he slowly lowered his mouth to hers.

Her free hand shot up and pushed on his chest. "Wait a minute. Did you say in *fifty* years?"

"Yes." He frowned. "I'm not dallying here, Henriette. I want you, for more than a fling or a flirtation. I'm in."

She blinked at that.

Usually he could tell what she was thinking by her expression, but he had no clue right now what was in her mind. "Tell me now if you aren't interested in something serious, Henriette."

"This is that serious to you?" she asked in soft wonder.

"Yes."

"You know we have logistical problems, as I mentioned before."

"I'm hoping we can come to mutually beneficial terms regarding that," he said as formally as she had.

She nodded. "Okay."

"Okay." He nodded too, then he frowned again. "What does that mean?"

"We'll discuss logistics at a later date. But I'd like a kiss. Now," she added, lifting her chin again.

"Okay," he replied, with a smile this time. Before she could say another word, he quickly pressed his lips to hers.

The sparks he'd felt at their hands flared at their mouths. She must have felt them too, because she gasped, a hushed breathy sound that felt like a caress, her mouth opening.

He tasted her, careful to keep himself from pressing his body to hers. He didn't think she'd mind knowing how she affected him, but he didn't want to tempt either one of them. He could feel the passion barely banked beneath the surface. One gust of wind and they'd ignite into an inferno—he had no doubt of that.

He wanted it. He wanted *her*.

But not tonight. He didn't want to chance rushing into anything and having their relationship burn out. He wanted a slow, steady flame that was going to burn for a lifetime.

For that, he was willing to rein it in.

He felt her hand spear into his hair, pulling him closer, taking more. Her breasts brushed his chest, and they both moaned.

He broke their kiss, already breathing heavily, searching her face. Her eyelids were lowered, sexy, and her cheeks were flushed. She was breathing heavily as well, and her lips were red and shiny and tempting.

He dropped one last sweet kiss on them. "I'll see you in the morning, Henriette. If you need anything, I'll be in that room there." He pointed to the door where he'd left his bag.

She looked to where he pointed. "What if I need another kiss?"

He grinned. "You'll have to wait until tomorrow night for that, when I walk you to your door again."

An inquisitive light flared in her gaze. "You're going to leave me in anticipation all day?"

"Yes, but I'll be right there with you." He kissed her again quickly, stepping back before she could deepen it. "Good night, Henriette."

"Good night, Liam." She gave him a look that was mysteriously female as she backed into her room and closed the door behind her.

Picking up his bag, he retired to his room, wondering what he was going to do with himself. A long, cold shower seemed like a good place to start.

CHAPTER 12

*M*aeve paced in front of her bed, holding her robe closed in case Evan walked back in. He couldn't actually be serious about spending the night in her room, could he?

He'd meant it when he said he'd help her get a room ready for Liam—he'd assisted putting sheets on the bed before escorting her back to her room.

She'd never have thought he'd know how to put sheets on a bed.

As she was about to tell him to stop the charade now that they were alone, his office rang with an emergency. She let him use her office so he'd have privacy to handle it, grateful for the respite from being around him.

The entire evening had been *fraught*. That was the only word for it: simply fraught.

She'd been out with many men—some of the most

eligible, charming bachelors in the world—but none of them had discomfited her the way Evan had simply by holding her hand.

The way he'd rubbed his thumb between her knuckles had turned her on beyond belief. If it hadn't been for the years of hiding her emotions in business, she'd have gone to pieces at the kitchen table.

And he knew how he'd affected her. She saw that in his eyes.

The sparkle of the ring he'd given her caught her eye. For the millionth time since he'd slipped it on her finger, she held her hand up and gawked at it.

It was absolutely beautiful.

What did he mean, giving that to her? Was it just for veracity? She didn't think that a man could pick a ring as perfect as this one for show.

But if that was the case, he'd stop pretending behind closed doors.

That was the problem, wasn't it? She wasn't certain what he was going to do once he returned to her room.

So she'd showered, taking care of herself in the shower to take the edge off, which was laughable because it'd only ratcheted up the tension in her body. And then she'd put her most covering robe on—and a nightgown under, just in case he did aim to sleep in her room. She wasn't going to sleep nude like she normally did if he was staying in there.

He better have brought pajamas too.

There was a soft knock at her door.

She froze, her hand gripping the top of her robe closed. She composed herself, forcing her hands to her sides. "Come in," she called.

Evan stepped in, closing the door behind him. His hair looked like he'd run his hand through it over and over, and he'd undone another button on his shirt. When he faced her, she saw the tight lines around his mouth—she wasn't sure if it was anger or exhaustion.

She went to the small rolling cart in the corner of her room and flipped open the top. Aware of him watching her, she poured a couple fingers of bourbon in a glass and took it to him.

He just stared at her.

She lifted a brow. "It's not poisoned."

His lips quirked as he accepted the glass. "You wouldn't use poison. You're more hands on."

That conjured thoughts of where she'd like her hands to get on, which made her turn and pour a generous dollop of bourbon for herself.

He was still studying her, his drink untouched, when she turned around. She gestured to her fainting couch. "Sit."

A smile threatened his lips again, but he went over the chaise. She pulled over an ottoman for herself, but she was aware of him taking his shoes and socks off, neatly tucking them under the couch before reclining on it with his legs up.

She pretended to settle herself on the large footstool, but really she was just trying not to stare at his bare feet. Feet weren't supposed to be sexy, so she wasn't sure why the sight of his made her fidgety, like she needed another shower.

He lifted the glass to his nose. His brow furrowed. "This is Blanton's."

She nodded, taking a sip of hers.

"It's my favorite."

"I know." She met his gaze. "Did you get your situation taken care of?"

"Yes. Finally." He closed his eyes in bliss as he tasted his drink. When he reopened his eyes, he looked straight at her. "I'm sorry for the interruption."

"There's no need. I understand business. Sometimes there are interruptions."

He swirled the bourbon in his glass. "I've been rethinking that."

"How do you mean?" she asked.

"I've been thinking of selling my business."

She frowned. "To do what?"

"Anything. To take some time. To focus on my personal life." He looked at her with his customary dry humor. "This is where you say, 'What personal life?'"

"I'm not one to talk," she said, lifting her glass to her lips.

"Don't you want a family?" he asked, studying her with his usual intensity.

"It's a bit late for me," she replied as casually as she could.

"No, it's not."

She felt something leap in her chest at the certainty in his tone.

"My mother was forty-five when she had me, and that was in a different era," he said. "Not to mention that you still look like you did the day I met you."

She smiled. "Is this where you tell me forty-seven is the new thirty?"

"You look like you're thirty." His gaze traveled from her head to her toes and back. "No, that's not true. You're more beautiful than when you were thirty."

She felt her cheeks flush. She hadn't blushed since she was seventeen, and now in a span of several hours, he'd made her blush a half dozen times. "Flattery, Evan? It's not necessary since we're already getting married."

"Not flattery. Truth." He smiled. "Come sit with me."

Her breath hitched, and she had to force herself to stay put and not jump up to join him. "There's no one here to make a show for."

"Exactly." He shifted on the couch. "Come sit with me."

She wanted to so badly. "What is this about, Evan? I know we didn't talk about it, but you don't need to act affectionate while we're alone."

"Who said anything about acting?" he said, taking another sip of his bourbon, his eyes steady on hers.

She cleared her throat. "For that matter, you weren't really serious about dinner tomorrow night, were you?"

"When have you known me not to be serious?"

True—he never said what he didn't mean. "I can't believe you had the audacity to instruct me to wear that red dress."

"I didn't instruct. It was a request." He smiled a little. "I've thought of you in that dress often. You looked stunning in it."

Before she could think of what to reply, he asked, "Maeve, can you say that in all these years you've never wondered about us?"

"There is no us," she said automatically.

"Yes, there is. We're getting married."

"That's for convenience."

"It doesn't change the end result."

She buried her nose in her glass, hoping the fumes would clear her head. "We need to talk about what we're going to do with our business relationship."

"There's nothing to discuss if I sell my company."

She sat up. "You're serious about this?"

He cocked his brow. "When have you known me not to be serious about something I said?" he asked again.

"A valid point." She frowned. "You aren't an impulsive person. You've been thinking about this a while."

"Yes." He stared at her. "Does that change your thoughts about me?"

Nothing would change her thoughts about him. He was the most attractive, incredibly smart, insanely hot, and utterly kind man she'd ever known. "Why did you agree to marry me?"

"Because when I see an opening, I take it, and I've been waiting for an opening for you for twenty years, Maeve." Sitting up, his feet on the floor, he shot back the rest of his drink and set the glass on the table next to the couch. "Is it okay if I take a shower?"

She almost choked on the words in her throat. She waved her hand toward the bathroom, trying not to visualize the reality of him naked in her shower. She was sure he'd find the extra towels in the cabinet by the bathtub.

As he walked to the bathroom, he pulled his shirt from his slacks and began to unbutton it. She stared at the sight, disappointed when he closed the door behind him before taking it off.

She downed the rest of her bourbon too.

She was still pondering another shot when he emerged from the bathroom in a cloud of steam, wearing nothing but a towel.

She looked him up and down, because only a fool would waste that sort of view. "Isn't this taking our engagement too far?"

"It's not nearly as far as I'd like to take it," he said, going to his bag.

"You better have brought something to sleep in."

He looked at her over his shoulder, brow raised. "Wouldn't you be disappointed if I did?"

Yes, she would. "If you stay in the spare bedroom—"

"I'm staying in here," he said with finality. "I'm your fiancé, after all."

She flushed, trying not to imagine what that entailed. "Where are you sleeping?"

"I'd like to sleep in your bed, but I'm happy sleeping on the floor if that makes you more comfortable. For the time being." He withdrew something from his bag and headed back to the bathroom. "Think about it."

She waited until he closed the door to pace back and forth. She couldn't let him sleep in her bed. It was inappropriate.

She snorted—since when did she act Victorian? She wanted him, and apparently he wanted her. For God's sake—they were getting married.

Except they hadn't talked about what that was going to mean. Were they going to go about their own business? She lived here in Westport mostly now; Evan lived in London.

Unless he was serious about selling his business.

She frowned. What was he going to do if he did that? She couldn't see him sitting idle at home. Would he be fulfilled?

Would being with her be enough?

She leaned into her dresser, tapping her fingers rapidly on the top surface. She was a risk taker. For the span of her career, she'd been known as a maverick, with a sexy portfolio of companies. She was used to assessing the gamble in a position, and she was expert at coming out on top.

She wasn't sure she'd come out on top with Evan.

But—hell—with him, she had a feeling she wouldn't mind being on the bottom.

The thing was, since the botched engagement in her late twenties, she'd ruthlessly protected herself against being snubbed by a lover. If they showed any sign of being unpredictable, she walked past them. If they were high maintenance, she ran in the opposite direction.

It was simpler and happier being on her own.

The real question here was, would she be able to return to her uncomplicated, peaceful life if this gambit with Evan didn't work?

"It comes down to one thing, Maeve."

She turned around slowly, taking him in. He'd put on some comfortable-looking baggy pants that looked soft to the touch, but his chest was bare and broad and utterly mouthwatering. He was rubbing his shoulder, rotating it a bit as if trying to loosen it up, and the play of his muscles was breathtaking. "I was just thinking that," she managed to say.

"Do you trust me?" he asked, his voice husky.

"You know I do." She could feel the weight of her ring heavy on her finger.

"Then you know I'd never do anything to push you into a corner." He advanced toward her, coming to stand a breath away.

"I know," she whispered.

He bent his head, kissing her altogether too briefly before saying softly, "Do you want me to outline the rest of the evening for you? Will that help?"

"I like knowing."

"I know you do." Smiling, he ran his hand over her hair. "We're going to climb into your bed, and I'm going to wrap my arms around you, and we'll talk about little nonsensical things from our day. I'll kiss your neck once or twice because I won't be able to help myself. Then I'm going to tell you to close your eyes and go to sleep, and you're going to resist until finally you fall asleep." He kissed her forehead. "And I'll fall asleep holding you in my arms, and when I wake in the morning I'll think that my greatest wish has finally come true."

Frowning, she stared at him. "You can't mean that."

"Maeve, you know I never say a word I don't mean."

Swallowing thickly, she grasped at the last straw. "Liam—"

"Based on the way Liam was looking at Henri, I don't think they're going to be aware of anything but each other." He kissed her forehead. "Get in bed."

She didn't know what to do but to take her robe off and climb under the covers.

CHAPTER 13

*H*enri always had a plan, but with this wedding and everything that had happened since she'd arrived, she was flying by the seat of her pants.

It was exciting, but it was also scary. She'd had trouble sleeping last night, although she knew her insomnia was less about baking Maeve's cake and more about a certain hot chef.

Liam wanted to *woo* her.

Alone in the kitchen, which was surprising in itself, she clutched her coffee cup, reliving their conversation and kisses from the night before for the hundredth time. *Delicious* didn't begin to describe it.

Putting the cup down, she took her mobile out of her back pocket and texted Vivi.

Henri

Panties can't actually melt, can they?

Her cousin responded instantly.

<u>Vivi</u>
Not if they're cotton.

Setting her phone aside, she took a deep breath and looked at the five sample cakes lined up side by side on the counter. Her tasting was today. She needed to take the delicious feelings on the inside and apply them to the cakes. She needed to keep her eye on the prize, and that was all the new customers Maeve's wedding was going to bring her.

Henri had known what frostings she was going to make for each one, but now, looking at the cakes, feeling what she still felt from last night, she knew she had to up her game. The simple frostings she'd expected to make weren't going to stand up to the tension abounding in this household.

It wasn't just her and Liam, either.

She'd crossed paths with Maeve and Evan earlier this morning. Evan had gone out for a run, and Maeve had retired to her office, but the push and pull between the two had been stark. Henri wondered why they didn't just lock themselves away until it was time for the tasting. Maybe they were trying to be polite or circumspect while she and Liam were here. She didn't know why, though—it wasn't fooling anyone.

Maybe it had to do with how Liam watched Evan last night, like he was making sure the older man didn't steal his sister's virtue. It was kind of sweet, even if she didn't understand it. Wouldn't you want the person you loved to be not only in love with her chosen partner but also in lust? That was the epitome of having your cake and eating it too.

She took out the bowls she'd need for each frosting, trying not to think about having *her* cake (Liam) and eating it (hold it together, Henri).

Pushing that daydream aside, she began measuring out the ingredients. She hummed as she whipped together each frosting, taking care as she quickly spread them on the cakes. Because presentation was important, even at this stage, she got out the gold leaf she kept on hand and began to lay out a simple design on each small cake.

She stepped back and looked at the five small cakes. For some reason, she felt uncomplicated was the key here, despite what Maeve said she wanted, so that was what these cakes were: elegant and simple but full of spice.

Perfect for Maeve and Evan.

She set the kitchen back to rights and then loaded a large tray she'd found, taking everything to the living room just off the foyer. Normally she'd have set the tasting up in the dining room or something comparable, but she felt like the more casual living room was where they should do it.

It wasn't at all like what she would have expected Maeve's living room to look like. There was a lot of texture and color, soft dreamy fabrics, and plush furniture to relax on. Instead of a table, there was a large rectangular tufted ottoman in the center of the room. Henri set the tray on there, the little forks and small plates neatly stacked by the spot she intended to sit. She arranged the cakes in the middle with a small vase of daisies she'd repurposed from her bedroom.

She loved daisies. They were such cheery flowers.

Lastly, she set champagne glasses in a cluster to one side. She didn't like drinking champagne on its own, but with cake it was transcendent.

"There," she said, standing back to look at it all. Satisfied, she went upstairs to change into nicer clothes. She shimmied into the dress Vivi had made her buy to wear for more formal meetings and slipped into the low mules Vivi picked to go with the outfit. She fastened on her favorite earrings, a dangly lace pattern dotted with diamonds that her parents had given her for a birthday, and pronounced herself ready.

She checked herself briefly in the mirror, wondering what Liam would think about how she looked. She tried to think if he'd ever seen her in anything but her chef's clothing or jeans. She didn't think so.

She'd seen him for a lust-charged moment this morning in the kitchen. He'd had to run to his restaurant to take care of a delivery issue, but he assured her he'd be back in time for the tasting.

She was getting a bottle of champagne out of the refrigerator when he strode into the kitchen. He wore jeans, a white shirt, and a leather jacket that was worn in the right way. He came directly to her, taking her by the waist and putting a lingering kiss on her cheek. "You look like heaven, and you smell like dessert."

Grinning, happy, she set the bottle on the counter and put her arms around his neck. "I'm a pastry chef."

"Hmm." His fingers tested the silky fabric of her dress. "I like this."

She shivered, her body perking up all over. "The tasting is in ten minutes."

He hummed again. "Are you telling me to behave?"

She laughed. "Will that work?"

Holding her face, his lips moved over her skin in kisses that were like delicate spun sugar. He stopped at her mouth for the briefest taste. "Like sugar and spice," he murmured.

She'd done a cardamom frosting for one of the cakes. "Come on. You'll like what I have going on."

"Yes, I will." He picked up the champagne, took her hand, and let her lead him to the living room as he told her about his morning.

The tasting wasn't scheduled to start for another ten minutes, but Maeve and Evan were already there, sitting on one of the couches close together. Evan was holding a fork up to Maeve's lips, which were open and waiting. Henri stopped short when she realized that was her cake he was feeding her. She looked at the cakes and saw he'd dipped the fork right into the cake itself.

She blinked. *Well.* She should have been affronted, she supposed, but it was hot. And perfect—the way cake *should* be eaten—so she couldn't fault them. She was tempted to grab a fork and dig in herself.

Maeve and Evan were so engrossed in each other that they didn't hear Liam and her enter until Liam coughed loudly.

"We decided to start early," Maeve said, not looking away from Evan's pinning gaze.

Henri grinned as she took the bottle from Liam's tight grip and stuck it in the ice bucket she'd staged earlier. "You're missing the champagne."

"We're not missing anything," Evan said, his focus trained on his fiancée. He dipped the same fork into the next cake and held it to Maeve's lips.

She wrapped her lips around the tines, drawing out the bite.

Liam cleared his throat loudly, his gaze narrowed. "Don't have too much sugar, Maeve. You don't want to get hyper."

"I'll help her come down if she does," Evan promised.

Henri snorted as she sat on the couch across from them.

Maeve looked at her and rolled her eyes.

Liam dropped next to Henri, arms crossed, glaring at his soon-to-be brother-in-law.

Because she understood the power of cake, Henri sliced a piece of one of the cakes, put it on a plate, and handed it to Liam. "Stick this in your mouth. You'll like it."

He looked torn between keeping an eye on his sister and focusing on her cake, but food was always going to win out with him. He held it up to his nose, inhaling the aroma before dipping his fork in and taking a bite. He hummed, a low, private sound that she'd never heard him utter.

Her panties went damp at the sound.

She crossed her legs and reached for the champagne to uncork it.

"Saffron and cardamom," Liam muttered from next to her, shaking his head as he took another bite. "Evocative and exotic, but not so much that it's over-powering."

"It tastes like Rabat," Evan said.

"You've been to Rabat?" Maeve asked, looking at him curiously.

"I have a house close to there."

Her brow furrowed, much like Liam's did. "I didn't know that."

Evan smiled faintly. "I have to have some mystery to keep you interested. Here." He held out another fork of cake to her. To Henri, he said, "What aphrodisiac do you put in the cake?"

She laughed. "Cake is naturally an aphrodisiac in itself. There's a reason 'cake by the ocean' is a synonym for sex."

"Is this apple and pepper?" Maeve asked, pointing to the one Evan had fed her.

"Apple and cayenne," Henri said. "With a touch of ginger."

"I love it." Maeve motioned to Evan to give her another bite. She speared Henri with a look. "How is it I've never heard of you?"

"I've only officially been out on my own for the past six months, with the exception of a few commissions here and there while I was at Papillon, and I haven't been a chef long enough to have the write-ups needed in order to become known." Henri glanced at Liam. "Though there was the *Esquire* article that one time."

He nodded. "That was owed to your vanilla and violet cake."

"And your *coq au vin*."

"Which you helped perfect," he countered.

Maeve hummed, looking back and forth between them. "We need to change that," she declared, tapping the couch's armrest.

Evan smiled at Henri. "That's her strategizing face."

Maeve raised her brow at him.

"Don't look at me like that. I know what you look like when you're plotting how to get what you want."

Liam glared at Evan, arms folded tight. "You think you know her that well?"

Evan met Liam's challenge head-on. "Yes."

"Down, boys," Maeve said lightly, putting her hand on Evan's leg, her ring sparkling in the light streaming in from the window despite the gray outside. Her fiancé immediately covered it with his.

Henri sighed.

"What?" Liam said.

Shrugging, she poured more champagne for everyone. "I always know when a couple is going to last forever, and I can tell that about Maeve and Evan. It's just nice."

The silence that filled the room was striking. She looked up. "What?"

Liam looked like he wanted to ask her something, but he shook his head. Maeve looked shell-shocked and Evan just looked hungry for Maeve.

She needed to wrap this up so Evan could carry his fiancée off to bed. "Since you need such a large cake, I can incorporate any or all of the cakes here together into your tower. If you prefer mixing and matching, we can discuss that."

"Maeve likes variety," Evan said.

"Variety is the spice of life," Henri said over Liam's growl. She shot him a look and focused on his sister. "You mentioned that you wanted cornelli on the cake."

"Cornelli?" Maeve asked.

"Piping that looks like fancy lacework," she explained. "If I can see your wedding dress, I'll make sure the cake and your dress have complementary patterns without being exact or too disparate. That way you won't clash or disappear in your photos."

Maeve frowned. "I haven't thought about a dress. I'll probably just wear something I already have."

Henri frowned. "You're having two hundred guests, but you aren't wearing something special?"

"I see the event as being a big celebration more than anything," Maeve replied without really answering.

"Of course it's a celebration." But people who went to all the trouble to have a cake this fancy didn't scrimp on the rest of the details. "I'll contact your coordinator to get information on the decorations and flowers then. I can make sure to decorate the cake in sync with that." Henri picked up her mobile to put it in her notes. "Can you give me her or his name?"

"I don't have anyone yet."

Henri dropped her hand. "The wedding is in a little over a week."

"I'll contact my assistant next week," Maeve assured her smoothly.

She shook her head. An assistant might be able to organize an event like this for two dozen people in a week, but not two hundred. "If you don't mind, I'll put my cousin Vivienne in touch with you. Vivi can help get everything in order, because with two hundred people, you'll need a wedding coordinator, at least for the day."

"Talk to Vivienne," Evan said to his fiancée.

The look Maeve gave him would have shriveled a lesser man. Evan merely returned it.

Henri watched them, seeing their unspoken communication but not sure what they were saying. Her mother and father were that way.

Could she communicate like that with Liam? She looked at him and raised her brows. He shook his head, obviously telling her he'd talk to her later.

"I'll speak to your cousin, Henri," Maeve said, standing. "I loved everything about what you did here, so I'll put the cake in your hands. Ask Liam for confirmation on anything you need." She headed out of the room. At the threshold, she stopped and looked over her shoulder. "Evan, are you coming?"

"Soon, I hope," Henri heard him say softly under his breath as he stood and stalked out after his woman.

Henri sighed as she reloaded the tray. "They are so hot together."

Liam growled.

She turned to him. "What's going on with you? You're acting like you aren't happy that your sister is so loved."

"There's loved, and then there's loved." He stood and began to pace. "I really don't want to think about either in concert with her."

Henri got up and put her hand on his chest to stop him. "Help me take this stuff to the kitchen. You can tell me what you thought about the cake."

As he focused on her, the tension melted from his

• shoulders. He hesitated, but then he covered her hand with his and nodded.

She felt a sharp need to take him into her arms and comfort him, to ask him what was going on. But her job was the wedding cake, so she picked up the tray and tried to distract Liam with small talk about spices and unusual combinations she wanted to try one day.

CHAPTER 14

While Henriette cleaned up after the tasting and organized her notes, Liam took the opportunity to steal into Maeve's office and text Áine.

<u>Liam</u>
Maeve needs an intervention.

<u>Áine</u>
Why? She's never exhibited obsessive behavior.

<u>Liam</u>
You haven't seen her with Evan.

<u>Áine</u>
How's that?

<u>Liam</u>
They've been holding hands.

<u>Áine</u>
They're getting married. It's allowed.

<u>Liam</u>
He made her blush.

<u>Áine</u>
Maeve never blushes.

<u>Liam</u>
She does now.

<u>Áine</u>
I'll call her.

Right as he put his mobile away, Maeve stormed in, closing the door firmly behind her. "We need to talk."

He crossed his arms and perched on the edge of her desk. "That's what I'm thinking too."

"I just talked to Henri's cousin, Vivienne." Maeve took a stance in front of him, hands on her hips. "They're under the assumption that we're having a big wedding because of the cake. So now I'm having a two-hundred-person wedding in a week. I don't know two hundred people I'd want to invite to my wedding. A wedding shouldn't be a spectacle, but that's what this is becoming."

Rubbing his neck, he winced. "That's a little sticky, isn't it?"

"It's more than a little sticky. This is completely out of hand, Liam. The woman is coming here to plan a wedding for me. She's on her way here, with God knows what kind of help to get this farce of a wedding on track." Hands on her hips, she glared at him. "So where do you stand with Henri?"

"I don't know," he answered honestly. "I want to think that Henriette would think me going through the trouble of hiring her for a cake is charming, but I forgot to factor in professional pride. She's counting on this to drive more visibility and customers to her business."

"Well, fuck," Maeve said succinctly.

"Exactly." He rubbed the back of his neck. Things were not going the way he'd planned.

"How the hell did you not think of her pride?" his oldest sister interrupted. "You've got it in spades. If she'd hired you with the same intent, and you were counting on it for more business, wouldn't you feel duped or, at the very least, let down?"

He winced again. "I don't want to ever let her down."

"Which means we need to make sure she gets what she needs." Maeve began to pace back and forth, her arms crossed as she thought.

"We need to make sure you get what you need too," he said, matching her stance.

Stopping, she frowned at him. "What?"

"I didn't just do this for Henriette. I wanted to help you too." He rubbed his neck. "Except I think I've made things worse. I've seen the way you look at him, Maeve. I saw how you held his hand."

"I—" She shook her head. "Liam, this is—"

He took her hand, pausing abruptly when he saw the stunning ring on her finger. That wasn't the sort of ring you gave someone in an arranged marriage. He looked his sister in the eye. "Are you falling for him?"

Her dark eyes narrowed. "Liam, *you* were the one who suggested this scheme. Don't try to make me out to be wrong here."

"I'm not. I'm just asking you to be more cautious." He squeezed her hand. "Have you thought that this might be an advantageous proposition for him?"

She breathed a harsh laugh. "Of course it's advantageous for him. He has to have something to gain from this as much as I do for it to work."

"Are you sure what he's gaining isn't your bank account?"

Her laughter cut off. "Because why else would someone want to marry me?"

He winced once more. "That's not what I meant."

"I think you did," she said, her back stiff. "Is that how you see me? Is that the only reason anyone would have to be with me? For my money?"

"Of course not." He waved at her. "You're gorgeous."

She cocked her brow.

"You know you are." He glared at her. "You can't blame me for the fact that you've cut yourself off from everyone. You even hold Áine and me at arm's length these days."

"I do not," she bit out succinctly. "You and Áine just don't need me like you used to."

He raked his hair back. "Our relationship isn't about needing you. It's about loving you."

There was a knock at the door.

He and Maeve both turned and yelled, "What?"

It opened and Evan stepped inside, closing it behind him. He first looked at Maeve, his gaze taking her in. Liam saw the moment the man saw that Maeve was upset by the way his jaw tightened.

Liam frowned. If he didn't know better, he'd think Ward had genuine feelings for his sister—especially when the man speared him with his cold pale eyes, like he wanted to reproach Liam.

When Evan spoke, his voice was measured. "I could hear your yelling in the hallway."

Liam rubbed his neck, already feeling bad enough. "We weren't yelling."

Maeve nodded. "We were expressing."

Evan looked at her with part disbelief and part humor. "I came to make sure you had the knives locked up, just in case, but since you two weren't actually yelling at each other, I guess that's unnecessary. Maybe you'll come for a walk with me, Maeve. The sun's come out."

Maeve looked outside and then back at Ward. Something passed in her eyes, but Liam couldn't decipher it. Then she nodded at the man. "I'd love to. I'll just change my shoes."

Evan gestured to her to walk before him. Liam glared at the man to let him know he knew what he was about.

At the door, Maeve glanced at Liam over her shoulder. "We need to figure out how to resolve this situation, Liam. Before it gets any more complicated."

This part of the situation was already more complicated than he'd anticipated. He waited in there, watching from the window as Ward held his sister's hand and led her down the shady path beyond the garden.

CHAPTER 15

*M*aeve stood in her walk-in closet, eyeing the red dress Evan had instructed—*requested*—her to wear. She actually had it here instead of leaving it in her London closet, which was amazing given that she'd only worn it once.

It was one of her favorite dresses. She hadn't been able to bear leaving it behind, even if she never wore red. The color and style caused too much attention when she'd been trying to downplay her femininity in business. She'd worn it that one time in a moment of defiance, to make a statement as she celebrated winning a bid over a competitor.

And she'd obviously been right, because Evan remembered the one time she couldn't resist putting it on.

She touched the silk fabric. Normally, she would have told him she'd wear whatever the hell she wanted, but she longed to put it on, for him *and* for herself. Normally, she didn't have much cause to dress fancy here in Mayo—if not tonight, then when?

She took it from its hanger and stepped back into her room. After their walk (which had been lovely, by the way), Evan had showered, dressed, and gone downstairs to make a call while he waited for her to get ready.

God, they were already acting like a couple.

She'd never admit it, but she liked it. On their walk, they'd talked about random things. Nature. Art. Food. Music—he liked *opera*. He taken her hand and he'd walked so close that their shoulders brushed, but he hadn't tried to kiss her again.

What was that about?

Her mobile rang, a welcome distraction from her thoughts, especially when she saw it was her sister. "We had the cake tasting today," she said the moment she answered it. "Liam's Henri is amazing. You'll love her spicy apple cake. A good thing too, because you're going to have to eat enough for at least fifty people."

"It's a good thing that I have a sweet tooth. But I'm wondering something else," Áine said in the serene therapist's voice.

"What?"

"Where did Evan spend the night?"

"With me." She raised her eyebrow even though her sister couldn't see it. "Nothing happened."

"Define 'nothing.'"

"No penetration."

"Maeve, we both know there's a world of other things that have just as much meaning as penetration."

"Is that the reason you called?" she asked. "To check up on Evan and me? We're grown adults, and we're getting married. I don't think we need a chaperone."

"I called because Liam is having a fit over the fact that you're apparently gaga over a man you've never exhibited a *tendresse* for."

Maeve made a face in the mirror. "I'm angry at Liam. He said some highly unflattering things to me about being easily taken advantage of, so he deserves to be hit over the head with a frying pan."

Áine gasped. "He didn't!"

"Yes, he did." It still stuck with her that he thought she was closed off to them.

"Well, in that case, Liam does deserve a good wallop." Her sister paused. "But there's one thing that he said that struck me."

"What?" She bent to slip her shoes on, anchoring her mobile in place with her shoulder so she could buckle her ankle straps.

"Liam said you blushed."

"I don't blush," Maeve replied, feeling her cheeks flush and glad Áine was in Dublin and not in Westport.

"Exactly. So either Liam lied, and we both know he'd never lie," Áine continued in her reasonable you-can-trust-me psychiatrist's voice, "or an anomaly occurred and you actually blushed regarding a man. Who's staying in your room with you."

"Nothing happened." So far. But this morning when she'd woken up with Evan wrapped firmly around her (emphasis on the "firmly"), it'd taken everything in her not to turn around to see what *could* happen.

He'd known it too, damn him. He'd murmured good morning in a husky voice and ran his hand over her hip to her leg, touching her skin where her nightgown had ridden up. There was no telling what would have happened if she hadn't hopped out of bed.

"You said no penetration happened," Áine pointed out.

She startled, thinking that Áine was questioning that. "It didn't."

"Penetration is the least frightening thing that can happen to a woman like you."

She cocked her brow. "A woman like me?" she said distinctly.

"One who's spent her life avoiding additional encumbrances," her sister clarified. "I'm a psychiatrist, Maeve. I see people's motivations. Plus, you and I have had too many cocktail nights together for me not to know that you purposely isolate yourself to avoid adding responsibility to your life."

"You make me sound…" She searched for the word.

"Human?" her sister asked with humor in her voice. But when she spoke next, sadness had replaced the humor. "Darling, of course you'd want to avoid more responsibility. You've had to take care of me and Liam since you were eighteen. I can't imagine what it was like for you to take that burden on when you were so young."

"It wasn't a burden." She cleared the emotion from her voice. It tasted like guilt, stuck there since the day she'd sold her dad's dream instead of trying to make it work.

"Yes, it was," Áine replied softly. "One that I've never taken lightly, and neither has Liam."

Rolling her shoulders back, Maeve blinked her eyes against the unaccustomed moisture. "Don't start on this now. My mascara will run, and I need to finish getting ready for dinner."

"With Evan?"

She hesitated a moment before she said, "He's taking me to *A Ghrá.*"

Áine laughed. "What did Liam say about that?"

There was a light knock on her door. Evan—she recognized his touch. "I have to go," she told her sister.

The door opened and Evan stepped inside. He took her in with one comprehensive head-to-toe appraisal. His approval was blatant in his gaze as he approached her.

"I have to go," she said to her sister again.

"He's there, isn't he? How hot is he exactly?" Áine whispered, more like a teenager than the professional she was, as if Evan could hear her.

"Blazing," was all Maeve could say, ending the call

and swiveling around on the bench she perched on to face him. "Am I late?"

"No," he said, taking her hand and helping her to her feet. His thumb touched the ring he'd given her. "I just missed you."

Her heart flipped at that, but she managed to outwardly keep her cool. "You've only been downstairs a little while."

He didn't say anything to that, instead lowering his head until his mouth hovered just above hers. "Can I kiss you?"

She glanced at his lips. She could still feel the imprint of them from the last kiss he'd given her. Last night, when they'd crawled under the covers, she'd wanted him to kiss her so badly. Usually she took what she wanted, and she'd thought about turning over and kissing him, but she wasn't certain she was ready to take that step.

Who was she kidding? It was less a step than one gigantic leap, and in the light of day it seemed wiser that nothing had happened. There would have been no coming back from kissing him in bed. There would have been penetration, and a lot of it.

Her body wanted that bad.

Her mind wasn't sure it did, though, and she wasn't one to leap before she was one hundred percent on board. So instead, she'd let him hold her, spooned behind her, until she fell asleep.

She slept all night. She couldn't remember the last time she hadn't woken up at all.

Evan touched a lock of her hair. "In that case, I'll wait to kiss you."

She frowned. He could read minds now?

"I have a sixth sense when it comes to you, Maeve," he said, smiling wryly. He took her hand and kissed just above the ring before turning it over and kissing the inside of her wrist, lingering on her pulse until she felt breathless. "Shall we go?"

She shook her head to clear it, trying to gather her wits. "I need my necklace."

Before she could move, he reached behind her and picked it up off the vanity. "Turn around."

"Are you trying to seduce me?" she murmured, giving him her back.

"I'm not trying," he said softly, pushing her hair to one side. "But if all I wanted was a seduction, I wouldn't have agreed to get married."

She shivered at the touch of his fingers on her neck, gathering her hair out of his way. "What do you want then?"

"Forever." He clasped her necklace, placing a kiss on her nape. "Now, before you freak out, let's go eat. You're hungry."

She wanted to deny it, but her stomach grumbled right then.

Holding her hand, he led her out of her house. Maeve didn't see any sign of Liam and Henri, which was just as well. She could imagine what Liam would say if he saw what she was wearing.

"They're in the kitchen," Evan said as he helped her into her coat.

"You really can read my mind," she muttered, tucking her clutch under her arm.

He untucked her hair from under the collar. "It's not magic, Maeve. I just know you."

She stopped and stared at him.

He smiled dryly. "Don't puzzle it out now. Let's just have a nice dinner together."

"Nice?" she repeated. "'Nice' isn't a word I've ever associated with you."

"I can be very nice," he said softly, close to her ear as he escorted her to his car. He opened the door for her and waited for her to settle inside before gently closing the door and going around to his side.

He didn't seem to need directions to Liam's restaurant. "You know the area well," she said, surprised that he knew his way around Westport.

"My property is close to here," he said, his eyes on the road. He pulled into a parking space across from the restaurant and got out to open her door.

She put her hand in his, aware of his gaze on her legs as she swung them out of the car. He kept her hand and walked her into the restaurant.

The hostess greeted them with a smile. "Welcome to *A Ghrá*. Do you have a reservation?"

"For Ward," Evan said.

Maeve glanced at him but he kept his focus on the hostess.

"Oh, yes." The young woman beamed at them and motioned with her hand. "This way."

They walked through the dining hall toward an empty table in the back, but then they walked past it.

Maeve frowned. The only thing back here was—

"Here's the tasting room," the hostess said, making a sweeping gesture. "Please make yourself comfortable, and if you need anything, there's a buzzer right here by the door. Someone will come answer right away."

"Thank you," Evan murmured as he helped Maeve out of her coat and handed it to the hostess.

Maeve slid into the seat Evan pulled out for her. "You reserved Liam's tasting room? Just for the two of us?"

"I wanted the undivided attention of my intended," he said as he took the seat next to her. Before she could figure out how to feel about that, he took her hand again.

She looked at the way his fingers twined with hers. "Are you going to hold my hand all through dinner?"

"Yes." His look dared her to say otherwise.

Fortunately, a waitress came in with a bucket of ice and a bottle of champagne. Maeve recognized Marie and winced.

"Maeve!" the young woman exclaimed with a delighted smile. "I didn't know you were the one who'd booked the tasting room tonight."

"I wasn't," she replied.

"Oh." Marie's lips formed a moue as she looked curiously between Evan and Maeve. Then she turned and focused her attention completely on Evan as she popped the champagne cork. "I'm Marie. Welcome to *A Ghrá.*"

"Thank you," he murmured politely.

"Liam isn't here tonight, as you probably know, but we have a wonderful menu prepared for you." Marie smiled at him. "Shall I wait a bit or get you started?"

"Maeve is hungry, so let's start," he said pleasantly.

"Maeve is sitting right here," she said, accepting the glass of champagne Marie poured for her.

Evan kissed her hand again. "A fact for which I'm grateful."

Marie sighed dreamily and then excused herself.

Maeve faced Evan.

Instead of explaining what was going on, he simply held up his glass. "To my fiancée, the most beautiful and clever woman I've ever met."

She frowned at him, not taking a sip of her wine. "You don't have to pretend like this, Evan."

"I'm not pretending." He looked right in her eyes. "Do you remember that benefit ball two years ago at Convent?"

She shook her head at the non sequitur. "What?"

"The benefit two years ago for single mothers," he replied patiently.

"Vaguely." Actually she remembered every moment

181

of it. It was the first time she'd seen him in black tie and she'd almost swallowed her tongue, he'd looked so dashing. She'd spent the entire evening trying not to stare at him. And then a few people started to dance, and suddenly he'd been in front of her, hand extended. He'd led her into the small crowd and into a slow, sensual whirl.

It'd been the most erotic moment of her life—until he'd kissed her when he'd arrived at *Cois Dara*.

She cleared her throat. "I was surprised to see you there."

He nodded. "I normally stay in the shadows at events like that. I let the people who need to see me catch sight of me and fade out of the spotlight otherwise. But that night I didn't care who watched. I just wanted to dance with you."

She sipped her champagne, staring at him over the top of the rim. "That was the only time we've danced."

"Until tonight." He stood up and helped her to her feet, much like that night long ago. He drew her into his arms and led her smoothly into a turn before swaying with her sensuously in the open space of the tasting room.

Without thought, she eased into his hold, feeling comfortable, like they'd done this hundreds of times before.

Evan obviously felt it too, because he said, his voice low and intimate, "You feel right in my arms. I always knew you would. I always knew we'd fit together like this."

She looked up at him. "What are you doing, Evan?"

He met her gaze, unflinching honesty in his. "I'm showing you we could be good together. I'm asking you to give us a chance to see if there couldn't be something more between us than a year and a half of a convenient marriage."

"I—" She swallowed thickly. "I didn't know you felt this way, Evan. When did this happen?"

"Twenty years ago, Maeve," he said, bringing her closer.

She gasped softly, feeling his hardness brush against her belly. She gawped at him.

"It happens around you. Don't worry." He smiled ruefully. "I'm not pressuring you into anything. I just want to be honest about where I stand."

She turned her head and rested her cheek against his shoulder—the better not to see his expression. "I don't know where *I* stand at this moment."

"The ground's shifted under your feet, hasn't it, love?" he murmured against her hair. "I won't pressure you, Maeve. If you want more from me than a show for other people, you'll have to make the move."

She looked up at him. "What if I don't make a move? What happens then?"

He brushed her hair from her face. "Why don't we set that aside for tonight? We'll dance a little, share food, and discuss the mundane things that people normally talk about on dates."

"I'm not certain I know what people normally discuss," she said, frowning. "I don't do dates."

"Then I count myself lucky to be here with you," he said.

"Do you go on a lot of dates?" she asked, hoping she didn't sound as jealous as she felt.

"Not anymore," he said with a quirk of his lips. "Except with you."

She harrumphed. But the idea of going on more dates with him captured her imagination, especially if there was more dancing. She could get used to dancing with him.

The thought was both lovely and haunting.

She pushed it aside. She just needed to get through the next nine days intact.

"Intact" was the key here. She trusted Evan implicitly with everything that she had, but she could see that her heart was going to be a completely different matter.

CHAPTER 16

enri curled into the turquoise chair in the kitchen, her legs under her, her sketchbook balanced on her thigh. She'd had an idea for the cake's decoration, but the more time she spent with Maeve and Evan, the more she was reconsidering it. An elaborate cake layered in heavy lacework didn't feel right. She was doodling some other designs, hoping to find the one that'd satisfy what Maeve said she wanted and what would actually suit them.

Out of the corner of her eye, she was aware of Liam. He'd brought over a comfy chair for himself and was flipping through a food memoir, looking for something based on his intent expression. She wondered if he knew what he was looking for. He kept glancing at the clock above the stove, scowling when he saw no time had passed.

He was worried about his sister. Henri smiled. It

was adorable, his concern for her when she was out with her fiancé. She wondered if he reacted this way here, how would he be if he had a daughter. She flipped the page of her notebook and began sketching him.

"Why are you looking at me like that?" he asked suddenly.

"Like what?" she said, penciling in his disheveled hair.

"Like I'm mental." Sighing, he lowered the book and rubbed his neck.

"Maybe because you are." She shut her sketchbook and set it aside. "You do realize that when Evan brings Maeve home, he's probably going to kiss her?"

Liam growled, closing his book with a little more force than necessary.

Chuckling, she leaned back in the chair. "I don't think you dislike Evan, so what is this about?"

"I'm worried about Maeve."

Because it was such a change from how their relationship was before, she hesitated, but then she went for it and reached for his hand. She took a moment to feel it, the texture of his skin and his calluses and the strength. Then she looked him in the eye. "Explain to me why."

"It's not rocket science," he said, leaning forward and putting his other hand on top of hers. "I don't want her to be hurt."

"For what it's worth, I don't think Evan would ever do anything to hurt her."

Liam didn't look convinced. "You really believe that?"

"I wouldn't say it if I didn't."

He stared at her longer. Then he said, "Would it help you if Maeve invited someone she knows from *Vogue* to the wedding?"

Henri froze. "A friend?" she asked, not wanting to read too much into this.

"Friendly enough." Liam shrugged. "Maeve knows a lot of people. When Maeve asks for something, people tend to jump to deliver."

"It's Maeve's wedding," she said carefully, trying to stay neutral. Somehow, she didn't feel like Maeve would like a random person there on her wedding day. "She should invite who she wants."

"It'd help you though, wouldn't it?"

It'd be the biggest boon *ever*. "It certainly couldn't hurt," she said, trying to downplay it.

"I'll talk to her then." He flashed her a smile that didn't reach his eyes. "She did the same for me. She asked a food critic to come to my restaurant the first week I was open. I didn't know it at the time. It was a gamble, given that a lot of restaurants are still working out their kinks the first few weeks, but fortunately my crew was ready."

"But Maeve loves you. I'm a stranger she just met. She has no incentive to help me."

"She'd do it because it'd make me happy."

She gripped the armrest, trying not to get too

excited about the possibility. That's all it was: a possibility. It seemed to be a big ask considering Maeve didn't know her and hadn't even had more than a few sample bites of her cakes.

Liam glanced at the time again.

Regardless, it was sweet of Liam to think of it. Anyone else and she would have hugged them. With Liam, she wasn't sure where she stood.

But she recognized that he was in a funny mood and needed diversion, so she swung her legs off the chair. It was the least she could do when he'd done so much to help her. "Walk me to my room?"

"Yes." He stood, picking up his book.

Leaving her sketchbook where it was, she got up and waited for him to take her hand. She frowned a bit when he just gestured to the hall. She walked ahead of him, wondering if he was going to kiss her again like he had last night.

She'd thought about what he'd said to her the night before. She'd gone to sleep hearing the words on repeat, and today they'd played on repeat as she'd iced her cakes. She wasn't used to distraction like that. Usually her focus was razor-sharp; when she was measuring the sugar for the frosting, she'd had to dump it out and remeasure it because she lost track of how much she'd put in.

It wasn't normal, and she was at war with herself about it. Part of her wanted to revel in the delicious anticipation of Liam's attention; the other part of her worried that she could lose her edge and end up working in a Tesco bakery.

She was still wrapped in her thoughts when they stopped at her door. Liam drew her toward him, finally taking her hand. "I was lousy company tonight. It's not what I wanted."

She tried to smile. "You love your sister. It's sweet, how you worry about her."

"I wouldn't be where I am without her." His brow furrowed. "I know the talent is mine, and I've worked to have what I have, but Maeve made sacrifices when she was younger to make sure Áine and I were taken care of. I was too young to help her then, or to look out for her properly. That's not the case now. She may still give to me, but I like to think I give her as much back."

"You're a good brother," she said, feeling that way about Chloe, though their relationship was less complex.

"Family is important." He looked at their clasped fingers, obviously thinking about something. "In the past eight months, that's been stark. When I came to Ireland to open *A Ghrá*, I thought I was doing it to be a rebel, to get what I wanted on my own terms. I was wrong."

Frowning, she tipped her head, trying to see him better in the dim light. "How so?"

"My priorities were mixed up. I was living for my passion instead of living." He looked at her like he wanted to say something else, but he shook his head.

"Passion is important, but the thing about it is you don't have to succeed in the fast lane. Passion just is, and if you believe in it and yourself, you'll do fine. It's the people around you and the time you spend with them that are more important."

"But you work hard at what you do," she insisted. "That's why you're where you are."

His grin was wry. "I owe luck and fate for what I have. I just have the good sense to use what was given to me. You're the same."

She wasn't sure she agreed. She scratched her forehead as she thought about it.

"You can't take your pans to bed with you, Henriette. They're a cold companion." Liam leaned in to press his lips to hers. It flared hot despite the fact that he kept it brief. "Let's get out of here for a bit tomorrow. Go into town with me," he implored.

"Where?" she asked, looking at his mouth. She wanted it back on hers.

"To *A Ghrá*. My restaurant."

She ran through her day. She needed to finalize how she was going to do the cake, check her supplies, make a list of everything she needed to purchase—

"I'm not asking for that much of your time, Henriette." He lowered his head and started kissing her again.

Each brush, each lick, made her feel more and more juicy, wishing and wanting. She arched into him, letting go of the lists in her head so she could concentrate on his lips.

"Think about it," he whispered with one last kiss before he took a step back. "Good night, Henriette."

Leaning in the doorway, she watched as he entered his room and closed the door. She stayed there, her fingertips tracing her lips, his words playing in her mind.

You can't take your pans to bed with you, Henriette.

Frowning, she went inside and closed the door. It wasn't wrong to want to succeed. He must not think so either; otherwise, why would he have offered to have Maeve arrange something with her contact at *Vogue*?

She took a shower and climbed into her bed, trying to visualize what she needed to do tomorrow. When she couldn't fall asleep, she pulled out her mobile.

<u>Henri</u>
Miss you! You and Mum good?

<u>Papa</u>
What's wrong?

Her chest tightened. Her parents always knew.

<u>Henri</u>
Just tired. There's a lot of work to do next week before the wedding.

Papa
Are you sure that's it?

You can't take your pans to bed with you, Henriette.
She shook her head and replied.

Henri
Is it lonely being good at what you do?

Papa
Not since I've had your mother.

Papa
Are you lonely?

Henri
I hadn't thought so...

Papa
This has to do with that chef, doesn't it?

Papa
Tell him I know how to use knives too.

She laughed out loud.

Henri
I love you, Papa.

<u>Papa</u>
I love you too, darling.

She put her mobile aside, warm with emotion. But the unease caused by Liam's statement crept back in, haunting her all night while she was awake and then straight into her dreams.

CHAPTER 17

*L*iam didn't fall asleep until after Maeve and Evan returned home. When he heard their car pull up, he furtively peeked out the window.

Evan got out and went around the car to help Maeve out. Liam snorted. Maeve never accepted help from anyone. Even in agreeing to his plan to help her acquire their father's business, she'd taken it over and run with it.

To his surprise, Maeve put her hand in Evan's as she stepped out of the car. Liam goggled as he watched Maeve lean into the man, her hand on his chest. He couldn't hear what they were saying, but he saw Evan's charmed smile as he gazed at Maeve with what looked like genuine fondness.

Liam squinted to decipher Maeve's reaction. He'd never seen that peculiar expression on his sister's face. If he didn't know better, he'd say it was infatuation.

Well, fuck.

Neither had he ever seen his sister look that young and hopeful, particularly around a man. Not even when she'd been briefly engaged twenty years ago.

Liam returned to his bed, trying not to listen to them as they entered the house and walked up the stairs, but he couldn't help hearing Evan's low voice and Maeve's hushed laugh. He heard them move down the hall toward Maeve's wing, and then her bedroom door closed and there was just silence.

Maybe Henriette was right. Maybe Evan *was* good for Maeve.

Well, *fuck*.

HE DIDN'T KNOW what time it was when he woke up. He felt like he hadn't slept. He threw on the first thing he found and went downstairs.

It was his luck that Evan was in the kitchen at the nook, reading the newspaper. The man looked up as Liam walked in. "Good morning," he said.

Liam mumbled as he poured himself some coffee. He remembered what Henriette said about him being bad-tempered when he woke up, and his scowl deepened. He wished she had firsthand knowledge of that, but after last night and her inability to even commit to going to his restaurant, he wasn't sure that was ever going to happen.

That just made him grumpier. Sitting across from Evan, he glared at the man as he sipped his beverage and attempted, unsuccessfully, to shake off the morning.

Evan folded the newspaper and set it aside. "Do you want to ask me what my intentions are and get it out of the way?"

Liam grunted.

Maeve's *fiancé* looked amused. "Since you asked so nicely, I'll let you know that I intend to encourage her happiness for the rest of our lives together, however long she allows that to be."

Confused, still frowning, Liam studied the man. The guy meant it.

Liam recognized that with sudden clarity. What a twist. Slumping against the chair's back, Liam took a long sip of his coffee, grimacing at the heat. "Does Maeve know?"

"I think she suspects, but you know Maeve," the man said calmly and without judgment.

"I do know Maeve. What I can't believe is that you know her too, but you do." Liam shook his head. Then he held his palm out. "Welcome to the family."

They were shaking hands when Maeve walked in. She was glowing—he'd never seen her look so incandescent—and Liam felt a pang of gratitude toward the man. He looked at Evan, who nodded, almost imperceptibly, to let him know they understood each other.

"This is cozy," his sister said, eyeing them. "I hope Henri hid the knives."

"We're gentlemen, love," Evan said mildly, his gaze following Maeve. "We use our fists."

Liam snorted, lifting his coffee cup to his lips.

Maeve made herself a cup of tea and then joined them, sitting next to Evan. The man took her hand and held it resting on his leg. Once again, Maeve's cheeks pinkened.

"I need to call Andrew again," she said, accepting the section of the newspaper that Evan held out. "The water's dripping still."

Liam perked up. If Andy had to shut the water off, he could convince Henriette to take a break with him. "I'll text him right now."

"Do I need to worry about my house?" his sister asked with an arched brow.

"Of course not." He took his mobile out and sent off a quick message. "It's in good hands."

Evan turned to Maeve. "Go for a walk with me today."

"It's Friday," she replied, her brow furrowed. "Don't you have work you need to get done?"

"Work isn't as important as spending time with you," Evan said softly.

If only Henriette had that perspective. Liam picked

up his cup. "I'll just leave you two to whatever you decide to do."

Maeve gave him that maternal look she had. Evan winked at him before raising Maeve's fingers to his lips to place a kiss on them.

At least that was turning out better than he imagined. As he turned to leave, he remembered something. "Maeve, you have a contact at *Vogue* still, don't you?"

"Yes." She eyed him suspiciously. "Why?"

"I wondered if you could contact them for Henriette." He held his hand up. "I know it's a lot to ask, but—"

"You love her," Maeve finished for him. "I was already thinking of doing it. It's not a problem. I was going to suggest they do a feature for their wedding edition."

He went back to her and kissed her cheek. "Thank you."

She smiled tenderly at him.

Since when was Maeve tender? He shook his head as he walked out of the kitchen. If someone told him the earth started spinning in the opposite direction, he wouldn't have been surprised.

ANDY COULDN'T COME to Maeve's until late afternoon.

It wouldn't have made any difference if he'd come sooner. Henriette was in full planning mode, and she was ensconced in the kitchen on the damned chair he put in there for her, not aware of anything, least of all whether anything was amiss with the water in the house. He'd suggested a walk, because the weather was lovely for a change, but she demurred, saying she wanted to finalize her design for Maeve and Evan to approve.

By the time Andy arrived at the house, Liam was reduced to pacing in the front room, annoyed that he was annoyed. He heard Andy let himself in, his footsteps drawing closer.

His friend peeked in. "I'm here to look at Maeve's bathroom again."

Liam waved him on as he continued to pace.

Andy leaned in the doorway, his arms folded. "I told ya you should have taken her to a bookstore."

"How can I take her to a bookstore when she won't even go for a walk?" He gestured to the window. "It's sunny out. Do you see how beautiful it is out there?"

"Fucking beautiful," Andy agreed with a nod.

"And she won't stop working long enough to go for a walk with me." He shoved his hands in his pockets. "It's enough to drive a man to drink."

Andy reached into the inside pocket of his jacket and pulled out a flask. He uncapped it and held it out.

Liam took a swig and handed it back. "What are you doing tonight?"

"I've got to shave my legs," Andy said, putting the flask away.

"Seriously," Liam prodded.

His friend shook his head. "Don't be looking to me to fill her shoes. I service your plumbing; I don't *service* your plumbing."

Liam dropped on a couch, laying his head on the backrest. "This is my doing. I was entirely too clever."

"Now that's something I would never think to accuse you of." Andy waved at him. "Come along then."

He lifted his head. "What do you mean?"

"Come talk to me while I look at the shower. Grab my other toolbox." He left the room, clearly expecting Liam to follow.

Exhaling his frustration (it didn't work), he got up. Andy had taken his larger toolbox with him, leaving a smaller one behind for Liam. Swearing under his breath, Liam picked it up—Lord, what did the man have in here?—and trailed up the stairs after him.

He'd had to adjust to living in the country when he'd moved to Mayo eight months ago. It wasn't the fact that it was so rural; it was the fact that everyone just walked into your house. It was so different from London and Dublin—and the places he'd stayed in the States, where you could have gotten shot for walking into someone's home without notice. The first time his mailman had opened the door to his cottage to leave his mail inside had been startling—it'd been startling for his mailman too, since Liam had been in his boxer briefs.

Needless to say, Andy knew the way to Maeve's

bedroom. He charged in there and made himself at home in her bathroom, like it was his second home.

Given how often Maeve had to call him, the man might very well have thought of it that way.

Liam followed more slowly. Maeve's bedroom was sacred—no one was allowed in there without her express consent. One time, when he'd been eight, she'd yelled at him for hours for daring to taint her private domain with his presence. Rightfully so, he thought now. She hadn't known it, but he'd been dared by Tommy Sullivan to go in there and take one of her knickers to show the guys in school. He'd deserved every swear word she'd leveled at him.

Of course, they were adults now, and while he didn't go into her room often, he'd been in there plenty of times. Now, as he walked through, he slowed down, noting the differences in it: the men's shoes neatly lined up under one side of her bed, the cufflinks on the dresser, the expensive man's watch on a bedside table.

In the bathroom, Evan's presence was more camou-flaged, his toiletries discreetly tucked away in a leather carrier.

"Sit there"—Andy pointed to a girly bench in red and gold that Maeve had against the wall as he opened his toolbox—"and tell me what's going on in this house. You're complaining about being too clever, and Maeve has a man staying in her room."

"That's because she's getting married."

Andy goggled at him, a wrench poised in the air. "*Maeve?*"

He nodded. "Next week."

Without a word, Andy took the flask back out, took a swig, and passed it over.

Liam swallowed a mouthful before closing the top and setting it aside, just in case. "That was part of my cleverness."

He launched into a brief explanation of his plan—the wedding, the cake, and all. By the time he was done, Andy was sitting on the floor, grinning at him like a loon.

Liam frowned. "I'm glad you're so amused."

His friend shook his head, chuckling under his breath as he turned to the shower drain. "I can't wait to meet this Henriette."

"That's what I was too clever about," he grumbled. "In instructing Maeve to order a gigantic wedding cake with a lot of fancy design elements, I've put pressure on Henriette to do a lot of work in a short period of time."

"Hoist with your own petard," Andy said with a little too much glee.

Liam made a rude gesture.

Andy ducked his head in the shower and fiddled with something. There was a clanging sound, and then he swore like a sailor. "Seriously though," he said a moment later, sounding calm. "I don't understand what the problem is. Go to the woman and tell her you're taking her to dinner. She's got to eat, ya? Put her in your car and take her to *A Ghrá*. If she's at all worth your time, of course she'll yield once she's there. It'd be like handing your baby to someone. Unless she's a monster, she's going cuddle your baby and say it's the most beautiful one she's ever seen, even if it's ugly."

Liam raised his brow. "Are you saying my baby is ugly?"

Andy winked at him.

"Okay, I'll take her to see my baby," Liam announced. "Even if I have to throw her over my shoulder and carry her out."

"Good on you." Andy muttered under his breath as he ran the shower, shaking his head. Then he said, "I have one question, though."

"What?"

"Who's going to eat all that cake?"

Liam snorted.

Maeve walked into the threshold of her bathroom, looking over the scene with a careful eye. "Isn't this cozy?"

"Maeve, you need new pipes." Andy stood up and pointed to the shower with his wrench. "I can't do anything else about the leak; you aren't happy with them, and calling me all the time is wasting your money. The pipes were fine seventy years ago, but they don't suit now. It'll be worse now that you have more people staying here and using the water. Plus, there's rust buildup further impeding the pipes, and who knows what we'll find when we open it up. The leak could be causing mold."

Hands on her hips, Maeve frowned at him. "Andrew, I—"

"You've got more money than God," Andy continued, cutting her off. "So I'm going to bring you an estimate, and we'll sign a contract, and then I'm going to get the work done. You'll have a bathroom that pleases you, with pipes that actually work, and maybe I'll have some peace for a change because I won't have to come here every other day."

Oh boy. Liam pressed his lips together, hoping Maeve's explosion only hit Andy.

But then she nodded, though her mouth was still tight. "Fine."

"Fine." Andy gave her a look and then bent to put his tools away. "And I expect you to invite me to your wedding. I've got to meet the man who's taking you on for life. He's got to have the biggest balls ever."

She turned to Liam, her gaze like an angry laser.

He lifted his hands up. "I didn't talk about Evan's balls."

With a humph, she turned and walked out.

"And you." Andy picked up his toolbox. "Where's this baker of yours?"

"In the kitchen, I think."

Andy looked at his watch. "It's opening time at your restaurant. Fetch her and go. Pour her some wine and let her unwind. If she doesn't want to go, throw her over your shoulder. Once you stick something in her mouth, she'll forgive you."

Liam gave him a deadpan look.

"I meant your pork belly." His friend smirked. "You've got a filthy mind, my friend."

"I can't believe I'm taking romantic advice from you." He stood up, feeling much lighter. "Thank you."

"It'll be thanks enough when she moves in with you and you decide to finally update your bathroom." His friend nodded at him.

Carrying the other toolbox again, he helped Andy out to his van. He watched the man leave. Next time Andy came into the restaurant, he was going to make something extra special for him.

Dusting off his hands, he strode into the house, down the hall, and into the kitchen.

Henriette was still curled up on that chair with her notes and recipes. Her teacup was empty and the sunlight had shifted to the other side of the room, leaving shadows on her.

It was such a familiar scene, one he was used to from Papillon, that he'd missed once he came to Westport to open *A Ghrá*. He'd imagined seeing her in his home—*their* home—just like this. While this wasn't his house, it was close in feeling, because it was Maeve's and therefore still home. And to see her here, like this, warmed his heart.

He wanted to pick her up and hug her. He wanted to kiss her and show her the extent of the passion he had for her, that he'd been banking because he wanted their foundation to be based on love and not just sex.

He wanted her to be as interested in him as her notes—and maybe a little more than that for a little while.

He went directly to her and, hands on the armrests, dragged the chair to be angled toward him. He knelt on the ground in front of her and took her face in his hands. "Come have dinner with me."

Her eyes were glazed over with fatigue, and she shook her head as if she were trying to clear it. "Liam, I—"

"Next week you're going to be consumed by your cake," he interrupted. "You're going to obsessively check over the lists you've made. You're going to want to bake your cakes, sometimes twice if you aren't happy with the results. You'll need at least a day to assemble, but maybe longer if you decide to do a complicated tower."

"It's like you know me," she said softly.

"I know you." He caressed her cheeks with his thumbs. "And I'm asking you before all that happens, before you're too busy to think about anything else, to come with me to my restaurant. It's one night, Henriette. I want you to see it. It means a lot to me. I'm afraid if we don't take the opportunity now, you'll miss it."

"I—"

"Aren't you leaving right after that wedding?"

Her expression clouded. "I imagine so."

He wanted to ask her to stay—he wanted to tell her that she should come stay with him for a bit. But he needed her to want it for herself. He couldn't hold her here just with his will. She had to see that she could be happier and more fulfilled than in London.

Right now, that didn't seem possible.

She studied him for a long moment. He clutched—she was going to turn him down. He was going to have to throw her over his shoulder, after all.

Then she nodded. "Okay."

"Okay." He breathed a sigh of relief. He thought about letting her change, but he thought she looked lovely as she was and he didn't want to give her the opportunity to change her mind. So he said, "Let's go."

The drive into Westport was quiet. He didn't know what Henriette was thinking. For his part, he was thinking about the fabulous dinner he was going to make for her.

When they arrived at *A Ghrá*, it was already busy with the start of the night's business. Marie waved at him as she bustled around to make sure everyone was taken care of. As they stepped in, their customers greeted him. He always took time to say hello and inquire about their lives and families. He introduced Henriette to them, knowing they noted the proprietary hand he had on her lower back. Several of the men pounded him on the back, and the wife of one of his best customers winked at him.

"You know a lot of people," Henriette said as they finally wove their way to his kitchen.

"It's a small, close-knit community," he said. He nodded to a couple ensconced at their usual table in the back. "I've gotten to know most of the people around. In the summer months, it'll be a different story with all the tourists that flock into Westport."

She pursed her lips, taking in the details of the space. "It's different than Papillon."

"Very." He knew she'd appreciate the small touches —the bold colorful paintings he'd bought from a local artist, the deep jewel-toned walls, and the flickering candlelight. When he'd been deciding on the décor, he'd looked at it from her point of view. They'd talked about architecture and design often enough that he'd learned a thing or two.

He pushed the swinging door to the kitchen. "Come on back."

She stepped through.

He heard her breath catch, and he saw her inhale deeply, liking her half smile at the aroma of browned butter and sizzling meat.

His crew called out to him, a chorus of "Hiya, Chef!" He waved back, knowing that they watched Henriette with more than a little curiosity. After all, he'd never brought a woman back here.

Hand on her back, he gestured to the table at the far end. "Have a seat. Wine?"

"Yes, please."

THE WORDS YOU SAY

He went to the cellar and picked a French red wine he knew she'd love. He took it back into the kitchen, snagging a couple glasses along the way. He set everything down and pulled out his wine key from his pocket.

Henriette watched him uncork the wine, running her hand along the table. "Do you have this here for special chef's tastings?"

"I have a separate room dedicated to that," he said, testing the cork. He poured a bit in her glass and set it in front of her to taste. "I put this kitchen table here so that if someone felt lonely, they could come be surrounded by friends, be warm, and have a home-cooked meal. Anyone's welcome, though my friend Andy spends the most time here. You'll probably meet him before the wedding. He's always underfoot."

She lifted the wineglass to her nose and inhaled. She hummed, and then took a delicate sip. "I love it," she said, raising her gaze to his.

He knew she would. It was from a region in France that she loved. He'd stocked it with her in mind.

Sitting down, he filled their glasses and held his up for a toast. "Reunited, and it feels so good."

Humor lit her gaze, erasing the last remnants of her fatigue. "That's your toast?"

"That song is underplayed." Smiling, he tapped his glass to hers. After he took a sip, he said, "You think you can come up with a better toast?"

Shaking her head, she held her wineglass cradled

against her chest. "I'm sure that I'd be hard-pressed to beat that one."

"Try."

She pursed her lips. "*À chaque fois j'y crois, et j'y croirai toujours.*"

"Now you're just showing off," he said with a smile. "We should toast with lyrics more often. I haven't done that since the goodbye party we had when I left Papillon."

"That was an epic night." She flashed him a dreamy smile. "Remember the gnocchi Raoul made? I still get a little turned on whenever I think about it."

Before he could unswallow his tongue and comment, Deirdre came over with two small plates. "Chef."

He smiled at her as she set them down. "Henriette, this is my sous chef, Deirdre. Deirdre, Henriette and I worked in London together."

The young woman's eyebrows disappeared under her dark bangs. She turned to Henriette, her hand extended. "You're a chef too?"

"A pastry chef," Henriette said pleasantly. "I can't wait to try this. Gougères?"

"With a mushroom filling," Deirdre said. "Chef's special recipe."

Henriette glanced at him. "He does the best mushrooms."

Deirdre turned to him, spearing him a look. "I

didn't know you were coming in. I suppose you'd like if I served you tonight, then?"

He'd planned on doing the cooking for them, but maybe Deirdre had the right of it. He nodded at her with as much docility as he could manage. "That would be brilliant."

She arched her brow at him and then turned a sweet smile to Henriette. "Enjoy."

He waited until she was gone to focus on Henriette. "She has attitude, but she's one of the best chefs I've ever met. She doesn't have your sense of adventure with flavors, but she's close."

"And you feel comfortable leaving her in charge on your days off," she said, lifting her wineglass to her lips.

"Generally we work all week. The restaurant isn't open on the weekends."

Henriette's eyes widened in surprise. "That's unusual."

He shrugged, turning his chair so his back was more fully to his crew. He didn't mind them watching him, but he didn't want them to think he was keeping tabs on them. He knew they did just fine without him. "I love to cook, but I don't want to do it nonstop. That's a sure way to burn out. This way, everyone is balanced and has weekends to spend however they wish."

"Your patrons don't mind?"

He shook his head. "They come in when I'm open."

"Interesting." She picked up a gougère and bit into

it, still thinking about it. Then her eyes closed for a moment and she uttered a low moan under her breath.

It went straight to his groin.

He distracted himself by having one too—he needed to tell Deirdre she needed to add the slightest bit of allspice to it—and then refocused on Henriette when he was sure he had himself under control again. "The meal is momentary. You forget the taste of what you ate after a while. You forget how it was plated and what was served with it.

"But you always remember who you shared it with, and you remember the feeling of being with them. I wanted to make sure I wasn't always behind the counter in the kitchen but with the people who matter to me, experiencing the moment." He nodded at her. "What's the most memorable cake you've ever had?"

She hesitated for a moment, but then she said, "My aunt Portia's birthday cake when I was really little. When I concentrate on it, I can still taste the vanilla cream and a hint of orange."

"Why was it your favorite?" he asked, watching her steadily.

"Because it was my first," she said softly. "Because my family laughs when they talk about finding me, barely able to walk, sitting on the table with fistfuls of cake."

He nodded.

She gave him a look. "I understand what you're saying."

"What?" he challenged her.

"That my experience was enhanced because of others. That if I work too hard, I'll miss those instances in life." She made a face. "But that's easy for you to say. You realized your dream. You have a successful restaurant that runs without you. I haven't gotten my business off the ground yet. Once I do, then I can take my foot off the pedal."

"And when you get to where you're going, what happens if no one's there with you?" He felt disappointment cloud some of the happiness he'd been feeling, seeing her disbelieving look. He pushed that feeling aside so they could have a nice evening, making himself smile. "I hope you're prepared to eat. I have a feeling they're going to try to impress you."

She leaned in, propping her elbow on the table. "It must be nice that they do that for you."

"This is the first time," he admitted. "Usually, if Maeve comes in, I cook for her."

"But you haven't brought other—"

"Women?" He grinned ruefully. "No. There hasn't been anyone in a long time." Since he'd met her, actually.

Henriette's cheeks turned a little pink. "Oh."

"Pork belly," Deirdre said, setting two plates in front of them. She shot him another look before scurrying back to her station.

He wondered if she was trying to tell him to go for it or warning him to behave.

His crew kept bringing them course after course until Henriette complained that she was going to explode. He signaled them to stop, and they sat there nursing their drinks, talking about the past and their families and things that they wanted to make one day.

Occasionally, a customer would pop his head in to call out to Liam. He was used to it, but he saw the impression it made on Henriette. That sort of thing never happened in London. It heartened him to see that she liked it.

After they cleaned, he sent his staff home, saying he'd lock up. He waited until they were all gone to turn to Henriette. "Are you up for dessert?"

She perked up, all trace of being full gone based on the interested look that lit her eyes. "What do you have?"

"Let's make a lava cake together," he said, watching her for her reaction.

A flush suffused her cheeks, but this time it wasn't embarrassment. "Okay," she said, pushing her chair back to stand up.

They moved in tandem behind the counter. She preheated the ovens; he got out ramekins. He handed her the flour, the sugar, and the eggs. She blithely added them to a bowl, mixing them with a whisk.

He couldn't help it—he went to stand behind her, his hands on her waist. She paused for a second before she continued to whip the whisk. Then she slowly detangled herself from him to set up a *bain marie* for the chocolate and butter, but she came back, staying still until he put his hands back on her.

Leaning in, he inhaled the scent of the chocolate and vanilla and *her*, and he was sure he'd never be able to order a lava cake without getting hard ever again.

The silence was profound. Around it, he could hear her breath over the flame of the stove and the burble of the boiling water.

She reached for the ramekins, filling two before sliding them into the oven.

She turned to him. "I doubt you have tomatillos for the sauce."

"You'd be right." He took her hand and led her to his walk-in refrigerator.

They stood inside together, scanning the fresh fruits and vegetables in there. Then, at the same time, they both exclaimed, "Blood orange!"

They smiled at each other. Liam picked an orange and tossed it to her.

While the cake was baking, she quickly whipped up a blood orange cream sauce. She plated the dessert and he carried the plates to the table.

They both sat down, pulling their chairs closer together. He dipped his fork into the cake, watching the oozing center pour out. He lifted his fork, looked at it, and then held it out to Henriette.

She looked startled.

"A shared experience," he said softly. "One that you wouldn't have if you hadn't taken the time to enjoy it."

Henriette stared at him so long he didn't think she was going to accept his offering. But then she leaned forward and closed her lips around the bite.

Before she could do anything, he pulled the fork away and kissed her.

It was a rich kiss, one of chocolate and cream—earthiness and air. He tasted her cake and *her*, a combination that he hadn't realized could bring him to his knees.

She licked the corner of his mouth and whispered, "More."

He scooped more cake with the fork, knowing Henriette was waiting for another kiss, maybe even more than a kiss.

She wasn't ready. *They* weren't ready. He could see how it'd go: they would have sex (*really* good sex) and then once Maeve's wedding was done, Henriette would go back to focus on her career.

So he decided to distract them. "I talked to Maeve about *Vogue*. She's going to contact them to see if they'll feature you in their wedding edition."

Henriette froze mid-bite. "What?"

"She can't guarantee it, but she'll try. For what it's worth, I've never known her to go for something she wanted and not get it."

Whooping with excitement, she grabbed his hand and squeezed it. "Thank you so much!"

He smiled sadly. He'd do anything to give her what she wanted, but he had a suspicion this was going to work against him. Getting this article wasn't going to cause her to reevaluate how much she worked; getting this article was going to cause her to work more.

And still, he'd do it again to see her as happy as she was now.

"Go out with me tomorrow," he implored impulsively.

She grinned at him as she took another bite of cake. "To celebrate?"

"Yes. I wanted to show you a couple of my favorite local spots."

"Can I let you know tomorrow?" She had a faraway look, like she was seeing into the future. "I want to see if I can make a design idea work. It'd make for a stunning cake."

He shrugged, trying not to be disappointed.

Who was he kidding? He was crushed. He'd never thought he'd be jealous of a cake. It was a rude awakening.

He pushed the lava cake away.

Henriette motioned to the plate and then looked askance at him. "You've barely had any. Is it okay?"

"I had enough," he said, taking a drink of water to wash the bitter taste out of his mouth.

CHAPTER 18

*N*ormally Maeve would have been in her office, but that was the first place that Evan would look for her, and she needed some space away from his pheromones to think.

She'd spent three nights sleeping with him—*just sleeping*—and it was driving her insane. The way he curled around her, not sexual but not *not* sexual, was taking her to the point of madness. True to his word, he hadn't made a move to touch her beyond holding her hand and wrapping her in his arms at night. She'd never slept better—once she managed to calm the burning desire to a dull flame so she could actually fall asleep.

The problem: even away from him, she couldn't seem to think worth a damn. He'd gotten her hormones in a tizzy, and for the first time in her life, she couldn't force her focus on what was important: buying back her father's legacy.

Which was why she was in the sheep pasture behind her house, furtively hidden by the oak tree the property was named after, trying to be invisible.

She knew better than to think she was going to be successful. Evan made his living knowing everything about everyone. There was no way he wouldn't find her if he wanted to.

The fact that he was giving her this time to regroup annoyed the hell out of her.

She pulled her mobile out of her pocket and made the phone call she should have made days ago.

"Terrence Walsh," a brusque voice said.

She gritted her teeth. "Mr. Walsh, this is Maeve Buckley."

"Maeve, this is a surprise. I didn't think I'd hear from you again after our last conversation."

"That's precisely why I'm calling." In for a penny, in for a pound. She took a deep breath. "You said that you wouldn't sell the company back to me because I wasn't married, and you wanted someone to carry on the business who had values in line with those you've instilled there the past thirty years."

"Yes," he replied carefully.

"I didn't want to say anything until I'd spoken to my fiancé, as we were keeping our engagement quiet, but we've set a wedding date."

"Why, that's brilliant, Maeve," the man said, surprise lighting his voice. "When did this happen?"

"Just this past week." Which was completely true. "I'd have called sooner, but we decided not to wait, so there's been a lot to coordinate."

"When is the happy event?"

"In a week. Next Saturday," she said, wincing as she began to pace back and forth under the tree.

There was a startled silence on the other end of the line. "That's fast."

She rolled her eyes, knowing he thought she was pregnant. "Without any cause other than we're eager to make our union known and saw no reason to delay things any longer."

"Well, that's marvelous. Your father would be very happy."

Frowning, she pictured her dad meeting Evan and realized that it was true. Her dad would have loved Evan for his steadfastness and the way he never let anything stop him from achieving his objectives. "I'm calling about my father, actually."

"And the company, I imagine," Walsh said. "I'll be accepting the bids the Monday after your wedding, so I imagine you'll be on your honeymoon."

She stopped pacing and frowned. Honeymoon? She imagined her and Evan somewhere warm on a private beach, rolling naked in the surf, hands and tongues and moans. "We aren't leaving for our honeymoon right away. Besides, this is important to me, so I'll make time regardless."

"No need to do that. Can you get your bid together by the Friday before the wedding? I'll take yours earlier. Your father would have done the same."

"That'll work," she said without showing emotion. "Thank you, sir."

"My pleasure, my dear. I look forward to meeting your fiancé."

She murmured something appropriately vague before hanging up. Then she pumped her fist in the air. "Yes!"

"You look triumphant."

She whirled, her face flushing at the sound of Evan's voice as he approached the tree. "I didn't hear you coming."

"You were on the phone and I didn't want to disturb you." He had his hand on his shoulder, massaging it as he rolled it. Walking up to her, he dropped a drawn-out kiss on her lips. "Good news?" he asked softly against her mouth.

She nodded, the yearning for him kicking up all over again. Or still—she wasn't certain it ever stopped.

"Tell me," he said, taking her hand in his.

She'd never held hands as much as she had since Evan had arrived on Wednesday. "I spoke with Terrence Walsh."

"The CEO of Buckley Sinks & Taps." Evan nodded, his attention trained solely on her.

He never forgot a detail. "I told him our wedding"—God, that sounded strange—"was next Saturday. I'm fairly certain he thinks I'm pregnant," she said, watching Evan's reaction.

"We've never talked about children," was all he said.

"Because our marriage isn't traditional," she pointed out.

"It is if you believe that most marriages through time have been arranged," he replied, his mouth quirking with humor. "How do you feel about five?"

"Five?" She knew her mouth fell open when she realized what he was saying. "Five *children*? Do you know how old I am?"

"Age has nothing to do with it." He studied her steadily. "Don't you want children?"

"I've never thought about it." She'd raised Áine and Liam from the time she was eighteen. The thought of being responsible for more children made her heart clench.

"Hmm," was all Evan said. He squeezed her hand. "Come back home with me. I'll draw you a bath."

She narrowed her eyes suspiciously. "Will you be joining me in the bath?"

He looked entirely too amused. "Are you asking me?"

"No." She wanted to, but she was holding on to her equilibrium by a thread. The last thing she needed was to see him completely nude.

He chuckled, brushing her hair back from her face. "Then you're on your own for the bath. Come, Maeve."

She shivered, her mind going someplace illicit. She resisted when he tugged on her hand. "I have one more call to make."

He considered her for a long, quiet moment. Then he nodded. "In that case, I'll go for a walk." He lifted her hand and kissed her knuckle, above the engagement ring—he did that every chance he got. "Call me if you want me to draw that bath."

As he started walking away, she couldn't resist calling out, "Why are you being so nice to me?"

He looked over his shoulder, a frown furrowing his brow. "Why do you think?"

She just stared at him, not saying a word, until he turned around and continued on his way. Then she got her mobile out and called her sister.

Áine answered on the first ring. "What's the news from Westport? Are you hiring a circus to perform at your nuptials?"

Maeve put her hand on her hip. "I was calling to invite you to my wedding."

"Wasn't that implied?" Áine asked mildly.

Maeve rolled her eyes. "I was going to ask you to be my maid of honor, but I'm reconsidering that now."

"You don't have anyone else you can ask, darling," Áine said, her voice gentle. "You prefer to be alone than to have people around you."

"Because I don't like people."

"Yes, you do," her sister replied calmly, as if she were the older, more grounded sibling. "You're just selective about who you like. It's really quite wise of you."

"Feck off," she replied.

Áine laughed. "You like Evan."

Yes, she did, damn it.

"Tell me about him."

"There's nothing to tell." Less than the truth, but if she started listing his virtues and how he was so kind to her even though she was being beastly to him—and he was doing this for her—she was afraid she'd throw herself at him.

"How does he look naked?" her sister asked. "I bet he looks amazing."

If only she knew. "Áine."

"On a scale of one to ten, what's the sex like?"

Zero, and wasn't that a pity? She frowned, not wanting to go there. "The wedding is next Saturday. Don't forget to come."

Áine laughed as if Maeve had told her the funniest joke. "Darling, wild horses couldn't keep me away."

CHAPTER 19

When Liam walked into Maeve's kitchen, he found Henriette sitting on the turquoise armchair, her head buried in her notebook.

Again.

Last night, having dinner with her at *A Ghrá*, had been wonderful. The only way it could have been better was if he'd joined her in her room after he'd escorted her home. But she'd chosen cake over spending time with him, and it'd taken all night and most of the day to get over.

He tried to look at it from her point of view. Eight months ago, he'd have given his right testicle to get his restaurant up and running. He'd been exactly like Henriette. He understood what she was doing.

The thing was, now, his perspective was different. Plus, he wanted Henriette.

Despite his disappointment, he'd given her a good-night kiss, walking her to her bedroom.

Being a gentleman was killing him.

But he kept the higher vision in his mind. If you wanted a three-star dinner, you didn't toss ingredients together willy-nilly. You took care in picking the right things, adding them together in the right way to create the best spread, one that you'd remember forever. You made sure you plated it well, because a haphazard display could kill a person's appetite.

That was what he was trying to do with Westport. If he could show it to its advantage, maybe Henriette would find it as beautiful as he did and want to stay.

But it wasn't going to happen if she never left the kitchen. Last night, she hadn't said yes, but neither had she said no. He hoped, like him, she'd had time to think about things and today would let him sway her to go with him.

Which was why he decided to tempt her with a special whiskey tasting he'd arranged, with the intention that a drive in the countryside would get her excited about the area. If he was lucky, the fairies would shower them with rainbows. Everyone was enchanted by rainbows.

The whiskey tasting was scheduled in half an hour and they needed to get going. So he stepped up to her. "Henriette?"

"Hmm?" She turned the page in her notebook and began writing what looked like a list.

When they'd worked at Papillon, she used to get lost like that all the time, engrossed in her baking and notes. She had a singleness of purpose that he admired, though his perspective was different these days. "Henriette," he prodded again.

She looked up, obviously annoyed. When she saw him, she blinked the annoyance away. "Oh. Hi."

That was it? He felt a touch of irritation as well, but he pushed it aside and tried to smile. "Are you ready?"

"Ready for what?" she asked.

"For our outing." Frowning, he gestured with his hand to the back door. "Yesterday I said I wanted to take you somewhere."

"Oh. Yes." She winced, looking down at her notes. "I just have to get this planning done. I want to make sure I don't miss anything, that everything is absolutely perfect, especially if there's a chance *Vogue* might be there."

She didn't want to go.

It was shocking how deep the disappointment cut. He opened his mouth and then shut it.

Things happen, he told himself. He'd just realign his expectations for the day. Being with her was more important than the tasting. "Can I help you with anything?"

She looked at her notes. "If I decide to bake the cakes ahead of time, do you have freezer space where I can store them?"

"Of course." He hadn't realized until right then that

he was wishing she'd asked him for something more—something only he could give her.

She stood up, smiling bright. "Thanks, Liam. I know I'm being anxious about this, but I just want to make sure everything is especially perfect. You understand."

Unfortunately he did. He flashed a smile, but it felt hollow.

She pursed her lips. "Is something—"

Her mobile dinged before she could finish her question. With an apologetic glance, she picked it up. "Vivi's here," she said, her expression brightening even more as she read her text. She hopped up. "Do you remember my cousin? Come meet her."

He wished he'd put that happiness on her face. But then she took his hand and he told himself to stop brooding. Vivienne was her cousin, but he knew she was also Henriette's best friend, so he wanted to get to know her.

Henriette dragged him down the hall. In the foyer, she let go of him and rushed to the door to open it.

There was a large orange Lamborghini SUV in the drive, parked directly in front of the front door. A tall, elegant blond woman stepped out of the passenger side. She strutted toward them, sure in her heels despite the gravel.

"Henri," she called, smiling wide.

It was in the smile that Liam saw the resemblance between her and Henriette—until she got closer and he saw her blue eyes. He remembered that Henriette had once told him all her aunts and cousins shared the same blue eyes. He'd met a few of them, including Vivienne, before, but he'd never noted that for himself.

Henriette rushed forward, meeting her cousin with open arms. They both talked at the same time as an equally elegant man got out of the driver's seat.

When the man turned around, Liam saw his eyes and realized it had to be another cousin. The man strode toward him, his hand outstretched, a warm smile on his face. "Luke Waite. I'm Henri and Vivi's cousin."

"Liam Buckley."

"Ah. The chef." He nodded. "I've heard you can do things to pork belly that'd make a vegetarian rethink his stance on meat."

"Are you a vegetarian?" he asked.

"Hell no." He made a face. "My dad is from Texas. Steak is in my blood."

"Liam," Henriette said, beaming. She had her arm around her cousin's waist. "You remember Vivi?"

Vivienne stepped forward, her hand outstretched. "We met briefly a long time ago, and I'm sure I didn't make that much of an impression."

Luke snorted. Then he turned to Henriette, pointing at his cheek. "Henri, you gonna show me some sugar, or what?"

"Or what," Henriette said, arching her brows at him. Then she broke into a smile and rushed to give him a kiss. "What are you doing here?"

"Vivi needed manpower. I was the only one free, so she forced me to come along."

Vivienne shook her head. "He wanted an excuse to drive his new car."

Luke ran his hand along the curve of the rear bumper lovingly. "When you have a lady as lovely as this one, you ride her every chance you get."

Henriette snorted.

Vivienne smiled at her cousin. "Is Maeve home? We should go talk to her right away, to make sure everything is set for next week. Two hundred people, in a week! We have some work to do."

"This way," Henriette said, leading Vivienne inside.

Liam watched them disappear inside, frowning. So much for a special day to show her how much he cared about her.

Luke clapped him on the shoulder. "I guess we're unloading all this stuff. Then you can show me where we can get a pint, and you can vent about my cousin to me."

He looked in surprise at the man.

Luke just shrugged with an easygoing smile. "Henri's lovely, but her head is always in a cookbook."

"I like that about her." Mostly.

Luke didn't look like he believed him.

At the moment, he didn't believe himself either.

CHAPTER 20

*V*ivi slipped her arm around Henri's waist as they entered the foyer. "*That* was Hot Chef?" she said. "He's more than hot."

Henri shushed her.

"How is he?" her cousin asked in the same too-loud voice.

"Shh," Henri said, frowning at her. "This is his sister's house."

"I'd still appreciate that even if he were my brother." Vivi nudged her. "So how is he?"

She nudged her back. "What do you mean?"

Vivi rolled her eyes. "Come on. You know what I mean. Kisses, on a scale from one to ten?"

"Thirty-five," she replied without thought in front of Maeve's closed office door.

"Nice." Vivi nodded, impressed. "I would have expected nothing less, seeing him. He's got that sexy

Irish poet thing going for him. The real question is, how is he in bed?"

Henri gestured to the door with her head, lowering her voice. "His sister is in there."

Vivi whispered back, "Then you better answer before she opens it."

"How is it you're my best friend?" Making a face at her, Henri knocked on the door.

"Oh dear Lord, you haven't shagged him yet," Vivi said right as the door swung open. Without missing a beat, Vivi smiled at Maeve, holding out her hand. "I'm Vivienne Long, Henri's cousin. We spoke on the phone the other day."

"Maeve Buckley." Liam's sister glanced at Henri (oh God—did Maeve hear that question?) but then Maeve returned her attention to Vivi. "Please come in."

Her cousin swept in, confidence ringing in every clacking step. She went directly to a high-backed chair and perched regally on the edge. Taking out her ever-present portfolio, she opened it and began organizing her notes.

Henri knew to keep quiet—Vivi always took charge —so she sat on one end of the couch, smiling at Maeve as she took a seat at the other end.

"Time is critical, given your wedding is in a week," Vivi was saying. "It'd help if we went over what you've planned and what you'd like, and we can proceed from there. Is your fiancé joining us?"

Maeve looked lost for a moment, but then she

shook her head. "He's busy right now. We can discuss this without him."

"All right." Pen poised to jot down notes, she smiled at Maeve. "I know you have the cake taken care of and that you'd like a champagne reception. Where is this taking place?"

Maeve twisted her engagement ring. "Liam's restaurant."

"And the ceremony?"

"Will be private," she said firmly.

"Where is it taking place?"

"We'll do it here." She looked out the window. "Or by the big oak if the weather is nice."

"That sounds lovely," Vivi said enthusiastically. "I assume since it's such a large gathering you've already sent out invitations."

"I thought we'd open it up to whoever wants to attend the reception," she said smoothly. She'd given it a lot of thought, because she knew at some point she'd have to explain why they wanted such a big cake. "Including local friends."

"How lovely. Now, when we talked on the phone you mentioned that you didn't have a dress picked out. I know some people don't put stock into that sort of thing, choosing to wear something less ostentatious." Vivienne smiled conspiratorially. "I admit I'm biased toward wedding dresses because my mother is a designer, so I took the liberty of arranging for a viewing on Monday, if that works with your schedule."

Maeve shook her head. "I—"

Vivi held her hand up. "Before you protest, let me say that you'll wear whatever you wish. I'm just offering a choice. Take a look at the dresses first before you decide one way or the other. I contacted a designer from Dublin who does good work and gave her an approximation of your size. She'll come here so it won't be inconvenient to you and do any alterations needed on site."

Maeve sighed.

Henri tried to hide her snicker, but Maeve must have heard because she looked over with a look of retribution.

Henri just lifted her hands. "You're having a wedding. These are wedding things. But Vivi will make it a day never to forget."

"That's what I'm afraid of," Maeve murmured.

Vivi looked up from her lists. "It's natural to be nervous."

Maeve just stared at her.

Her cousin's lips curved a little. "Now, do you have a room where I can store a few things? And I'd like to arrange to see the restaurant. It'll be closed to the public on your wedding day?"

"It's not open on the weekends." Maeve stood.

"Excellent. I'll arrange that with Liam." Vivi closed her portfolio and stood as well. "I have a few more questions but perhaps I can contact you later to go over more."

Maeve nodded. "You can store anything you need in the room next to Henri's. I'll show you to it."

"I can do that," Henri said, jumping to her feet.

"We can all go up," Vivi said brightly. "I'd love to see more of the house anyway."

Henri trailed behind her cousin and Maeve to the second floor. Vivi kept up a constant stream of chatter. She wasn't sure how her cousin managed to do that without being annoying. It was some latent skill she had, like drawing or something.

Maeve guided them down the hall. Vivi saw the open door of Henri's room and went straight to it. "Oh, this room is lovely!" she exclaimed, breezing right in.

"That's Henri's room," Maeve said, poking her head in without entering it.

"It's absolutely fabulous. And look!" Vivi went to the windowsill where the potted flowers were. "How perfect. Henri loves plants. You should have seen her rooftop before she gave up her apartment when she went to France. Henri, these are edible flowers, aren't they? Did you pick them specially for her?"

"Liam did that," Maeve said simply.

Henri turned to the woman. "What?" She'd thought they were just in here as part of the décor.

Maeve nodded. "Liam wanted to make you feel welcome, so he came before you arrived and added some touches to make you feel more at home, like the plants and the flowers by your bedside. And the chair in the kitchen."

"Liam did all that?" Henri asked, rooted to the spot as she searched Maeve's face for the truth.

The woman smiled softly. "I'm sure it's not a surprise that he cares about you. He was the one who urged me to contact *Vogue* for you. Incidentally, one of their staff will come take photos on the wedding day. I can't guarantee they'll use them, or even do the article, but it's a good sign."

Henri glanced at Vivi, who just raised her brow before continuing her friendly chatter. What did that mean?

Henri was still glued to the spot, thinking about the article, when Maeve showed Vivi the room next door. She wasn't sure how long it was before Vivi returned, alone this time.

Her cousin closed the door and strode toward her. Her voice lowered, she said, "Okay, tell me what's going on really. When I texted you, I understood that you were still attracted to Liam, but you didn't give me the pertinent facts." She pointed at the potted flowers. "That is *not* the act of a man just looking for a good time in your pants, and neither is having his sister pull strings for you. Those are all acts of love, to show you he sees you and is invested in your happiness."

"I—" She wasn't sure what she'd been about to say, but nothing came out.

"Oh no." Vivi stood toe-to-toe with her. "What happened?"

"He wanted to take me someplace special today but I got lost in my lists."

Her cousin moaned, her hand on her forehead. "Henri."

She winced, remembering the look in his eyes when she'd said she was too busy to go with him. "He's been trying to get me to go places with him."

"Of course he has." Her cousin rolled her eyes. "He's trying to show you that you'd do well here."

"Here?" She gaped at her cousin.

"Yes, here. In Mayo." Vivi looked at her like she was mad. "Why not? You have your own business. You can work from anywhere."

"But here? In Ireland? Our family is in London."

Vivi shrugged. "Chloe moved to Ireland. Your parents would come visit, as would everyone else. What's the point of having your own business if you can't live where you want to live?"

"Would you live here?"

Her cousin shrugged. "If the man I loved was wedded to it, of course. Have you set your notebooks down long enough to look outside? It's glorious, despite the faint wafting of *eau de livestock*." Vivi grinned, patting her arm. "Now let's go downstairs and make sure Luke hasn't completely corrupted Liam yet."

Henri let Vivi slip her arm through hers and lead her downstairs. As they reached the foyer, the front door opened and a large broad man suddenly filled the doorway.

Vivi stopped cold, her arm tight on Henri's arm as she gawked at the man. He wore jeans that Henri would have called "lovingly worn in" (she had pairs just like them) and a blue T-shirt with words on it. She had to squint to read it.

YOU MATTER.
Unless you multiply yourself by the speed of light squared...
THEN YOU ENERGY.

Henri snorted a laugh.

Vivi, however, didn't look amused. She frowned at the man, though Henri would have called it more of a glare. "Who are you?" she asked like she was queen of the mountain.

"Who are *you?*" the large man shot back at her.

His gaze was narrowed, but Henri was struck by his eyes, which were a deep emerald-green color she'd never seen on anyone. "Do you wear contacts?" she asked, curious.

"No." He turned his attention to her for a moment before glaring at Vivi again.

Henri looked back and forth between them. If she didn't know better, she'd think that they were going to strip right there in the entryway and have hand-to-hand combat to see who could make the other climax first. "I'm Henri," she said, trying to disperse some of the energy.

"Andy," he muttered without taking his eyes off Vivi.

"Liam's friend." She snapped her fingers as she realized. "He's told me about you."

That finally drew his attention away from her cousin. His expression eased a touch. "Henriette. Yes, he's told me about you too. Is he here? Or Maeve?"

"Maeve is upstairs, I think. I don't know where Liam went." If he was with Luke, anything was possible. "Do you want me to fetch them?"

"No." He glanced briefly at Vivi, who was clutching Henri's arm for dear life. "If you can give this to Maeve, that'd be lovely."

She took the papers he held out. "I'll make sure she gets them."

He nodded, backing out the door as if he didn't want to turn his back on them. Though likely it was just Vivi he was concerned about—he'd barely given Henri the time of day.

"What *was* that?" Vivi said, her eyes still on the doorway even though the man was no longer there.

"Andy, Liam's friend."

Vivi faced her, her skin flushed like she had a fever. "Is that what men look like out here?"

She shrugged. "I haven't noticed." Frankly, she didn't think he was as hot as Liam.

Vivi fanned herself. "I need a glass of water, half an hour alone in my hotel room, and a smoke, then I'll be good to go."

"You don't smoke," she pointed out.

"I'd be willing to start for *that*." She pointed at the spot where Andy had been standing. "If only he weren't so rude."

"I thought he was nice," Henri said with another shrug.

"You thought he was nice because he dressed like you," Vivi clarified. She shook her entire body one more time and then said, "Come on. I have some calls to make, and I want to hear what cakes you're thinking of doing. Also, we need a plan."

"For the wedding?" she asked as they headed down the hallway.

Vivi put her arm around her waist. "For Liam."

She stalled. "I don't know, Vivi."

"I do." Her cousin gave her a patented Summerhill smile, the kind that had lured men for centuries—one Henri had missed out on.

"There are a lot of reasons not to go there," Henri said, because someone had to be sensible.

Vivi nodded. "And there's one *very big* reason to do it. At least, given the look of him, I'd assume it's sizeable."

Henri rolled her eyes.

"Don't tell me you haven't thought about him that way."

She shrugged. She couldn't deny it. "Liam's more than that."

Vivi squeezed her. "And that, my dearest cousin, is

exactly why you should go for it. If the way he was looking at you was any indication, he'd be very pleased by the effort."

But if things didn't work out—and how could they? —then she wouldn't have him at all, and that wasn't a place she wanted to go.

"Don't worry," Vivi said. "I know what to do about this."

"Oh God," Henri moaned.

CHAPTER 21

*M*aeve was used to being alone. She preferred it that way. She'd never had as many people in her home as there had been the past several days, and it seemed like every day someone new arrived. At least Henri's cousins were lodged at a hotel in Westport, but today Áine was due to arrive. She'd texted last night and said she didn't want to miss out on the excitement, so she was going to drive in from Dublin.

So Maeve stayed in her room. It was perhaps not the most enlightened way to deal with the intruders, but it was working for her.

She stretched out on her chaise, staring out the window. It was Sunday. By this time next week she was going to be married to Evan Ward.

If two weeks ago someone had told her that was going to happen, she'd have laughed herself silly.

The subject of her brooding knocked on the door at that moment. She already recognized his knock. "Come in," she called.

He opened the door and strode in. He was rubbing his shoulder, moving his head back and forth the way she'd noticed he did sometimes.

For a moment, at the first sight of him, her breath caught, like it always did. Part of her couldn't believe this gorgeous man was willing to marry her, all to help her acquire a company that was less a financially sound investment and completely an emotional purchase.

He came to stand next to her, surveying her. "Are you hanging in there?"

She pursed her lips as she pondered the question. "My house is taken over and my plumbing is failing. We're getting married next week. We're having a wedding with the biggest cake ever, and there are no guests. I'm looking at wedding dresses tomorrow, and by the end of the week I should own my dad's company again. I think I'm doing as well as can be expected."

"Put that way…" He flashed her his sexy grin. Motioning her to scoot over, he sat on the edge of the couch and took her hand. "What can I do?"

She frowned. "You're giving up your bachelorhood. Isn't that enough?"

"My bachelorhood doesn't mean anything to me." He must have seen her disbelieving look because he added, "I'm hardly a playboy, Maeve."

Averting her eyes, she cleared her throat. "We

should talk about what to expect after we get married, shouldn't we?"

"Are you asking if I'm going to be faithful?"

She lifted her gaze to his, hearing the hint of anger in his voice. "That's not what I meant precisely."

He studied her for long moment. "Let me be clear, Maeve. I will mean every one of my vows, and if you don't want me sexually, then I'll go without." His gray eyes blazed hot. "I expect the same of you. If that isn't what you want, tell me now."

She sat up, glaring at him. It was exactly what she wanted, damn him. "That wasn't what I was saying."

"What were you saying?" he asked.

She wanted sex—with only him. It shocked her how much. "I just want us to be on the same page going into this, especially since you're doing me a favor."

He barked a laugh. "Maeve, I'm not doing you any favors," he said, and then he took her mouth.

That was how it felt: he *took* it. There was no dithering, no pretense of anything—only pure heat.

She gave herself up to it, moaning into him, even though he'd barely touched her.

His fingers wove into her hair, holding her close as he leaned into her. She reclined until he was pressed against her, not quite on top of her.

"Ask me, Maeve," he said, his lips moving over hers. "Tell me you want this as much as I do. Invite me into you."

She looked him in the eye. Her heart thundered,

and her breath caught in her throat. She should stop this now and preserve what little there was left of her sanctuary.

But then he placed the sweetest, lightest, least demanding kiss ever on her lips, and she couldn't say anything to him other than, "I want this, Evan. Please."

He didn't gloat. He didn't celebrate. He just dove in.

She wound her arms around him, pulling him closer. She wanted to feel him cover her, to feel every inch of his body on hers. "Yes," she murmured, tipping her head back as his lips traveled down her neck.

He pushed her loose cashmere sweater off her shoulder so he could taste her there. "Maeve, you aren't wearing a bra."

"Have I ever told you what a good private investigator you are?" she replied.

He nipped her collarbone, his chin rasping against her skin, and then he put his hand on her, over the soft sweater. As he massaged her breasts, he watched her expression as if gauging to see what she liked.

Frankly, she liked it all: the luxurious feel of the cashmere he was working against her skin; the way he rolled her nipples firm, but not hard, until the tips were hard and aching; how he paid attention to her as if she mattered.

"In a moment I'm going to take your sweater off," he said, his voice a husky promise. "I'm going to touch you like this until you can't stop making those little sounds, and then I'm going to kiss you here." His fingertips closed on the tip of her breast, teasing it until she was writhing under him.

Like he vowed, he sat up long enough to get rid of her sweater. When he left her skirt on, she looked askance at him. "You don't want it off?"

"No." He pulled his shirt off over his head using one arm, and then he unbuckled his belt. His shoulders and chest rippled with the movement. He took a couple condoms from his pocket and dropped them on the side table next to them.

"Ever ready?" she asked, raising her brow.

"Ever hopeful," he corrected. "I didn't want to be caught flat-footed."

She stilled, watching him lower the zipper and step out of his pants.

He wasn't wearing boxers or briefs.

She gasped at the sight of him. He was long and thick, so erect he was pressed to his belly. She'd never seen a man so virile, so absolutely *male*. She wanted to run her hands over his ridges and valleys, to feel the supple strength of those muscles. She wanted to lick him where his skin was a shade lighter below his waistline.

Really, she wanted to lick him everywhere.

Covering himself with one of the condoms, he lowered himself on top of her, taking care not to crush her. Without thought, she ran her hands along his shoulders. She felt something along the back of one, and she frowned as she traced it. "Is this a scar?"

"I was discharged from the special forces for an injury," he said, kissing his way down her neck and chest.

She knew that, but she didn't know what the injury was. She blushed with shame—she should have asked him. "That's why you rotate your shoulder sometimes?"

He hummed against the curve of her breast, right over her heart. "To keep it loose."

She bit her lip as his stubble rasped close to her nipple, her body arching up. "Was it bad?"

He lifted his head and looked at her.

She held his face. "Will it help if I massage it for you later?"

He blinked, his thoughts shadowed. But then he nodded. "I'd like that."

She brought his lips down to hers and kissed him. She felt him groan into her mouth, his hands suddenly as insistent as his hardness pressing into the vee between her legs. She wrapped her legs around his, holding him there.

Supporting his weight on one elbow, he used his other hand to snake under her skirt. His smile was wolfish when his fingers found her without knickers. "I knew it."

She arched her brow.

"You realize from now on, I'm going to speculate about what you have on, or don't have on, under your clothing," he said, his fingers exploring her gently. "It's going to drive me crazy until I can check for myself.

It's going to drive me crazy thinking about all those meetings we had in the past and wondering if you were sitting there bare the whole time."

Her legs fell open of their own volition, and her hips pushed up at him to encourage more. "Maybe," she teased him.

He groaned, taking her mouth again. Then he pushed her skirt up, glancing down to look at her. His hand fisted in the fabric, and then he took hold of himself and notched himself right there. He looked deep into her eyes. "If you want to stop, tell me now."

She slipped her hand between them, grasping him in her palm, and placed him exactly where she wanted him.

His breath left his body in a deep *whoosh*, his eyes closing. It was her turn to watch him, panting, feeling the incredible stretch as he slowly slid into her. His hardness prodded a delicious spot, and she gasped, surprised by the intensity of it.

Evan stopped his unhurried plunge, pulling out and then pushing back over that spot.

She moaned, gripping his waist. She knew her nails must be biting into his skin, but she had to hold on.

Then he opened his eyes, and she fell.

Her climax hit her by surprise, fast and forceful. She cried out; her neck arched back. She felt his mouth on her breasts, licking her nipples, and she undulated against him, feeling another wave of pleasure fast on the heels of the first one.

"Again," he said against her skin.

Writhing under him, she came again, her head spinning, calling out his name.

He lifted his mouth to hers for a voracious kiss. She tangled her fingers in his hair, holding him to her as he thrust more and more enthusiastically into her.

Just when she thought she was going to die, he slipped his hand between them and touched her, and she screamed as she hit another peak.

His movements became insistent, and as she rode out another orgasm, she felt him get impossibly harder inside her before he threw his head back and came too. He kept rubbing into her, his groans exciting her, and she rocketed one more time.

After what seemed like a long time, he relaxed on top of her, his weight to one side so she could breathe. She wrapped her arms around him, closing her eyes, holding him tight, feeling her heart pounding, more evident than she'd ever felt it. She wondered if it was because his heart echoed its beat back at her.

He nuzzled her neck, dropping a kiss on her shoulder. "Stop thinking," he said drowsily, holding on to the condom as he carefully withdrew from her.

She snorted. "Or what?"

"Or I won't start all over again."

Her eyes popped open. "That's an option?" she asked, intrigued.

"It's more an inevitability than an option." He

moved his lips over her rapidly beating pulse at the base of her neck.

She arched, stunned that after all that she could still want more.

"It's how we are together," he said, caressing the side of her face like she was precious. "Inevitable."

———

MAEVE HAD NEVER FELT so languid. She poured herself into clothing, but she couldn't yet make herself get off her bed.

They'd had more sex on the chaise, and then on the floor. From there they moved to the bed.

Then there was the shower.

Fortunately Evan had more condoms in his bag, but they got creative a few times anyway.

She'd never known sex could be that way. She'd always had to work for her pleasure, or take matters into her own hands, but with Evan it was as natural as breathing. She wasn't even sure she'd call it sex. It was heaven.

And sometime in between, she'd massaged his shoulder like she'd promised. He'd practically purred under her touch. She'd loved that.

Evan strode out of her walk-in closet, where she'd made room for him to hang his clothing. Buttoning up his shirt, he stalked toward her.

Her body sparked at the memory of everything

they'd just done, excited at the thought of doing it over again.

He smiled, obviously seeing it in her expression. "If your sister weren't about to arrive, I'd strip the clothes off you like you're silently asking me to."

She stretched like a cat, liking the way his gaze roamed over her. "I'm surprised that'd stop you."

"Only because I know you're looking forward to seeing her." He put his palms on either side of her head and dropped a kiss onto her mouth. His right hand moved down her leg, to the hem of her skirt and under. His fingers trailed up the inside of her thigh to her core.

She smiled as he realized she still wasn't wearing knickers. But when his thumb feathered over her, her smile faded and she moaned.

He grinned, straightening, tugging her to her feet. He brushed her hair from her face and rubbed his cheek against hers. "Maeve—"

"Maeve!" her brother yelled from somewhere downstairs. "Áine just pulled up!"

Evan smiled ruefully. "We'll finish this later."

"I'd like that." She put her hand in his and walked alongside him to greet her sister.

The front door was open and she could hear Liam's low rumble just beyond it, followed by Áine's lighter, even tone. Smiling, Maeve led Evan outside.

Liam was leaning into Áine's Audi, getting her bags out while Áine stayed out of his way. The moment she heard their footsteps on the gravel, she looked up. Maeve watched her younger sister take in all the details: the way she and Evan held hands, the ring on her finger, and their expressions (probably a dead give-away of how they'd spent the past three hours).

"There they are," Liam said, straightening, a bag in each hand. He looked them over too, arching his brow at Evan, who merely looked smug back. Maeve swore she heard her brother mutter, "At least someone's getting lucky," as he walked past them to take Áine's things to her room.

Maeve let go of Evan and came forward to hug her sister. "You got here sooner than I expected."

Áine looked much like her: straight dark-red hair that was usually in a complicated twist, milky complexion, tall and thin. Her eyes were golden like Liam's, as opposed to dark brown like hers, and they saw everything. She dressed conservatively, whether in suits for work or casual like she was today.

Áine held her out at arm's length, examining her, her head tilted.

Maeve rolled her eyes. "And what is the prognosis, Doctor?"

"Marriage looks good on you," her younger sister said with a faint smile. "No wonder they call it wedded bliss."

"I'm not married yet," she pointed out.

"Semantics at this point, apparently." Áine looked past her at Evan, approaching him with her hand out.

"I'm Áine, and you're Evan. I've heard so much about you over the years."

The corner of his mouth hitched as he took her hand. "I hope that doesn't deter you from becoming friends."

"I think that makes me more inclined," she said, a glimmer of her wicked humor shining in her eyes. "In any case, I've always wanted a brother."

"I heard that," Liam said, coming out of the house. He tugged on Áine's ponytail, winding his arm around her waist. Then he frowned. "You're too thin."

Maeve and Áine exchanged an amused glance. Liam may have been the youngest, but he was always fussing over them. Not that she didn't agree with him—Áine looked thinner than she had when she'd been here a month ago. To distract him, she asked, "Where is everyone?"

"Henriette is with her cousins at their hotel," he replied. "I'm to meet them later to give them a tour of *A Ghrá*, since that's where your champagne reception is taking place." He gave her a pointed look.

"Did I forget to tell you about that?" she said, knowing perfectly well that she had.

Evan touched Maeve's back. "What can I do to help? It's my wedding too, after all."

"That's kind, but I've got this." She smiled at him. "I'm sure you have other things to do anyway."

He tipped his head without saying anything. Then he turned to Liam. "How about a pint?"

Liam perked up, though he looked confused. "Sure."

Maeve frowned, not sure what Evan was doing. But before she could suss it out, Áine put her hand on her sleeve. "I have a dress question, Maeve. About what I'm wearing as maid of honor."

She took her attention off Evan and looked at her sister. "What?"

"I brought a dress I thought you'd like, but if you want something else, I can go shopping. Let's go to my room and I'll show you." She took Maeve's arm, practically dragging her inside.

Maeve dug her heels in. Since when did Áine care about a dress? "What are you doing?"

She made cow eyes at her, unrelenting in her grip until they were ensconced in the privacy of her room. Áine closed the door, leaning back against it. "Tell me the truth."

"Okay." Maeve didn't make a habit of being dishonest.

She lowered her voice to almost a whisper. "*Sex.*"

Maeve raised a brow. "Pardon me?"

"Sex," Áine repeated. When Maeve didn't say anything, she waved her hand. "You know what that is. Where tab B is inserted—"

"Is that what they taught you in school?" Maeve sat on the edge of the bed. She had a feeling she'd be happier if she was comfortable for this conversation.

Áine joined her, curling her legs under her like she

was twelve again, asking her about boys. Her sister grabbed her arm. "Tell me the truth, Maeve. Is it *good*?"

Maeve thought about earlier and all the times she'd climaxed, and she felt her entire body heat up. When would Evan be home? She wondered if he'd come home early if she texted him.

"Damn." Áine sat back, openly impressed. "That good?"

She nodded. "Better than that good."

"How many times?" Áine asked, her eyes wide.

"Too many to count."

"Damn," she said again.

With a happy smile, Maeve pressed a kiss to her sister's forehead and stood up. "Champagne, darling?"

CHAPTER 22

*M*aeve was in her office, pacing, when Liam opened the door and walked in. He stopped abruptly when he saw her. "I thought you were trying on dresses," he said.

"No," she replied with exaggerated patience. "Right now, I'm *hiding* from trying on dresses."

"Ah." He dropped onto her couch, letting his head fall back. "It all makes sense now."

She frowned at him, that look she got when she put her maternal hat on. She came to sit next to him, taking his hand. "Tell me," she said simply.

"I can't get Henriette to spend time with me. I devised this entire scenario to bring her here, to show her how wonderful life could be, and she's still too distracted to see it." Closing his eyes, he shook his head. "Andy said I was hoist with my own petard, and he's right. I was too clever."

"I'd never call you too clever, darling," she said with a slight smile.

He probably should have volleyed an insult back at her, but it felt like too much effort.

Frowning, she squeezed his hand. "Maybe you need to stop being gallant and just tell her what you want."

He opened his eyes, staring into hers. "Is that what Evan did?"

"Evan and I are different than you and Henri."

"How is that? I don't see any difference. Stubborn woman"—Liam gestured to the ceiling, where Henri's room would be, and then he gestured at Maeve—"stubborn woman. Guy in love"—he pointed at himself, and then he nodded at the window, beyond which Evan's car was visible—"guy in love."

"Evan's not in love," she protested.

He stared incredulously at her. Was she mad? Lifting her left hand, he held her ring finger up so the day's light reflected off it. "I'm sure he had this lying around for the off chance that he'd want to suddenly propose to someone. How lucky it was just your size, not to mention completely your style. Yeah, he didn't go through any trouble to pick out the perfect ring for you."

"Liam—"

"Not to mention that he agreed to marry you without any fuss, because men are always willing to jump into a marriage," he continued with dry sarcasm.

There was a knock at the door, and then Áine

poked her head in. "I was asked to fetch you, Maeve. They're ready."

Liam squeezed her hand and then pushed her up to standing. "Go pick a dress, for Christ's sake. Drink some champagne and celebrate that the man you love wants to be with you."

"I—"

Liam cut her off. "If you tell me some nonsense about you not loving him, I swear I'll swat your bottom. Go."

She was pale, and the corners of her mouth were taut, like she was scared. Because of a dress? But she went along with Áine without a fuss.

What a pair they were. Liam plopped back against the couch. Maeve was scared to try on a wedding dress for fear of getting what she wanted, and he was whining because he was frustrated for not getting what he wanted. What was he doing? He never whined.

It was time to take action.

At some point he'd probably figure out what that was.

CHAPTER 23

Áine kept shooting sidelong glances at Maeve, but at least she kept quiet. Finally, when they were on the stairs, her sister cleared her throat. "Liam seemed to have been in a mood."

Maeve gave Áine a quelling look as they entered her suite.

It felt like there was a crowd of people waiting for her: Henri, Vivienne, the dressmaker, and her assistant. Someone had set up an extended sitting area around her chaise. There was soft music playing and champagne in an ice bucket.

The doors to her closet were open, and through it she could see a fluff of white hanging in there.

Her diaphragm seized, and for a second she thought she was going to vomit with fear. She'd never vomited from fear, not even when she was in her early twenties and had been given hundreds of millions of dollars to invest for other people.

How did life get so out of control? Because the very definition of "out of control" was standing in your bedroom—the most private of all rooms—with strangers hovering about you as you were about to get naked.

Vivienne glided over, the epitome of elegance and competence. In her hands she held two crystal flutes, which she handed to Áine and Maeve. "In our family, wedding dresses are a sacred event," the younger woman said. "It's as much a celebration as the wedding itself."

Henri snorted from where she was sprawled on the floor, her glass on the floor, her notebook open to a list next to her. "You should count yourself lucky. With the Summerhills, it's usually standing room only."

"Really?" Áine went over to one of the plush chairs and daintily perched on the edge of the seat. "And how do you feel about that?"

"There's always cake, so I feel good." Henri grinned. She patted Áine's leg. "Don't worry. I've got that covered today."

The designer clapped her hands together as if she were bringing a class to attention. Maeve had the odd compulsion to queue. "You're the bride, yes?"

Why that brought another wave of panic to her, she had no idea. She nodded, not trusting herself to speak.

"This way." The woman tipped her head toward the closet.

Maeve looked at the glass of champagne Vivienne had put in her hand and downed it.

She entered the closet. She'd had it built specially, spacious and open. She'd always loved it in there, but today she hardly recognized it. In one corner, Evan's things were neatly tucked out of the way, and in the other corner there was a profusion of white.

"Vivienne estimated your size and what you may like," the designer was saying, holding one of the dresses out by the hanger. "I brought a few different choices in style. What do you envision yourself wearing?"

She'd never imagined herself getting married, so she didn't envision anything. Not that she was going to admit that to this woman, certainly not with her specter-of-an-assistant lurking in the shadows.

Setting her empty glass down, she strode over to the dresses and looked at them as critically as she would have inspected a company. She immediately vetoed the first one—she wasn't Scarlett O'Hara. The second one was a clingy silk charmeuse that would have looked lovely on her, but she had dresses like that already.

The third one captured her imagination. It was a lace sheath, simple but elegant. It had a slight fishtail in the back, and the neckline was low with fitted sleeves.

She touched it—it was soft rather than scratchy the way some laces were. "I'll try this one."

"Wonderful. Alison." The designer waved her assistant over to prepare the dress. Then she looked at Maeve, frowning. "Down to your underthings. Now."

No one had told her what to do in so long that she almost took offense. She stifled the urge, but she almost wished she hadn't worn lingerie today, just to be contrary. Quickly, she stripped out of her clothing, neatly folding it to put on top of a chair.

The assistant had pooled the dress on the floor, gesturing Maeve toward it. Maeve carefully stepped into it, letting the girl help shimmy it up her body.

It fit like a dream.

"A little long," the designer mumbled. She tugged here and there, muttering to herself. "Shoes," she ordered, snapping her fingers.

The assistant helped Maeve into a pair of her own heels, a dressy pair of red shoes she'd never worn. "A splash of color is not remiss," was all the designer said. Then she made a shooing motion. "There's a mirror set up in the bedroom."

Áine, Henri, and Vivienne were clumped together. Their cousin Luke had joined them, telling Áine a story as he was handing out plates with what looked like cake. Vivienne was ribbing him, while Áine listened quietly, sipping her champagne and logging everything the way she always did, though her gaze followed Luke very closely.

They all turned to her, going silent when they saw her.

"Well?" she asked, touching the dress. "Does it look ridiculous?"

Luke whistled, long and low. "You look smashing, love. Your fiancé is going to swallow his tongue when he sees you."

"You look like a princess," Áine said reverently, coming to stand before her. She took both Maeve's hands in hers and led her to the mirror.

Maeve faced it, blinking in surprise when she saw herself. She did look like a princess—a sexy one with the way the lace bodice hugged her chest.

Vivi came to flank her. "And what girl doesn't want to feel like a princess at least once in her life? How do you feel?"

Overwhelmed. Terrified. Excited. Randy.

The door to the bedroom opened, and Evan stood in the threshold. His gaze fell on her, going up from her red shoes, taking in her dress and every curve of her body, and then continuing all the way up to her eyes. "Out," he ordered, his voice low and intent.

Maeve shivered, feeling the tips of her breasts react.

From somewhere in the periphery, she heard the designer gasp. "Is this the groom? He can't be here. It's bad luck."

"You can't have bad luck looking upon something so beautiful," Evan said, never taking his eyes off her. "You all have three seconds to leave."

Luke herded the women toward the door. Maeve faintly heard the designer say that she'd already marked the dress for alterations, but she'd need it ASAP, followed by someone (probably Vivienne) assuring her she'd drop it off.

Maeve couldn't care less about any of that—not when Evan was looking at her like *this*.

He locked the door behind them and then stalked toward her. "This is the dress you're going to wear?"

"Do you like it?" she asked, her voice sex-husky even though it'd been *hours* since they'd been intimate.

"Like isn't the word for it." He walked around her once and then stopped in front of her to gather her in his arms. His voice was a naughty whisper close to her ear. "Are you wearing knickers?"

She reached under the skirts and shimmied out of them, holding them up for show before dropping them on the floor. "Not anymore."

Evan growled, sweeping her into his arms and carrying her to the bed.

CHAPTER 24

*I*n the end, Henriette helped him with an excuse to show her around Westport.

<u>Henriette</u>
I need supplies for the cakes.
Want to go shopping with me?

<u>Liam</u>
I'll pick you up in fifteen.

He got there in record time.

Henriette was outside, wandering in the front of the house, checking out the flowers. He enjoyed the sight of her there, taking in her love of gardens.

And then he saw that she was wearing a skirt.

He knew he had to be gaping at her, but he'd never seen her in anything but jeans. Her legs were creamy and long, and he would have given anything to feel the softness of her skin.

He parked over to the side, taking the opportunity to pull himself together as he walked toward her. "You should see the flowers at the back of the property."

She turned to him, a smile curving her lips. In the daylight, they shined like she'd just been kissed. "I haven't had the chance to explore anywhere yet."

"Maybe we can remedy that." He held his hand out. "Ready?"

Her brow furrowed, but she put her hand in his.

He helped her into his car and after conferring about what she needed, they took off. He drove them out along the Wild Atlantic Way for a bit so she could see the craggy coast before turning inland and heading toward Patrick Smith's farm.

"I've always thought Ireland was so green, but the blues are very stark, aren't they?" she said, looking at the passing scenery.

He pulled into the drive and went all the way back to the cottage.

Patrick came out of the shed at the back, a big grin on his face, followed slowly by his dog. "And if it isn't himself," the older man said as Liam and Henriette got out of the car. He shook Liam's hand enthusiastically before turning to Henriette. "Why, she's a picture, isn't she?"

"She needs a lot of eggs, Pat," Liam said, leaning down to scratch the dog behind his ears.

Pat began to ask Henri about herself. Somehow they got on the topic of France, and she charmed him with a story about the time chickens started chasing her and she fell and broke all the eggs she'd just gathered from them.

"I loved him!" Henriette exclaimed as they got into his car.

She said that about every farmer he took her to. By the end of their expedition, she had a soft glow on her face. "I can see why you love it here. The people are amazing. So friendly and genuine. You wouldn't find that in London."

He glanced at her as he drove. "There's a lot to recommend it here."

She frowned at the road. "This isn't the way back to Maeve's house, is it?"

"We have one more stop," he said.

"I did all my shopping. I don't need anything else."

He shot her a smile. "If you don't like it, we'll leave."

She was silent the rest of the way until they pulled into his drive.

His cottage was set a ways back from the road. Every time he came home, he took a moment to appreciate the utter beauty of the land. It struck him every time.

"This is your house," Henriette said suddenly. She leaned forward. "Lovely."

"I think so." He pulled up to the front.

Undoing her seat belt, she followed him out of the

car. She turned in a slow circle, surveying the garden and the host of trees surrounding his land.

"It's absolutely beautiful," she said with quiet awe.

He took her face in his hands and kissed her.

She took his hand. "Take me inside and show me your home, Liam."

He led her inside, feeling a peculiar sense of rightness that she was there. He could see her coming home to him, her hair tangled from the wind, a basket of wildflowers and herbs in her arms.

She went from room to room, sometimes touching a random knickknack, sometimes just looking and moving on. In the kitchen, she ran a hand over the counters and eyed the oven suspiciously.

"It's old," he said.

"I can tell." Her lips quirked.

"I wanted to remodel but I thought to wait." Because he wanted her to be there, and she'd want to have a say in how it was designed.

"How's your plumbing?"

It took him a moment before he realized what she was saying. "Andy is taking care of it. He's been busy, and since I've been staying at Maeve's, it's been low in priority."

She hummed and moved on to the next room.

His bedroom.

CHAPTER 25

*H*enri leaned against the doorframe of Liam's bedroom, relaxing her grip on it when she realized she was holding it so tight the wood was probably imprinted with her fingerprints.

There was a lot of light in his house, and his bedroom was no different. Light poured in from the windows, illuminating the entire room. It was simple, the room of a person too busy to decorate, with a large four-poster bed, a dresser, and a colorful rug on the floor.

She was aware of him behind her as she looked around in his space, aware that his attention was trained on her. He always had such a focused look, like nothing else existed except what was in front of him—and right now, that was *her*.

The red in his hair glinted as he stepped into a ray of light, and his eyes seemed to glow as they raked over her. He was used to seeing her in jeans and T-shirts, and she wondered what was going through his head as he looked at her. She wondered what he'd think if he knew how hard her heart was beating and that her knickers were damp from the touch of his gaze.

All she wanted to do was pour herself all over him.

"Henriette," he said, a question, a plea, and a command all at once.

She remembered Vivi's encouragement. She remembered the conversation they had the first night, in the hallway outside her bedroom in Maeve's house. She thought about how he wanted to make sure sex wouldn't ruin their friendship and what they might have.

She still had reservations. Plus, she'd been so busy...

But today had been so lovely, and this seemed like the perfect—the only—way to cap it off.

She wanted it so much. She wanted *him*.

So she stepped toward him, taking hold of the bottom of her shirt and pulling it over her head. Next she unhooked her bra. Tossing it aside, she shook out her hair as she moved to slip out of her skirt.

He stepped up to her, his hand reaching out, but he stopped short of touching her.

She would have thought that he would have divested her of her skirt immediately, but he didn't. His hand hovered between them, close enough to her stomach that she could feel the heat emanating from him, and then he moved it up, tracing a line up her body without contact, between her breasts where he paused.

She gasped, feeling her nipples harden even though he hadn't done anything other than allude to touching her. "Are you going to put your hands on me?"

He paused, and then he shook his head. "Not yet. I'm going to make this last as long as I can."

She put her hand on the bedpost, needing to hold on to something. "I may pass out. FYI."

"I'll revive you." The back of his hand brushed her neck. "But you only get one chance at a first time, and I want to make sure ours is perfect."

She arched into the caress of his fingers down her collarbone and over the curve of her breast. "I have a feeling this will feel pretty damn perfect."

He nodded, slipping two of his fingers into the waistband of her skirt and pulling her toward him. He caressed her skin there before slowly tugging the skirt all the way down the length of her legs.

"Do you believe in love at first sight?" he asked.

"Sometimes. Do I believe it for myself?" She stepped out of her skirt, pushing it aside with her foot. "When I met you, I had lust at first sight."

He chuckled, and she felt the rumble of it through his chest and into her heart.

She looked him in the eye, her fingers tangled in his hair. "Did you feel love at first sight?"

"I felt lust, certainly, but it had to be more, because I wanted more than a few nights of sex with you."

She swallowed the full feeling that admission gave her. "What did you want?"

"All of it." He kissed her, stealing her breath. He trailed his lips down her neck. "Have I told you how glad I am you came here?"

"To Westport?" she asked, running her hands down his back to slide into the waistband of his pants.

"To my home. Take these off." He tugged at her knickers.

She pushed her underwear down her legs and kicked them aside too, watching Liam as he took her in from head to toe. She wondered if she should have felt funny, standing there naked while he was completely dressed, but instead she felt powerful. She was like anyone—sometimes she looked at herself and saw the things she'd have liked to change. But Liam was looking at her like she was perfection—like she was the most scrumptious dessert he'd ever seen and he couldn't wait to taste her.

And then he brushed her belly with his hand.

She couldn't help it—she moaned, her head falling back, her hands fisting in his hair. "Again," she commanded.

He did the same thing, and she moaned again, writhing against him. She wanted to tell him to touch her properly, but this slightest touch of his fingers was so intense she couldn't form the words.

His other arm wrapped around her back, and he walked her toward the bed, easing her onto her back and crawling up with her until she was in the center and he was balanced over her. His gaze ate her up hungrily.

Then his hand slid lower, into the vee between her legs.

She cried out as he ran the tip of his finger over the perfect spot. He circled it once, twice, and she cried out again, her body arching up as an orgasm surprised her.

"Henriette," he groaned, bowing his head to lick first one nipple and then the other. His finger kept rubbing over her, gentle but persistent, until she felt another orgasm begin to grip her.

Eyes closed, she held on to him, moaning his name.

"Again," he said, his voice a dark whisper against her skin.

She climaxed again, a hand fisting in the sheets as she reached over her head to brace against the headboard.

The wave of pleasure swept over her, building up again as his fingers slipped inside her. Her body writhed against him, wanting to feel more of him against her. "In me," she said, panting, tugging at his clothes.

He chuckled, kissing her, his fingers wreaking havoc with their steady press into her. "I am."

She reached between them, sliding her hand into his pants and taking hold of him. He felt hard and long and thick and deliciously silky. She squeezed him, heard him groan, and felt him arch into her touch.

"You're making a compelling argument," he murmured against her lips.

She rubbed the wetness at the tip, wanting to lick him. He'd taste like her vanilla *fleur de sel* savarin, with its salty sweetness—she just knew it. "Haven't we waited long enough?"

He lifted up. "You win," he said as he hastily unbuttoned his shirt and pushed it off his body.

Henri undid his pants, letting her hands glide across his hips before returning to his hardness. Groaning, he hurriedly shoved his pants and boxer briefs down before covering her. "I have condoms." He kissed her. "Wait here."

She laughed as he launched off the bed. "Where would I go?"

"Nowhere, I hope." He grinned at her as he held up a pack in triumph. Opening it, he took one and tossed the rest on the bedside table, close to them.

She watched him roll it on himself, holding her arms when he turned back to her.

He covered her body with his. "I want this, Henriette, and not just for tonight."

"Okay." Touching his face, she moved her hand between them to take hold of him. She hooked her leg on his hip and guided him into her.

It was the most deliciously decadent feel, filling and hot and exciting. He eased all the way in, slid out, and then thrust back into her.

"Good?" he asked, low and focused on her.

"Yes." She moaned again, her body moving of its own accord. "Do it again."

Humming, he eased in and out of her, his entire attention centered on that place inside her that made her cry out each time he rubbed himself over it.

Her fingers bit into his back, and her hips undulated in time with him. "Liam," she gasped again.

He kissed her neck, his teeth nipping her just below her ear. "You like it?"

She moaned, unable to form proper words.

"I knew you'd taste like vanilla and sex," he murmured almost to himself. He held her face, his mouth on hers. "Henriette."

She opened her eyes and looked at him.

"Now," he said softly, pushing into her.

As if by magic, the pleasure rose up and crashed over her. She gripped his hips with her legs, shaking, holding on as he kept up the steady thrusting inside her. Afraid she was going to scream, she muffled it against his shoulder, biting him.

His hands tightened on her. "Henriette," he groaned as he lost control and began to plunge into her with less finesse. "Can you come with me again?"

"I'm not sure I could stop it." Why would she want to? She wrapped her hands in his hair and pulled him closer.

His cry was muted by her mouth. He angled her hips up with his hands, thrusting and rubbing at the same time, inciting her both on the inside and out. Just as she felt the rise of another wave, his fingers tightened on her and he called out her name as she felt him get harder inside her and the pulses of his own orgasm.

He rolled her on top of him, disposing of the condom before pulling the covers over them.

She kissed his shoulder where she'd bitten him and rested her hands on his chest to use as a prop for her chin. "That was like the best kind of *mousse au chocolat*."

He raised his brow. "You realize *mousse au chocolat* is just a fancy term for pudding?"

"Not if you do it right." She ran her hand down his body, tracing the trail of hair that led to his stirring—

He rolled them over again, rubbing himself against her center. "You're playing with fire," he said, smiling as he kissed her.

"I like it hot," she told him.

"That's the only way I serve it," he said before they got lost in each other all over again.

CHAPTER 26

*T*he day before the wedding, Maeve realized two things.

One: everyone was in her house, and where a week ago it'd been annoying, she kind of liked it now. She'd never had very many friends—she worked too much—but having her siblings and Henri's clan here made her want to do this more often.

Two: they didn't have someone to officiate the wedding.

She was walking with Evan, the way they did every morning since he'd come to stay, when she realized she'd forgotten to book someone to conduct the ceremony. It hit her so suddenly that she tugged him to a stop.

"What is it?" he asked, looking at her concerned.

How could she have forgotten something that important? She gaped at him, not sure what to say.

"What?" He stepped closer, holding her hand against his chest. "Are you feeling okay?"

"Yes. It's nothing." She started to walk again. She'd take care of it as soon as she got back to the house.

He held her fast, not letting her walk away. "You're obviously upset about something. Tell me. Maybe I can help."

"It's just a detail I forgot." When he didn't budge, she sighed. "I forgot to hire someone to officiate the wedding."

He looked at her steadily, his gray gaze implacable. Then he began to walk again.

She walked next to him—he was holding her hand, after all—and shot him a sidelong glance. "You're upset."

"Of course I'm upset, Maeve." His voice was even, but she'd known him long enough to hear his anger under the calm.

"I'll talk to Vivienne and take care of this," she said. "It's not an issue."

He stopped and faced her. "You're a woman who knows what she wants and always acts toward it. You don't miss details, especially important ones."

She frowned at him. "What are you saying? That I deliberately forgot to book someone?"

"I'm saying that if you didn't arrange someone to marry us, you must have a subconscious desire not to get married."

"Have you been talking to Áine?" she tried to joke,

but by the look on his face it fell flat. She exhaled. "Evan, I promise I'll take care of this."

He didn't look thrilled, but he began to walk again. The tension stayed between them though.

"I'm sorry, Evan," she said, because she didn't know what else to say. "I really didn't do it on purpose."

He was silent for so long that she thought he wasn't going to respond, but then he asked, "Why don't I take care of this?"

"I'll do it. It's my wedding, after all," she said as blithely as she could.

Evan said nothing.

As soon as they got back to the house, Maeve found Vivienne and pulled her into her office. She closed the door and turned around to face the younger woman. "I realized I forgot to book an officiant for tomorrow."

Vivienne gasped, her complexion going white. Then the efficient wedding planner fell back into place. She took out her mobile and held it ready. "I can't believe I overlooked that very important detail. Do you have someone you want?"

"At this point, I don't think it matters as long as we have someone." She paced back and forth, wondering if she'd forgotten any other crucial detail.

In all the fervor of the week (read: lots of monkey sex with Evan) she'd almost forgotten to submit her bid to Walsh. She'd sent it to him yesterday, but she had a feeling he wouldn't accept it until after the nuptials.

"Let me call around and see what I can do," Vivienne was saying, scrolling on her mobile. "I'll let you know what I find, though I feel I should just book anyone who's reasonable."

"That's fair." Maeve touched the woman's arm. "I'm sorry about this."

Vivienne shook her head. "I should have checked. We'll take care of it."

The wedding planner strode out of the room, her head bowed over her mobile.

Maeve leaned against her desk, rotating her ring as she thought about Evan. She wondered if she shouldn't find him and offer him a massage to make up for the glitch.

Just as she was going to find him, her mobile rang. She frowned. It was from Buckley Sinks & Taps. "Maeve Buckley," she said crisply.

"Maeve, it's Terrence Walsh. I wanted to let you know I received your bid."

"Great. I'm sure you'll be pleased with the bottom line, not to mention that I grew up working at Buckley Sinks & Taps and have unique knowledge of the company."

"When I saw the bid, I got to thinking about your wedding," Walsh said, as if she hadn't spoken. "I'd love to attend if you don't mind."

She blinked. "Attend? The wedding?"

"Unless you see a reason I shouldn't be there," he said, sounding offended.

"Not at all." She pressed a hand to her forehead.

"The ceremony is private, but the reception is an informal one at my brother's restaurant *A Ghrá* in Westport."

"Excellent!" he exclaimed. "I'll see you tomorrow."

Hanging up, she groaned. What else could go wrong?

CHAPTER 27

"*D*o you need help?"

Smiling, Henri shook her head as Liam nuzzled in behind her. "Don't knock my hand," she ordered as she steadily piped cornelli on the cake.

During the past couple days, Henri had been busy in the kitchen, baking, with Liam closely pressed up against her, "helping." They'd had a shift in their relationship, though she still wasn't sure what they were going to do after the wedding was over.

It was tomorrow.

But she pushed all that out of her mind and focused on what was important: the cake. This cake was going to earn her a spot in *Vogue*. The *Vogue* photographer was due tomorrow to take a few pictures of the cake and such.

It was all happening.

In the end, she'd created a simpler design that included four asymmetrical layers in a deep red. For the piping, she used white. Instead of covering all of the layers in lacework, she did a trailing design that flowed down from the top in a delicate cascade.

She'd decided to add a few white roses to the tops for freshness. She wished she had her brother-in-law's flowers to work with—Oliver was world-renowned for his roses—but yesterday she'd gone for a walk with Liam and picked some roses from the back of the property.

"How much longer do you need to work?" Liam asked, kissing the nape of her neck.

"Almost done." She put the last few touches on the cake and then stepped back to see it from a different perspective.

Beautiful, even if she said so herself.

He walked around the counter where she'd assembled the cake, examining it. "It's gorgeous."

Beaming, she put her frosting bag down.

"Let me help clean up," he said, taking the empty bowl she'd made the icing in.

Chuckling, she began to pick up after herself. "Eager to retire?"

"Yes. Now that I've had my hands all over you, I don't like the idea of keeping my hands off you," he murmured against her skin as he reached around her for her utensils.

They finished putting the kitchen to rights quickly

since they were both doing it and they had incentive. Before they turned the lights off, she took one more look at her cake. She thought about moving it but ended up just adjusting it farther away from the edge of the counter. "I can't wait to watch people taste my cake, especially the saffron layer."

"It'll be a hit." He smiled as he reached for her, his mouth curving against hers. "I tasted your cake last night, and this morning, and I still want more."

She kissed him once more. "Do you think it'll be okay here on the counter? We could move it."

"It'll be fine," he assured her, his arm around her waist. "It's not going anywhere."

"Okay." She patted his arse. "Then walk me home."

This time when Liam walked her to her room, he followed her in and locked the door behind them.

HENRI WOKE up blanketed by the sun and Liam's long body. Smiling, she snuggled into him and sighed.

She could get used to this. Really easily.

Grumbling, Liam pulled the comforter up around their shoulders and burrowed into her, trying to get away from the sun. She chuckled softly. He really wasn't a morning person.

She could get used to that too.

It was startling how quickly everything changed. She didn't know how it was going to turn out, but for the time being, she was going to hold on to everything with both hands. She was going to enjoy Liam for as long as she could, and today was a new dawn where her business was concerned.

She could not *wait* for the *Vogue* photoshoot. She knew she shouldn't count on it going through—no one had promised anything—but she had a good feeling about it.

Liam stirred behind her, his arm snaking between her breasts. "Coffee," he groaned.

She grinned. "Say please."

He made a sound like a kraken.

Laughing, she took pity on him and got up to go make him some. She kissed his forehead and went into the bathroom to put some clothes on. Not bothering with underwear, she slipped on a pair of jeans and a T-shirt and headed downstairs.

The house was quiet, except for a dripping sound that got louder the closer to the kitchen she got. Strange. She hoped she and Liam didn't leave the faucet on the night before. She stepped into the kitchen and—

She cried out, her hand covering her mouth. There was water in a heavy drip from the ceiling, and part of the stucco had dropped.

Onto her cake.

She pressed her hand to her chest, stunned into paralysis. *Her cake.* Some of the stucco stuck out like blades from her masterpiece. Some had glanced off the surface and smeared the lacework she'd painstakingly done. All in all, the cake was ruined. With the water dripping onto it, it was all contaminated and not salvageable.

"Jesus," she heard from behind her.

She turned woodenly to see Evan enter the kitchen. He eyed the ceiling and then the cake. And then he put his hand on her back. "You have bare feet so stay back. I'll get Maeve."

She nodded dumbly, unable to look away from her formerly beautiful cake. Train wrecks had nothing on this.

Evan returned with Maeve, who gasped when she saw the state of the kitchen and her wedding cake. She lifted her mobile and made a call, crossing her arms and hugging herself tight.

Henri tried to tell herself that in the scheme of things, her situation wasn't the worst here. *Vogue* features weren't once in a lifetime things, right?

Groaning, she dropped her head in her hands.

"This is a sign," Maeve said, shaking her head. "I need to cancel the wedding."

"What?" Evan and Henri said at the same time.

Maeve nodded. "I'm going to cancel it. I shouldn't have gone along with the idea to begin with." She winced, clutching her mobile. "I should call Walsh and tell him I'm not getting married so he doesn't drive all the way here for nothing."

"What about me?" Evan asked, his jaw tight.

Henri looked at him, then shot a glance at Maeve. Of all the couples, of all the weddings, she'd never have thought Maeve and Evan's would collapse like this. Weddings that fell apart this colossally were usually because they were entered into for the wrong reasons.

Evan stalked toward Maeve. "From the beginning of this engagement, you've made me feel like I'm a prop in the whole thing. Other than the cake, have you asked my preferences for anything? Have you included me in any decision? Maybe I was mistaken thinking this was my wedding too."

Maeve frowned at him. "What are you saying? You didn't want to marry me, Evan. I pushed you into this because I wanted to buy my dad's company back."

Henri gaped at them. "What?"

Maeve didn't spare a glance for her, her attention completely taken by Evan. "You should be happy that you got out of this."

"Maeve, for a smart woman, you are an idiot." He took a step closer. "For twenty years, I've waited for an opening to be with you, my opportunity to show you we could be good together. I knew how you felt about our working relationship and I didn't want to jeopardize that. When you called me with Liam's scheme, I saw it for what it was, the perfect opportunity to make myself known. To show you I love you."

Liam's scheme? Henri frowned, moving closer so she didn't miss anything.

"You don't love me," Maeve protested, hand at her throat, her face pale. "How can you love me?"

"How could I not love you? How could you have been in that bedroom all week and not have felt how great we were together?" Evan put his hands in his pockets. "I know you, Maeve, but twenty years and you don't know me at all. The sad part is that to you I'm more expendable than that cake." Rotating his shoulder, he stormed out of the kitchen.

A moment later, Andy walked in carrying a toolbox. He whistled when he saw the damage. "You have a leak," he said to Maeve.

"No fucking kidding," she snapped at him, pushing her hair back. "It's a sign."

"Don't be an eejit. It's bad plumbing." Andy pointed at her. "I told you this would happen. You shouldn't have put it off like you did. Ignoring it won't make it better."

She glared at him, lifting her mobile to her ear. "Mr. Walsh, Maeve Buckley. I wanted to let you know that my wedding is canceled." She paused, obviously listening. "I understand but that can't be helped. And as I have an emergency on my hands here, I'll wish you well and hope we can come to a mutually beneficial agreement."

She got off the phone and dropped her head in her hands.

"Ya know, Maeve," Andy said, arms crossed. "Maybe this *was* a sign. A sign for you to stop being daft and to recognize that that man was the real thing." Shaking his head, he went to the counter to put a bucket under the leak. "Your poor cake, Henri. It looked good too. Oh well. The best laid plans and all that."

Suddenly she remembered what Evan had said. She faced Maeve. "What did Evan mean by 'Liam's scheme'?"

Maeve froze.

Andy made a face. "Oh boy."

She faced the plumber. "You know too? What am I missing?"

At that moment, Liam walked sleepily into the kitchen. "Where were you? You've been gone a lon— Oh shite," he said, shocked, gaping at the cake.

Henri met him head-on. "What scheme?"

He looked blank for a heartbeat, and then he winced.

That was an answer in itself. She winced too.

Liam took her hand. "Henri, it's not as bad as it sounds."

"Any explanation that starts off that way is a harbinger of bad news," she pointed out.

"I just made a plan to help you with your business and to spend time with you," he explained. "I knew you're independent and were going to get there yourself, but I didn't want to wait to see if we'd be happy together."

She shook her head. "Was Maeve's wedding part of the plan?"

"Yes," he said, rubbing the back of his neck.

She took a moment to breathe, to figure out how she felt. "I don't think I'm upset that you tried to help me, though the methods were questionable," she said slowly. "But I'm really upset that you didn't trust me with the truth. Why didn't you just tell me what you wanted?"

"Because you wanted something different, and I didn't want to take a chance that you'd veto us"—he gestured between the two of them—"before we could see how we'd be together."

Nodding, she took a step back. "I understand what you did and why, but I don't like it. Was the *Vogue* feature real?" she made herself ask.

"Maeve contacted them for me. I don't know for certain if they'd have run with the article, but there was a good chance. I believe in you, Henriette. I wouldn't have done any of this except I wanted to help you. I just didn't think you'd accept it."

"You have a point, but now we'll never know." She turned to gaze at her cake sadly. That *Vogue* feature would have been really nice.

They would have been too, she thought as she quietly left the kitchen to pack her things.

CHAPTER 28

*L*iam opened the door to Maeve's office and allowed Áine to enter first.

Maeve scowled at them from behind her desk. "Go away."

"Like hell we are," Liam said, crossing his arms and glaring back at her.

Áine primly perched on the couch, straightening her skirt. "We're staging an intervention."

His older sister cocked her brow in the iciest way he'd ever seen.

He stood unmoving in the face of it. "I'm sure that look terrifies most people, but I know that at its core there's a lot of hurt and probably a good amount of fear." He stared at her steadily. "But that's what Áine and I are for, to help you get over it."

Maeve crossed her arms too—gripping them so

tight her fingers were white. "There's nothing to get over."

Liam snorted. "What's Evan then?"

"You're still wearing his ring," Áine said, pointing to her hand. "If you're over him, why haven't you taken it off?"

Maeve closed her fist on it, protective.

Liam's heart broke, seeing the push-pull of love versus what she thought she wanted. It didn't escape his attention that he was facing the same thing with Henriette.

Looking at her hand, Maeve forced her fingers open, and she began to wiggle the ring off her finger. He wanted to stop her, but he didn't have to. When she got it to the first knuckle she stopped, looking up at them. For the first time since their parents' funeral, he could see all her feelings plain as day on her face, and it made him feel wretched that she hurt so badly.

"I don't want to take this off," she whispered, holding her hand against her chest.

"Because you love him," Liam persisted. When she didn't answer, he gave her a cross look.

"God, you look so much like Dad right now," she murmured, tears coming to her eyes.

That took the fight out of him. He went to her and helped her to standing, soothing her head, wishing he could shoulder her hurt.

"What would Dad have said to you?" Áine asked gently.

Her words were muffled into his chest. "He'd have told me love is the most important dream, and that nothing was worth losing that."

"Well then," Áine said, as if that was that. "I bet he would have felt that way about his company too. Do you think he wouldn't have sold it in a second if it afforded us security?"

Maeve lifted her head to look at their sister.

"I don't remember him much," Áine said gently, "but from what you've told us, he wouldn't have done anything differently than you did."

Maeve shook her head. "But—"

"But you tried, and that's all one can ask," Liam pointed out.

Áine nodded. "Now you need to decide if you're going to live in the past or embrace the future." She crossed her ankles, smoothing her skirt. "I can tell you, if I had that man in my bed, I wouldn't just embrace it."

"*Áine.*" Liam winced. Some things a brother just didn't need to hear.

"The thing about you, Maeve, is that you always make the right choice. So..." Áine reached into her pocket and pulled out a piece of paper. "You'll want this."

Liam looked at Áine. What was that? They hadn't discussed anything but having a talk with Maeve.

Maeve untangled herself and took the scrap. He peered over her shoulder as she opened it. On it, there was a postal code. Based on the similarity to his, it wasn't far from here.

"What is this?" Maeve asked.

"Evan's address. He may have left *Cois Dara*, but I doubt he went back to London." Áine straightened the hem of her skirt. "For when you go to him to ask him to marry you for real."

He heard Maeve's gulp.

Whenever he'd had doubts or moments where what he wanted didn't seem possible, Maeve was always there to help him overcome it. Because this was his turn to do it for her, he put his hand on her back and encouraged her toward the door. "Go. You've got this."

She flung her arms around him, holding him tight. With a quick kiss on Áine's cheek, she rushed out of the office.

They watched Maeve run out of her house, the door slamming in her rush.

Then Áine turned to him. "Now, you."

He frowned. "What about me?"

"What are you going to do about Henri?"

"What can I do? She left."

"You're just going to let her go?" his sister asked in a mildly curious voice.

"How many years did you go to school to learn to talk in that tone of voice?"

She just smiled. "Deflecting the question only confirms that you feel in the wrong."

"I don't feel in the wrong!" he yelled. "I tried to show her a life here that would be beyond wonderful."

"Yes, but did you tell her you loved her?" she asked reasonably.

Damn it—he hated when she had a point. "Stop psychoanalyzing me."

She smiled just enough to let him know that *she* knew she had him. "You just told Maeve that she needed to tell Evan she loves him, but you haven't told Henri? Really, Liam. When did you become daft?"

He glared at her. "You used to be my favorite sister."

Coming to him, she laughed. She kissed his cheek, laying her palm on it. "You've been waiting for her forever. Go get the girl. She's at the hotel in Westport with Luke and Vivienne."

"How do you know that?"

Her cheeks pinkened enough that he was suspicious. "I pay attention. But she won't be there for long, so don't tarry."

She wouldn't leave without her pans, and they were still in the kitchen. He'd had a moment where he'd considered holding them ransom until she forgave him for not trusting her with the truth—she was right about that—but he didn't want it to be about their careers. This needed to be about them and what they wanted.

He wanted her—more than ever.

He rubbed the back of his neck. "I need a plan."

"Enough with your plans," Áine said. "Just go with your heart for a change."

"Can that possibly work?" he muttered. He always had a plan for everything.

She patted his chest. "I have faith in you. Plus, you've got love on your side. How could you possibly lose?"

He studied her closely. She was only two years older than him, so their relationship had always been different than theirs with Maeve, who'd been a parent to them for so long. Maybe that was why he felt like he was seeing Áine anew: a strong, smart, beautiful woman.

One who was too thin. He tugged on her ear because he knew it annoyed her. "Come over and let me make you dinner."

She narrowed her eyes. "Why?"

"Because you live too far away and I miss you." He kissed her cheek. "But come in a couple weeks, because I'll want at least that much time alone with Henriette."

Áine laughed. "What a lucky woman."

No, *he'd* be the lucky one if she'd have him.

CHAPTER 29

The postal code Áine gave her (she had no idea how her sister managed to get it) took her to the coast, up a ways from Westport. The terrain was craggy, which suited Evan to a T.

She followed the winding road, until she reached a large house situated on a bluff overlooking the sea. It seemed to glisten in the light that reflected off the water, with lots of tall windows.

His car was in the drive.

Her heart tightened, and she slowly pulled in behind it. She had a compulsion to box it in so that he couldn't leave before she'd had her say, but she knew better. Evan didn't run. Evan faced his emotions straight on.

She could learn a thing or two about that.

Staring out the window at the door, she told herself she could do this. She got out and strode to the door, straightening her dress. Taking a deep breath, she knocked on his door.

There was no answer. She frowned—was he ignoring her? She was about to knock again when the door swung open.

The first thing she noticed was that he had no shirt on. She'd laid her head on that chest at night. The thought that she'd fucked up that privilege upset her.

He didn't look surprised to see her. Really, he looked blasé, like he was unaffected by her presence. The only evidence contrary was the momentary flare in his gray eyes as he took in her red dress—she wore the one he liked, not to pull him but because he liked it and she wanted to show that she did pay attention to him.

But just as quickly as it'd flared up, it was gone, replaced with blank politeness.

Not politeness, she thought as she looked closer. It was a protective mask.

That was her fault, she realized with a sinking feeling. He'd never worn any sort of mask around her.

She was just going to have to fix that. She lifted her chin. "I was daft."

He nodded. "Yes, you were."

"Andrew also said I was an idiot."

"Andrew is astute," Evan agreed.

"I don't want my father's company."

That set him off. Anger overtook the mask of disinterest, and he stepped forward. "Now you're lying to me, Maeve. Of course you want your father's company."

Some people might have backed away under the force of Evan's anger, but she was so relieved to see it that she almost went noodly right there.

She lifted her chin and looked him in the eye. "If it means not having you, I don't want it."

His brow furrowed at that, as if he couldn't understand what she was saying. "Why are they mutually exclusive?"

"I didn't want you to think I was here, asking you to marry me, because Buckley Sinks & Taps was my driving ambition."

He moved so fast, turning her so her back was against the house with him leaning into her, that she didn't have time to do anything except surrender. "What's your driving ambition?" he asked, his voice low.

"You," she said simply, looking into his lovely eyes. She put her hand on his face. "Us. A life together."

"I want children."

Somehow she knew he was going to say that. Her heart caught in her throat, and an overwhelming longing that she'd repressed for so long rose up. "Not five," she said. "But I'm willing to discuss it."

A hint of a smile touched his lips. "We'll live here in Westport, your place or mine, I don't care."

"Maybe your place until my plumbing is repaired." She shrugged. "I don't care as long as I'm with you."

"Tell me, Maeve," he said, his voice low and insistent and full of longing.

It felt like his fingertips brushing teasingly along her skin, and she shivered. "I love you, Evan." She got on her toes and kissed him. Then she kissed him again, deeper, because it was so right.

His hands stole into her hair, holding her close. "I'd started to despair that I'd ever hear you admit that to me."

"Admit it?" She frowned at him.

"I knew it was there. It had to be there, since I felt this so deeply." He took her left hand, kissed her finger below the ring, and cradled it against his heart. "But I didn't think you'd choose it. I thought, in the end, you'd choose being alone and content."

She shook her head, leaning into him, leaning into his heart. "If you hadn't agreed to marry me and shown me how it could be, I might have. But now there's only one choice, and I choose you. Marry me, Evan."

Smiling, he lowered his mouth to hers. In a whisper, just between the two of them, he said, "I thought you'd never ask."

CHAPTER 30

*H*enri lay facedown on Vivi's bed. It wasn't the first time she'd ended up in her best friend's room, upset over a boy, but this time felt different. This time it felt like her heart was never going to be the same.

Luke sat on the edge of the bed—she could tell by his weight and his light cologne. Her body rolled toward him.

He nudged her hip. "What do you know about Áine?"

"Seriously, Luke?" She lifted her head to glare at him from under her messy hair, which has fallen into her face. "That's what you're going to talk to me about in the face of my misery?"

Vivi snorted as she sat on the other side of the bed. "The guy went through mad machinations to help your business succeed, and you're finding fault with him?"

"He hid the truth from me," she pointed out.

Luke shrugged. "But he didn't lie to you, right?"

She glared at him. "Don't be a guy."

He glanced down at his crotch. "That's going to be really difficult, love. My manhood cannot be denied."

Vivi snorted. Then she turned to Henri. "As much as it pains me to say this, Luke is right."

Luke got out his mobile and held it up. "Can you repeat that so I can record it?"

Vivi pushed his shoulder. "Shut up. We're focusing on Henri right now." She faced Henri. "You're stubborn. That's not an accusation. It's one of those unavoidable Summerhill traits, like the blue eyes. If Liam had offered to help you straightaway, you would have turned him down. You've turned down all our help. And you're so determined to make your mark, that you would have let him pass by."

She sat up, frowning. "No, I wouldn't. I was attracted to him. I would have gone out with him."

"To what end?" Vivi looked at her frankly. "He wants a life with you. What would you have agreed on? Seeing him on the odd weekend when you weren't busy with a cake, until it became too hard to go back and forth between London and here? I hate to tell you this, Henri, but cake isn't that filling."

Luke edged away. "That's the sort of statement that would make her head spin."

Vivi pushed him, but she kept her gaze on Henri. "You're my best friend and I love you, but sometimes your focus is so absolute that nothing reaches you. Even me."

Henri sat up, upset. "No, it's not. I'm never that busy."

Vivi nodded sadly. "Last summer when I broke up with Riley I needed you, but you were busy with work."

"Really, Vivi, his name was *Riley*. That should have been your first clue he was a wanker," Luke teased, though he put his arm around her shoulders and cuddled her into him.

Henri thought back to that time. She'd been busy working at Papillon and baking on the side for the occasional wedding. She remembered Vivi calling, but she'd been hustling to get everything done and had had to cancel a few times on her.

Now she took Vivi's hand. "I'm so sorry."

"It's done now," Vivi said in her practical way, waving her hand. "But I don't think that's who you are or how you want to live, so think about all this and decide."

Vivi stood and nodded at Luke. "Go grab a latte with me?"

"Sure." He got up, straightening his pant legs. "Want us to bring you something back, Henri?"

"A bottle of whiskey?"

He grinned. "Careful what you ask for."

Still lying on the bed, she watched her cousins leave. Her mind churned over what Vivi had said, looking back at the past week and seeing it in a new cringeworthy light. They were right: she'd cut Liam down every time he'd wanted her to spend time with him. He'd had to almost threaten her to go to see his restaurant.

That made her not even a good friend, much less anything more serious.

She took out her mobile.

<u>Henri</u>
Am I too driven?

Her dad answered immediately.

<u>Papa</u>
That depends on what you want, doesn't it, love?

<u>Papa</u>
If you want only your career, then no.

<u>Papa</u>
But if you want your career and a life, then you may need to make adjustments.

"Oh God, I'm too driven," she said to the empty room.

<u>Papa</u>
Why? What happened? Is it that chef?

<u>Henri</u>
I didn't treat him well, Papa.

<u>Papa</u>
Do you want to?

<u>Henri</u>
Being with him makes my heart light.

<u>Papa</u>
Well, then.

Well, then. Was it that simple?

There was a knock on the door. She frowned at it. Did Vivi forget her room key? That wasn't like her.

Sighing, Henri rolled off the bed and went to answer it. "I can't believe—"

The words dried up in her mouth when she saw Liam standing there.

"Hello, Henriette." He motioned to the room. "May I come in?"

She stepped aside and let him enter. "How did you know where I was?"

"Áine told me." He took his jacket off and set it on a chair. "And the front desk clerk likes my roast chicken."

"Small-town charm." She should have been annoyed, but she was oddly grateful. "I'm glad you came."

Liam lifted his head, his gaze sharp on hers. "You are?"

She nodded, but she held her hand up. "First of all, I appreciate the sentiment behind what you did. It was sweet. But if you ever hide anything or mislead me ever again, I'll make sure you'll never be able to have children. I have a cleaver, and I know how to use it."

"I understand," he said, edging toward her. "Anything else?"

She took a deep breath. "It's been brought to my attention that I've been obsessive when it comes to cake."

He moved closer to her. "Cake *is* delicious."

"And very important to life, as it's a sign of fortune." She bit her lip and searched for what she wanted to say. Finally, she just said, "Cake punctuates life, it isn't life."

Liam took her hand. "What are you saying?"

"I'm saying I'm sorry my singlemindedness was out of balance." She put her hand on his chest. "I still don't know what to do about you being here and me being in London. My family is there."

"Your sister is here," he pointed out.

"True." That perked her up. "But I don't know that I can make my business work here."

"Would that be an option?" he asked, watching her carefully.

"I think it could be." She searched him. "Would you want it to be an option?"

"Henriette, I love you." He pulled her against him. "That's the only option I want."

She wound her arms around his neck, twining her fingers in his hair. "Did I say I was sorry?"

He brushed his lips against hers. "Did I say *I* was sorry?"

She rubbed her cheek against his, loving the gentle masculine rasp of it. "Let's just call it even and make up."

"I've always thought you were the wisest woman I've ever met." He dipped in, kissing her until she was breathless and weak-kneed. She held on to his hair, reveling in the silky feeling of it, the spring thickness. She moaned when his hands slipped under her shirt and up her sides until they touched her bare breasts. She'd gone braless because she hadn't had the energy to put one on, but now she congratulated herself on her forward thinking.

"I was scared I'd lost you, Henriette," he whispered against her lips. "It's been a wretched morning."

"I know." She pressed herself to him and poured her heart into the kiss. Then, because her father always said you have to be explicit when you mean something, she held Liam's face and looked into his golden eyes. "In case you wondered, I love you too."

His smile lit the room. He began to walk her backwards, toward the bed.

Right then the door to the room opened. Based on

their expressions, Henri wasn't sure who was more surprised: Liam or Vivi and Luke.

Vivi put her hands on her hips. "That's *my* bed. You're going to have to take this reunion elsewhere."

Henri glanced at Liam. She heard "reunited, and it feels so good" play in her head, and she laughed. He began to laugh too, and then he bent and lifted her over his shoulder, a hand on her arse to keep her balanced up there.

"Impetuous," Luke said, sounding impressed.

Henri squealed as Liam whirled around to face Vivi. "I'm taking her."

Henri raised her torso up enough to see an upside-down Vivi wave toward the door. "She's all yours."

"Yes, she is," Liam said, sounding pleased with himself as he carried her out of the room.

Henri was pleased with herself too, because she knew he was just as much hers.

EPILOGUE

*T*he bride wore white and a look of utter satisfaction.

Sitting at a table far from the center of festivities, Áine sighed as she watched Liam and his new bride Henri take the dance floor. The platform had been set up inside the reception tent, in the field by the old oak tree, behind Maeve's house. The tent had been in concession to the mercurial Irish weather, but Liam had said that it was superfluous, because the fairies would bless them with the perfect day, full of sun and warmth.

Liam wouldn't have had it any other way, not for his Henriette.

Áine sighed again. She'd been sighing a lot today, and that needed to stop. Determined, she lifted her champagne flute and took just a small sip so she wouldn't get sloppy. She'd focus on the happy things, like her brother being ever so happy.

He looked dashing in his suit, with his hair wild, the way it normally was, and that sparkle in his eyes. He held Henri close, as if he was never going to let her go.

Which was as it should be.

Not that Áine had had experience to that end, in her line of work or in her personal life.

Henriette was radiant. She wore a dress one of her cousins had designed (Áine thought it was Vivienne's sister, but there were so many Summerhills it was hard to keep them straight), a dress fit for a princess, with its fitted bodice and light, flowing tulle that floated around her legs as Liam twirled her. In her hair, she'd woven flowers. On her feet, she wore blue shoes.

That intrigued Áine. She looked down at her own feet, tucked together because of her crossed ankles. Serviceable black, fine of quality, heels not too high, not too low. Nothing too showy—she didn't want her clients to get distracted by her.

All her shoes were black. Her items of clothing were as monotone as her life.

The chair next to her moved, and she looked up to see Andrew taking the seat. "All's well that ends well," he said, holding up his pint glass.

She smiled and lifted her glass to gently tap his. "Even Maeve's plumbing."

He snorted at that, looking out over the party.

Everyone watched Liam and Henri sway to the music, supplied by a motley quartet of local lads. It seemed like all of Westport attended, and combined with the dozens of Summerhills that had descended from all corners of the world, it was a large gathering.

Áine frowned. No—it was a celebration. She'd never been to an event that had this much joy and laughter. It was quite educational. Most of her functions included other therapists, and all they did was discuss their problems and dissect their egos.

She glanced at Andrew to see what his reaction was. She'd expected his gaze to settle on Liam and Henri—Liam was his friend, after all. She was surprised to watch it zero in on Vivienne Long and stay there.

Interesting. Keeping her glass in her hand as a prop, she looked over its rim, seeing the moment Vivienne felt Andrew's gaze and the way the woman's shoulders stiffened, as if forcing herself to keep her back turned and engaged in the conversation she was having with a couple women from town.

She felt more than heard Andrew growl next to her. It was the sort of low, primal sound that she imagined wolves made when they identified their mates.

When he made it again, she rolled her eyes, because he was around so much he may as well have been family. "Why don't you go ask her to dance?"

Andrew looked at her like she'd suggested he strip and run naked through the crowd. "Dance?"

"Where you hold her entirely too close because it's the most polite way to feel her curves in public and pretend to sway to the music while you mentally undress her," Áine clarified. "It's the conscious way of giving in to an unconscious desire without risking hurt."

He arched his brow. "Well, when you put it that way..." He set his pint down with a bang and stalked off to claim his dance.

She smiled as Vivienne's posture became more erect. Based on Andrew's reaction, Áine was sure that wasn't going to be the only erect thing in that quarter.

Lucky them. Not that the sexual attraction would last or be ultimately fulfilling—at least not in her experience, with her own episodes as well as what she saw with her clients. But she felt glad for them, same as she felt for Liam and Henri.

Who would have expected that their little brother would have been the first of them to get married? Áine had thought it'd be Maeve, especially since Henri's business took her away much of the time, especially since *Vogue* had done a feature on her cakes and she'd become so busy.

Not that Maeve and Evan were far behind.

They'd decided to wait, planning a more formal event that was taking place in a month. It sounded like it was going to be the wedding of the decade, with all the people attending.

The real shock had been when Evan and Maeve had both announced that they were retiring, effective the beginning of their two-month honeymoon in Morocco. There was a lot of conjecture in the business world that Maeve would be back, but Áine knew her sister.

A two-month honeymoon...

That would have never occurred to Áine. Before, if someone had stepped into her office and told her they were going off to have sex for two months straight, she'd have treated them for sex addition. She couldn't imagine having sex for two continuous hours, much less two months.

There wasn't a doubt in her mind that Maeve and Evan would be having sex continuously. They *sizzled* together. Talk about utter satisfaction. Sexual fulfill-ment *rolled* off Maeve.

She also didn't doubt that they were completely sane, grounded in their relationship, and healthy in their desires. There wasn't a whiff of dysfunction around their sexual activity—and in the past weeks she'd really poked and prodded to check. Áine wasn't sure how that was, or why they were different.

It made her envious.

It also made her hopeful. If Maeve could find such repletion, maybe she could too.

Tugging her skirt down (why had she let Vivienne convince her to wear such a short dress?), Áine wondered what it was like to feel that kind of satisfaction. At her own hands (with her assortment of intimacy aids), she was fine. But she'd never been able to orgasm with someone.

She was a psychiatrist, and she could diagnose herself with any number of issues that could explain it. She listened to people with sexual dysfunctions all day long. However, she knew she didn't fit any of those profiles. She was a fully functioning adult woman who could achieve orgasm on her own—sometimes multiple times.

The problem resulted when she introduced a man into the scenario. Invariably she found herself trying to understand what her companion was doing, to the point where she'd become distracted and fall into analysis. She'd learned long ago not to question them during the act—men reacted aversely to that—which meant that she became an observer instead of a participant.

The death knell of pleasure.

Eventually she'd fake it so she'd be able to gracefully leave.

She knew overthinking was on her, but she knew the men she'd been with were equally at fault.

Look at Maeve. At forty-seven she'd finally picked a man who equaled her, and their chemistry was palpable. Áine was surprised the drapes hadn't singed, they were so hot together.

Where did one find a man like Evan?

The chair scraped next to her again. She startled, for a second wondering why Andrew had come back, but then she looked up to find Henri's cousin, Luke, looming over her.

"May I?" he asked, gesturing to the chair.

"There aren't other chairs?" she said, trying to calm her suddenly rapidly beating heart. He was gorgeous—the kind of handsome that belonged on the movie screen or big billboards advertising men's underwear.

She was *not* going to imagine Henri's cousin in underwear. Áine folded her hands in her lap.

"This chair has the best view," he said as he angled it to face her.

She sympathized with Vivienne, feeling Luke watching her and trying to remain unaffected by it. She focused on Evan, because he was very grounding and settling.

"Do you like him?"

Frowning, she faced Luke. "Who?"

"Evan." Luke nodded in the man's direction.

"Of course I like him." Was he daft? "He's marrying my sister."

"I meant, *like* him, as in have feelings for him." She must have looked horrified, because Luke shrugged and said, "The way you were looking at him, you can't blame me for asking."

"Not at all!" She gaped at him, appalled. "Is that what it looks like?"

He shrugged. "Most women would think he's attractive."

She shook her head, clutching her hands. "Yes, but not like that, at least not to me." Watching someone didn't mean she wanted him. It was just what she did.

Luke nodded. As if that appeased his curiosity, he turned his attention to Liam and Henri.

Henri's father stepped onto the dance floor. He was a broad man with keen eyes that saw everything. Áine wasn't used to that; *she* was the one who noticed everything. She wondered what it would have felt like to have a father like that. The thought made her chest feel tight—with sadness, she realized after briefly touching in with herself.

Today wasn't a day for sadness, so Áine set that feeling aside.

Liam kissed Henri sweetly and then let her father sweep her into his arms. Smiling, he went to Maeve and drew their sister into a dance with him. Maeve smiled, so happy and glowing in her red dress—*red!*—that it brought tears to Áine's eyes.

She picked up her champagne and took another sip, to give herself time to regroup.

"Don't you like it?"

Blinking, she swung her gaze to Luke. "Pardon me?"

"The champagne." He nodded to her glass. "You haven't had much."

"I've had as much as I need," she replied. "What makes you think I need more?"

"It's not what you need." He put his elbow on the table, resting his chin in his hand as he leaned toward her. "Do you want it?"

Why did that sound naughty? Why did she feel like he was asking her a different question?

Why was she tempted to say yes?

Before she could decide how she wanted to answer, a server came to them and offered a plate. "Cake?" the young man asked.

For their wedding cake, Henri and Liam had decided on lava cake, which they'd made together in advance. Liam's pastry chef had taken over and baked them today, so everyone would have a fresh cake. Henri said it wasn't bad luck, because she wasn't making her own cake: that she and Liam did it together was an intention of their partnership in life as well as a conscious sharing of the sweetness of their life with their guests.

"We'll share one," Luke said.

She frowned at him.

He just smiled winningly. "You'll like it. Trust me."

She was sure she would—too much.

The server, unaware of their byplay, set the cake and two forks closer to Luke. Luke pushed aside one fork and took the other, cutting into the cake so the center oozed in a delicious rich rivulet of chocolate.

He lifted the fork to her lips. "Open."

She felt herself flush, the heat rising up her chest at

the command. Pressing her knees together, she debated whether or not to do it.

For goodness sakes, she scolded herself. She was a professional; she knew how to handle men like this. She put on her placid mask and said, "Do you always expect women to obey your commands?"

He looked startled for a moment, and then something shifted in his gaze. It wasn't challenge, though—she knew what that looked like and what was behind his eyes definitely wasn't that. To her, it appeared to be awareness and curiosity, and a lowering of defenses. In a session, this would have been the point where she knew she'd be able to really connect with her client.

Holding his gaze, she continued. "You speaking like that makes me wonder about your childhood and how your parents affected your development."

He laughed.

She blinked, the unabashed sound cracking her mask for a second. But she quickly put it back in place.

"You'd be right," Luke said, wiping tears from his eyes. "My mother says I'm a holy terror, and that it's all my father's fault. He takes that as a point of pride, though. He's very proud of my brother and me."

She took in the warmth and love in his tone, surprised by both. "You're close to your family," she said, somehow shocked.

"Very." He said it definitively.

It wasn't the comportment of a playboy. At least not according to her textbooks.

Still smiling, he held the fork out again, his voice gentle. "Have some cake, Doc, not because I'm trying anything but because I want to share it with you."

"Why is that?" she asked, suspicious.

"I have no idea," he said, shaking his head with honest bewilderment. "Maybe you can help me figure that out."

Because she was curious, because she wanted to explore all of this more (including the feelings he was stirring within her, which were *not* normal), she took the fork from his hand and ate the cake before handing it back to him.

"I like a woman who knows her own mind." He smiled, scooped another bite, and handed her the fork again.

They shared the rest of the cake that way, with him taking a bite and then handing her the fork.

It was oddly erotic.

She touched her collar, wanting to unbutton the top one to give herself room to breathe. Only he was too close to her personal space.

"Dance with me," Luke said suddenly.

She glanced at him, startled. "I don't dance."

"Don't you think it's time to start?" he asked with mild curiosity.

She recognized that tone of voice—she used it all the time herself, when she wanted to point out someone's intractability. She narrowed her gaze at him. "I know what you're trying to do."

"Then that makes one of us," he said with another smile. He stood and held out his hand. "Tell me what I'm up to while we dance, Doc."

She couldn't help herself—she put her hand in his and let him guide her onto the dance floor.

The first thing that struck her as he took her in his arms was his scent. It was clean and crisp and citrusy rather than cloying or overwhelming like other men she'd been close to. When she smelled heavy cologne, she always wondered what the man was hiding. Luke didn't appear to be hiding anything.

The second thing was that she fit perfectly into him. She didn't feel awkward or like she had to figure out how to adjust to dance with him. She just stepped into him and it felt right.

"Nice," Luke murmured against her hair. "I thought it would be."

"You thought about this?" she asked, looking up at him to read his expression.

"Is that hard to imagine?" He looked at her askance. "You're beautiful."

She arched her brow. "I'm already dancing with you. You don't need to give me lines."

His brow furrowed. "It's not a line."

If she didn't know better, she'd have said he looked disturbed. It must have been a trick of the fading evening light.

He swept her into a turn, twirling her, and then

brought her back to the circle of his embrace. "Was it one man?" he asked suddenly.

She gaped at him. "Pardon me?"

"Or was it more than one?" he asked. "Who told you that you were lacking?"

She turned her head, looking past his shoulder.

"Whoever led you to believe there was something wrong with you should be taken out back and taught a lesson," he murmured. Then, louder, he said, "You know the first thing I thought when I met you?"

"What?" she asked, looking up at him again.

"I thought you were stunning and elegant, very smart and eloquent." He held her gaze. "You know the second thing?"

Caught in his blue eyes, she shook her head.

"I thought that I'd never met a more sexy woman, and I wondered what you wear underneath those very proper clothes," he said in the same even tone.

She opened her mouth but nothing came out on the first try. She swallowed and tried again. "You're going to have to keep wondering. I'm not the type of person who uses a wedding as an excuse for a bad sexual decision."

He frowned at her. "I'm going to ignore that you think I'd lead you into a bad decision, since you appear to have only known wankers in the past. I'm not a wanker, Áine, and sex with me wouldn't be bad."

She shrugged, feeling remorse over hurting his feelings.

Luke stopped abruptly in the middle of the dance floor. "You do think it'd be bad. Tell me why."

Bad was a judgment; saying it would be unfulfilling was more accurate. She looked around, conscious of the curious stares. "Everyone's watching."

"I don't care about them." He pulled her closer. "I care about you."

"You don't know me," she pointed out.

"I know," he agreed. "That's what makes this confounding. Why would you imagine sex with me would be bad?" he persisted. "There has to be a reason."

She shook her head. "It's not you."

"Which means you think it's you." He studied her intently, as if trying to look under the surface for hidden answers.

She returned his look with one of her own, the one that never failed to put her clients back in line. "I didn't think anything other than we should finish this dance."

He continued to study her, but then his intent gaze gave way to a smile, one that was astonishingly sweet and full of promise. He pulled her into him, cradled against him unequivocally, as if he wasn't going to let her go. "Doc, this dance has just begun."

Did you know that each time you leave a review, a rainbow brightens the sky?

Leave a review for THE WORDS YOU SAY and get ready for the magic!

Want more? Keep reading for a preview of THIS COULD BE THE NIGHT, book two in the Summerhills Next Generation series.

THIS COULD BE THE NIGHT

CHAPTER 1

Luke Summerhill Waite glanced at his mobile for the hundredth time since he'd sat down in his parents' parlor for tea. Still no text from Áine.

He knew the package had been delivered to her by now because he'd received a notification. He'd had it sent to her psychiatric office this time instead of her home because he hadn't wanted to wait all day to hear from her.

He shifted on the chair, impatient. What would she say? Today's gift seemed a little more normal, if more intimate, than the other three he'd sent her. He'd hesitated in sending it because of that, not certain how she'd feel. But he'd meditated about what to send each time, and each gift had been very clear. He knew to trust his gut instinct even when he didn't understand it.

Still, even he'd questioned sending her a large

unicorn last week. Áine had just texted him with, *Latent childhood desires?*

He'd replied, *Or just a new friend.*

She'd been quiet since—like every time after she'd thanked him for his gifts.

Dr. Áine Buckley was a confounding woman.

God, he wanted her.

"The usual with your tea?" his mother asked.

"Yes, please," he replied, still looking at his mobile. In a sea of disillusionment, Áine had appeared like a bright light, giving him hope for a different future, one that focused on growth rather than destruction.

He used to think his career did bring growth, but a few months ago he'd seen firsthand the destruction he'd unknowingly wrought. It'd rocked his world off its axis.

An email popped up on his mobile from the office about the latest company they were investing in. Luke had spearheaded the whole process, certain in his gut that it was the perfect business to give capital to—they had solid leadership, vision, and an excellent product.

He was doing exactly what he'd always done, but he wasn't sure he wanted to any longer—not after he'd seen what the end results could bring.

His dad had impressed on both him and his twin brother Trent that the measure of a man was more than physical things—it was what was in his heart. Right now, Luke's heart was a mass of longing and confusion. Longing for Áine, and confusion because of what he was faced with at the office.

He tucked his phone in his pocket. He'd read the email later. After he'd talked to Áine.

"You're distracted, Luke."

He looked up to see his mother studying him as she ever-so-properly prepared his tea. Wincing, he tugged his sleeve down over his watch. "Sorry, Mum."

"I'm here having tea with my son," Portia said with a smile, "but my son is somewhere else entirely."

He smiled apologetically at her. "I'm not the best company, am I?"

"You're always wonderful." She handed him the cup followed by a plate laden with finger sandwiches, biscuits, and cakes. They had formal teatime rarely these days, since their schedules were busy, but when they did it, Portia Summerhill Waite insisted on doing it properly. "You just have something heavy on your mind."

"It's that obvious?"

"Your father gets the same line between his brows when something isn't going the way he wants it to go." She settled back against the cushions, her fingers touching the pearls around her neck. Portia loved pearls. His dad had given her this necklace when they'd married; it'd been originally from the collection of the Duchess of Windsor. His dad had bought it at auction for a small fortune. He always said it was perfect for his wife, who was the director of a very posh auction house in London. "The Duchess's pearls for my duchess," he liked to say.

Pearls wouldn't suit Áine at all; Áine needed mystery. Luke would have loved to see her in champagne diamonds—the same color as her eyes—cool and fiery at the same time. It'd look lovely against her milky skin.

Not that jewelry was the thing to give her yet—that much was clear even without meditating. The last thing he wanted was for her to think he was plying her with what was in his "playboy" arsenal, as she would see it, instead of giving her what he thought would bring a smile to her lips.

She was incandescent when she smiled.

She'd look lovely wearing a necklace of champagne diamonds and nothing else—that'd bring a smile to *his* lips. He wondered if she'd be willing to put her pragmatism aside long enough to indulge him in something that sensual. Did her analytical psychiatrist self ever go off the clock?

He spent too much time wondering all sorts of things about her, and it was driving him mad.

"Is it work?" his mother asked, pulling him out of his reverie. "You've been checking your mobile every five seconds."

He smiled at her canniness. "Everything at work is going like clockwork. I closed the deal I was working on last week. There's a few loose ends to tie up, but it should all work out."

Fingers crossed.

What he was beginning to suspect wouldn't work out: continuing as a venture capitalist.

How did he tell his parents—especially his dad—that he was disenchanted with his career? They wouldn't understand. He'd been born with business in his veins, after all. His earliest memories were of himself at four, sitting on his dad's lap and poring over contracts. Being a successful venture capitalist was second nature to him.

It'd been a logical, easy decision to join his dad at his firm. He'd deliberately chosen that path. Luke had been handed a golden life, one that a lot of people would kill to have. He was smart enough to value and nurture it. Plus, he got to be with his dad every day. His dad was his hero—of course Luke would want to spend every day with him.

Hence why he went into business with his dad at Waite Venture Capital instead of pursuing music, his other, more illicit and tumultuous love.

His mother watched him closely. He braced himself for her to probe deeper, but instead she asked, "Is it Trent? I've been very worried about him."

In the same way Luke took after their dad, with his single-minded focus as well as a talent for making money by finding risky ventures to invest in, his twin Trent had inherited their mother's love of antiquities and unerring knack for knowing how to find them. He'd struck out on his own, though. Trent had always been independent, preferring to forge his own way. He and his roommate from uni had opened what Luke jokingly called "Treasure Hunters, Unlimited," locating and acquiring antiquities for their clients.

Portia, being the head of an auction house, had a deep understanding of Trent's field. Which was why she was so concerned about what had happened to him two weeks ago on a buying trip in Egypt.

"Trent will weather the storm and come out on top," Luke said, lifting his tea, even though he wasn't sure how Trent was going to get out of the trouble he'd landed in. "You know how he is."

"I'm still worried about him. It's not like him to distance himself in this way."

"I'll talk to him," he promised. Though he wasn't sure what good it'd do. Trent had been uncharacteristically closemouthed about getting arrested as he was leaving Egypt. He'd only been in jail for two days, but still. Wanting to defend his brother, because anyone with sense would know that the charges had been trumped up, Luke had offered help in getting it all resolved. But Trent had turned him down, saying he was taking care of it. "You know Trent is dogged once he's set on a course."

"Yes, but what *is* his course here?" His mum worried her pearls, her brow furrowed in concern. "His reputation is in tatters after that article about the alleged fraud. I'm not sure he can weather that."

Luke just wasn't certain either, but he didn't want to worry his mum more than she was.

"And being in an Egyptian jail…" His mum clutched her necklace.

"He was only in two days, Mum."

"Two days can be an eternity."

True. "Trent is resourceful, but I'll talk to him," he assured her again.

However diverging their paths were, they'd always talked things out together.

Until now. Despite living together, Trent had been scarce since he'd returned from being released from an Egyptian prison. Yes, it'd been just two days, but their mother was right; Trent hadn't been himself since he'd been back.

Although he wasn't one to talk. He'd been just as reticent as Trent. Since he'd come back to London from his cousin Henriette's wedding in Ireland three weeks ago, he'd had a lot on his plate with work and Áine the past three weeks. He knew he wasn't as present to his brother as he usually was.

He felt a twinge of guilt. He'd correct that.

"I'm worried about you too," he heard his mother say.

He blinked back to the present. "Don't worry. I won't get arrested," he tried to joke as he picked up a raspberry *financier* from his plate.

His mum gave him a faint smile as she picked up her own teacup. "I appreciate that. You boys always celebrate milestones together, but I'd prefer you both jump into something happy instead of prison."

Happy was Áine.

He couldn't recall how many times his dad had told him and Trent about the day Portia Summerhill walked into his life and how he knew in that first moment that she was it for him. He said first he'd noticed her legs and her racy underthings, but then he'd seen *her*, and that was it for him.

It'd been the opposite for Luke. It'd been her eyes that had pulled him in—the way she'd watched everything like she was starving and there was a feast around her that she couldn't bring herself to partake in. Like she was on the outside of all the love and joy of the occasion, adrift.

Adrift like him.

It'd made him want to find out why she felt that way when there was obviously love between her and her brother and sister. It'd made him want to give her everything she thought she was missing.

That'd surprised him. He'd never felt that compulsion before.

And then he'd danced with her at his cousin Henriette's wedding, and he'd known for certain—she was it for him.

"There's something that has you bothered," his mum insisted.

"There's something I'm interested in," he capitulated. "I just haven't figured out how to convince the other involved party that it'd be mutually beneficial to undertake the deal." He bit into the *financier*, barely tasting it. The only thing he had an appetite for was a buttoned-up psychiatrist.

His mother tipped her head. "You'll figure out how to get what you want. You have your father's relentless charm."

He grinned ruefully. "You don't make it sound like a compliment that I'm like Dad."

"What do I make it sound like?"

"Like I inherited a genetic disease from him."

She laughed.

"That's music to my ears," Jackson Waite said as he strode into the parlor. Even at almost seventy, his dad was still vital—tall and strong, with a twinkle in his eyes, especially when he saw his wife. Despite living in London for the past thirty-five years, he still had his Texan drawl and still wore cowboy boots.

His dad sauntered straight to Mum, leaning down to give her a lingering kiss before smiling at Luke. "Can anyone join this party?"

"This party wouldn't exist without you," Luke pointed out, standing up to give his dad a hug.

His dad held him at arm's length, looking him over with his shrewd gaze. "What's going on? They didn't back out, did they? I thought we came to an agreement about the investment and that the papers are being signed tomorrow."

"They are."

His mum tugged at Jackson's shirt. "We discuss business at the office, not at home."

His dad snorted as he dropped down next to her, his arm easing smoothly behind her across the back of the couch. "You and Trent discuss antiques all the time."

"That's because we share a love of *objets d'art*, not an office."

Luke caught the look his dad sent him, that they'd talk about this later. Having worked at his dad's investment capital firm since before he graduated from uni, he was fluent in his dad's silent conversation. It came in handy when they were in meetings together.

He just wasn't certain he wanted to talk later. He loved his dad, and his dad loved his firm. Telling Jackson Waite that he was disillusioned by work would be a blow, and Luke was loath to deliver it.

He wondered what Áine would say about that. She'd ask what had caused his feelings about work to change.

That was easy.

It was that night a few months ago when he was in Manhattan on business. He'd gone out to dinner and been chatting with his waiter, a very pleasant older woman, when she'd mentioned that she'd only been working in the restaurant a few weeks because she'd been laid off when her company, where she'd worked for seven years, had downsized and gotten rid of some of the middle management. She'd had to resort to waiting tables because she said at her age it was hard to find a new position.

It'd been a company he'd helped restructure as part of an investment.

He hadn't told her his part in any of that. All he'd felt like he could do was leave her an exorbitant tip, like a rich wanker.

And now he was doing the same with another company. How many people's lives were going to be destroyed because of what he did? How many people landed in an office like Áine's because of what he did?

Shaking his head, he pulled out his mobile, willing Áine to text him so he could focus on something positive.

"Waiting for a call, son?"

Luke met his dad's curious gaze. "I'm more hoping than waiting," he said, setting his mobile down.

His dad grinned, a knowing spark in his bright eyes. "It's a girl then."

"Jackson." Portia gave her husband a look as she handed him the old Summerhill china. The china had been in the Summerhill family for five generations, but Portia insisted that something so dear should be used every day. Her father had sold off much of the Summerhill artifacts before he'd died, but Jackson had tracked the set down and given it to her for an anniversary. "Do I need to remind you how you hated having your father meddle in your love life?"

"Now why would you want to spoil my fun,

duchess?" his dad replied, playing with the clasp of her necklace.

Portia Summerhill Waite gave her husband a look.

His dad chuckled. "You know when you look at me like that it only encourages me to be bad."

Luke cleared his throat. When he and his twin brother were younger, they were embarrassed by their parents' playful relationship. Now it just amused him—and it filled him with longing for that sort of companionship himself. "Do you two need to be alone?"

"Yes," his dad said as his mum said, "No."

They exchanged a private smile.

He could see looking at Áine that way—now and after thirty-five years of marriage.

Luke had been attracted to her from the first moment he'd seen her, but attraction didn't always rate action. It was that day at Henri's wedding, when he'd danced with Áine and felt her in his arms, that he'd realized he was more than just attracted to her.

That day, everything about her had been spectacular—from her fiery hair, so neatly contained, to the provocative dress he knew his cousin Vivienne, as wedding consultant, had coerced her into wearing. But it'd been the way she played tug-of-war with the hem of her short dress and the longing in her eyes as she watched her brother Liam marry Henri that tugged at Luke's heart.

It'd come out of nowhere. One moment he was tagging along with Vivi to Ireland to stave off the unrest he'd been feeling because of work, and the next he was obsessed with a woman who didn't think sex with him was going to be good.

She'd said as much while they'd danced at Henri's wedding reception. Why would she think that before even kissing him? Especially when dancing together had felt so incredible.

She'd fit him like a piece he hadn't known was missing.

Something foreign tightened in the pit of his stomach. He realized it was uncertainty. Everything had always come to him easily, but this was different. She wasn't falling into his arms like most women did, a fact he actually appreciated. But he couldn't convince Áine to want to be with him—she had to want it herself.

So far, her texting because of his presents encouraged him. But he wanted more.

He wanted it all.

His dad faced him. "Is Trent coming for tea?"

"Not today." Luke sipped his tea. "I think he doesn't want to bring his mess to your doorstep."

"Might be the best thing," his dad said as Portia snuggled next to him. He gave her a lazy, adoring smile. "Your mama would set them all straight. She's already got her mama bear face on."

His mum's expression *was* fierce. When Portia Summerhill Waite looked like that, you didn't mess with her.

Sitting up ramrod straight, she said, "They've not only impugned Trent, but the Summerhill name."

His dad cleared his throat. "Last I saw, the boy was also a Waite."

Luke exchanged an amused smile with his dad.

Still grinning, Jackson eased Portia back into him. "So tell me about this girl who has your knickers twisted."

"Jackson," his mum chided, elbowing him lightly. She faced Luke. "Are you accompanying Vivienne to Ireland? Liam's sister Maeve is getting married Saturday, isn't she?"

"I'm thinking about it." Because it meant Áine would, of course, be coming down from Dublin to visit. Helping Vivi with the wedding gave him a valid excuse to be there with her. He was desperate to see her again. "It's a good time to take a short holiday in Ireland. The area around Westport is beautiful. Spending time with Vivi and Henri will be nice."

"Vivi'll be busy a lot," his dad pointed out, reaching for a biscuit. "Won't you get bored out there? Westport is nice, but you're used to a faster life."

His life wasn't offering him the same sort of fulfillment as it once had. Since before he'd met Áine, he'd been thinking about making changes. He just didn't know what that looked like.

His guitar flashed in his mind. His fingers flexed of their own volition.

He cleared his throat. He wasn't certain he was

ready to plunge that deep. "I might ask Trent to go with me."

His mum smiled. "That's a wonderful idea. Getting out of town would be good for him, and the country air is clearing."

"Think you can do without me at the office for a bit?" he asked his dad, watching carefully.

"You know you don't need to be there as much as you are," his dad replied with a slight frown. "You set your own schedule. If you want to spend a week in Ireland, you do it anytime you want."

He thought about Áine, her golden eyes, and losing himself in the wonder of her arms. "I might take longer than a week."

His dad burst into laughter, nudging Portia. "I told you there was a girl."

"There isn't anyone," Luke said. Because a few gifts and bantering texts didn't mean anything.

"Yet," Jackson replied.

Yet. He liked that. He just had to convince Áine that she'd like it too.

———

Continue the dance with Áine and Luke in THIS COULD BE THE NIGHT.

———

Come hang out with Kathia on FACEBOOK and INSTAGRAM. She's fun and wacky, and she paints naked people and flowers—sometimes together.

Or subscribe to her NEWSLETTER for her sporadic musings and news on upcoming releases.

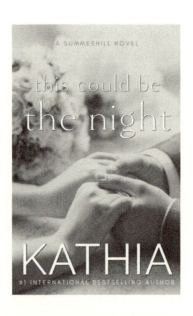

"Put simply, Kathia's novels are like a glass of champagne - heady, addictive and leaving one with a taste for much, much more."

— THE LITERARY SHED

"I find the Summerhill books filled with mirth, love, lust, passion, happiness and joy. I smile the whole time I read them."

— GOODREADS REVIEWER

Start smiling with THIS COULD BE THE NIGHT!

Available where books are sold.

PILLOW TALK NOVELS

PLAYING TO WIN

PLAYING DOCTOR

PLAYING FOR KEEPS

THE GUARDIANS

MARKED

CHOSEN

TEMPTED

WHIMSICAL NOVELS OF YOUNG LOVE

SWEET ENDEAVORS

UNRAVELED

PROJECT DADDY

For a complete booklist, check out Kathia's site.

ABOUT KATHIA

With over 6 million books sold (and counting), Kathia's novels have been #1 bestsellers around the world. They've received starred reviews from Booklist, have consistently earned Editor's Picks for Best Romance, and have been featured by *O, The Oprah Magazine*.

Kathia has written over 40 books so far, some translated into several languages, all about hope and dreams and the bonds of friendship and family. She's also written a couple screenplays and various poems (her ode to the color orange is particularly moving).

For more, check out...

www.kathiaherself.com

You can also find Kathia in all the usual places...

instagram.com/kathiaherself
facebook.com/kathiaherself
twitter.com/kathiaherself
bookbub.com/authors/kathia

DON'T FORGET TO SIGN UP FOR
KATHIA'S NEWSLETTER.

What do you get?
The latest on upcoming releases.
Bloopers and deleted scenes.
And a front-row seat to Kathia's adventures.

Do it. It's a piece of cake.

www.kathiaherself.com/newsletter

Made in United States
North Haven, CT
30 June 2023

38385240R00221